To Mary Lou.
Devoted wife, loving mother, best grandma,
kind friend, and avid reader.

LENORA BELL

Blame It on the Duke

Duke

The Disgraceful Dukes

piatkus

PIATKUS

First published in the US in 2017 by Avon Books,
an imprint of HarperCollins Publishers, New York
First published in Great Britain in 2017 by Piatkus
by arrangement with Avon Books

3 5 7 9 10 8 6 4 2

ISBN 978-0-349-41763-9

Printed and bound in Great Britain by
Clays Ltd, St Ives plc

Papers used by Piatkus are from well-managed forests
and other responsible sources.

MIX
Paper from
responsible sources
FSC® C104740

Piatkus
An imprint of
Little, Brown Book Group
Carmelite House
50 Victoria Embankment
London EC4Y 0DZ

An Hachette UK Company
www.hachette.co.uk

www.littlebrown.co.uk

Acknowledgments

"Begin at the beginning," says the King in Lewis Carroll's *Alice in Wonderland*, "and go on till you come to the end: then stop."

Thanks to my parents for reading out loud to me as a child. Thanks to my dear family and my wonderful friends for all the support and encouragement during the rough patches. Big hugs to my husband, who always knows just what to say—it's my turn to clean the cat boxes, sweetie.

To my editors, Carrie Feron and Amanda Bergeron, I'm so very fortunate to be able to learn from you and grow as a writer with your guidance. My everlasting gratitude to the entire fantastic, dedicated, and passionate team at Avon Books.

Huge thanks to my dream agent, Alexandra Machinist, and to all the friends who read early versions and didn't laugh too hard, especially Charis, Rachel, Lisa, and Neile.

Finally, to the Facebook commenter who wrote, "Please tell me Book Three is about Miss Alice Tombs . . ." Hope you enjoy!

Chapter 1

> Kama is the enjoyment of appropriate objects
> by the five senses of hearing, feeling, seeing,
> tasting, and smelling, assisted by the mind
> together with the soul.
>
> *The Kama Sutra of Vātsyāyana*

London, 1820
Ballroom of the Duke of Barrington's House

*V*enus rose from the undulating green waves,
naked save for her long red-gold hair and a serene
smile.

Ethereal harp music rippled through the air.

The small audience of titled gentlemen burst
into applause.

"Who is she, Hatherly?" Captain Lear asked.

"She's mine." Nick's gaze caressed the classical
lines of his soon-to-be mistress's lavishly curved
form.

Lear grinned roguishly. "Does she have a twin
sister?"

"How about the handmaiden?" Nick glanced at

the pretty actress with long, flowing brown hair, threaded with white roses, waiting to garb Venus in a robe of sheer pink silk.

"You make off with a goddess and I rate a mere handmaid?"

"What can I say, old friend?" Nick poured Lear more French Armagnac from a glass decanter on the round table in front of them. "It's my party."

Nick was infamous throughout society for his hedonistic entertainments. For tonight's festivities he'd recreated Botticelli's exquisite painting, *The Birth of Venus*, searching the opera houses of London for the perfect muse.

No matter that her name was Sally and she hailed from Liverpool.

Tonight she was Botticelli's Venus.

Art made flesh.

Temptation incarnate.

And tomorrow she'd be transformed back into the reigning goddess of the demimonde.

Lear chuckled, his gaze sweeping over the gentlemen seated around the stage Nick had constructed in the ballroom at Sunderland House, his father's palatial London mansion. "Just look at 'em. Rapt as babes with their mother's teat. You'll have trouble besting this one, Hatherly."

Nick nodded ruefully. "It's getting harder to devise new amusements. I've seen everything. Done everything."

"What you need is a change of scenery. Wide open skies, bracing sea air . . ." Lear winked. "Buxom barmaids at every port. Flexible flamenco dancers."

In polite parlance Lear was known as an adventurer; a ship for hire.

Others called him a pirate.

He certainly wasn't a true captain in the Royal Navy with his tanned skin, long black hair, and small gold hoop pierced through one ear, but he kept Nick supplied with this oak-aged brandy from France and spiced Portuguese wine, so Nick didn't ask too many questions.

Lear clapped a hand on Nick's shoulder. "Come with me on my next voyage. No, I'm serious," he said as Nick began to protest. "When was the last time you left London? You're suffocating here in this soot-stained city when there's a whole world to explore."

His friend's words conjured a long-buried memory. Salt spray crusted on his cheeks. Staring over a bleak, gray ocean. In the cabin below, his father, the Duke of Barrington and celebrated orchid collector, feverishly scribbling in his journal, pausing only to fill his inkwell. Endless cramped lines of gibberish, his mind gone murky and as unfathomable as the ocean they crossed.

Nick suppressed a shudder and swallowed the rest of the brandy in his glass, savoring the tart, sweet apple and caramel flavor.

"I'll never set foot on a ship again," he said, his voice low and even, but the words ripped from his soul. "Hate the ocean. Hate the boredom. Pacing the deck for months on end. I'd go mad. Only did it for my father."

Lear searched his face with a puzzled expression. With an effort, Nick restored his customary expression of amused carelessness. "Only ships I want to see are theatrical props, old friend," he said heartily, gesturing at the stage where the prow of a ghostly ship, stark against the blue backdrop, was rolling into view, signaling it was nearly time for Venus to sing.

Her talents had been completely wasted in the chorus of that halfpenny opera.

She had a smoky swirl to her voice that quickened a man's pulse.

This was where Nick belonged.

Here, in the depraved heart of the decadent kingdom he'd built for himself.

If the future held madness, he'd damned well drain every last drop of pleasure out of each moment left.

He'd go insane in grand style, the most envied man in London, with a voluptuous goddess in his bed, and a cellar full of expensive brandy.

"Besides," Nick said, "you know I can't leave the duke here alone. His mental derangement waxes and wanes. Today he's fine. Tomorrow he could be manic like poor old George. Rest his soul." Mad King George had gone to his troubled grave in the end of January, only four months previous.

"Where is Barrington?" Lear craned his neck, searching the room. "I haven't paid my respects."

"Left him slumbering in his chambers with his attendant, Stubbs, watching outside the door. No doubt the old man's dreaming of searching for elusive ghost orchids in tropical climes."

"I brought him some rare bulbs from Spain this time," Lear said. He brought the duke orchids every time he returned to London. "Packed them in bark and kept them warm and cozy so they should have survived. There's money in orchid collecting these days. May have to find a wealthy investor and hunt some myself on my next—"

A deep voice sounded from the stage, drowning his words. "Ho, there! Comely Venus! Have you seen my son?"

Nick glanced up sharply, sloshing brandy over his cuff.

His father balanced on the prow of the ship, swaying in time with the lengths of billowing silk waves. For some reason he was wearing evening dress, though his cravat had come undone and his white hair was standing on end.

Lear snorted. "Slumbering in his bed, eh?"

"How the devil did he climb up there? And where's his caretaker?" Nick scanned the room for Mr. Stubbs, whom he'd hired from an agency after too many nurses quit because of the duke's amorous advances. His father's mind may have weakened, but his predilection for buxom older ladies remained firm.

"Young lady, you ought to put some clothing on," the duke called to Venus.

Venus made surreptitious silencing motions, striving to maintain her beatific smile as the audience laughed.

"You'll catch your death on that clamshell in your altogether," the duke scolded loudly.

Her moment of triumph was quickly evaporating.

"He's liable to break his neck," Nick said. "The ship's not meant for anyone to stand on."

It was only a shell made from rotting old timber and mounted on wheels. Nick had rented the ship, as well as an entire theatrical troupe, for the evening from a theater on King Street.

"Help me fetch him down." Motioning for Lear to follow, Nick headed toward the stage.

"Thar he be!" the duke thundered, pointing at Nick.

"Come down from there," Nick called.

"Come and fetch me," the duke crowed.

More laughter from the onlookers.

Venus pouted and stamped a dainty foot on her plaster clamshell.

Which made the audience laugh even harder.

That's when the harpist seated to the left of the stage decided this had become a comedy and began improvising a rollicking sea shanty. The violins joined in, to the spectators' vast amusement.

Hearing the change in the music, the duke glanced up with a gleam in his faded gray eyes and began to dance what looked like it was meant to be a hornpipe.

Nick's blood froze as his father tottered precariously on the rolling deck.

He vaulted onto the stage with Lear close behind.

"Distract him," Nick said urgently. "Keep him talking. If he's talking, he's not dancing. If he's not dancing, the ship might hold."

"Aye." Lear nodded. "What are you doing up there, Your Grace?" he called. "Why don't you climb down?"

"Hullo, Cap'n," the duke said in a jovial, booming tone of voice. "I needed a platform. I've an announcement to make. Where's my son? Wasn't he with you?"

Nick's boot became tangled in the green silk stretched across the stage. He wrenched free and raced for the ship.

"Speech! Speech!" called someone from the audience.

The inside of the ship smelled like piss. An actor or two must have mistaken it for the privy. The smell made Nick's eyes water as he climbed the rickety ladder that the duke must have used to reach the deck.

"I played a game of cards tonight," Nick heard the duke proclaim. "Not supposed to gamble. 'Tis a sin, I know."

"Had a lucky night?" someone shouted.

"I lost." Nick heard the familiar sound of confusion in his father's voice. "Rather badly, I'm afraid."

The sound of the spectators' hilarity was muted from inside the hollow hull of the ship.

"How much did you lose?" Lear kept the conversation flowing, stalling for time as Nick had instructed.

"Not how much . . . *whom*," the duke replied.

Nick gripped the ladder's wooden slats. He'd have his father down within seconds.

"Fine then, *whom* did you lose?" Lear asked.

"My son," boomed Nick's father. "Gambled him clean away."

What in hell was that supposed to mean?

Nick took a deep breath. It couldn't possibly be true. The duke suffered from delusions and this was merely a new one.

Nick grabbed hold of the duke's boot, and his father stuck his head down the opening. "That you, Nicolas?"

"It's me," Nick said grimly. "Now clasp my hand and I'll help you down."

"No," his father said stubbornly. "I'm making an announcement."

"I'd rather you didn't."

"Hush. My audience awaits." His father popped his head back up the opening.

Nick sighed. Bodily force it was, then.

"As I was saying, I lost the marquess at cards," the duke proclaimed. "To a wealthy baronet. So you see, fair Venus, he won't be yours much longer. He's to be married to Miss Alice—"

The end of his announcement grew garbled as, with one swift tug, Nick grabbed his father's boots and pulled him into his arms.

Not a moment too soon.

The rotting deck splintered as Nick carried his father down the ladder.

Nick shielded the duke as a wooden beam jarred across his back.

Safely away from the collapsing ship and off the stage, Nick placed an arm around his father's shoulders.

"You're all right," he soothed, as his father stared wildly about him, frightened by the sound of splintering wood and the shouting from the gentlemen in the audience.

Captain Lear helped Venus off her shell and draped his evening coat about her shoulders.

She glared at Nick. Her expression did not bode well for the night of debauchery he'd planned.

Lear made a chivalrous bow and kissed her hand. "Captain Lear, at your service, Miss Venus."

"Sally's the name," she cooed in her smoky, sensual voice. "Though you may call me anything you like, Captain." She tossed her long gold curls and narrowed her eyes at Nick. "If you take me away from here."

"I believe that could be arranged." Lear glanced at Nick.

Nick gave his friend a brief nod. Who could blame the lovely opera singer for wanting to leave? They hadn't even become lovers yet. Nick had promised her sensational success and the adulation of every gentleman in the room, and delivered only farce. She'd no doubt be happier with Lear tonight.

Lear flashed Nick a triumphant grin as he led his prize away. *Goddess*, he mouthed. *Mine*.

Nick groaned. This evening was plummeting to hell faster than a bishop in a bawdy house.

Members of the acting troupe had already cleared away the ship's wreckage. Nick caught the manager's eye and gestured for the next act to begin.

The show must go on.

Nick placed an arm around his father's shoulders and helped him across the room, shielding him from the swarm of inebriated gentlemen who all seemed to be speaking at the same time.

"Did you truly wager the marquess, Your Grace?"

"Who's the lucky lady?"

The Earl of Camden's heavy jowls wobbled into Nick's peripheral vision. "Not to worry, Hatherly." He laughed. "I'm sure the girl will be gentle with you on your wedding night."

Loud guffaws.

Elbow jabs to the ribs.

Everyone howling with merriment.

Nick laughed along, pretending this was all a huge joke.

With such an unpredictable father, he'd learned to hide his emotions and appear cavalier no matter what happened.

"Back to your seats, gents," he called. "You won't want to miss what comes next."

When they were safely away from the ballroom, Nick relaxed his grip on his father's shoulders. "That was a fine show, Barrington. You could have injured yourself."

His father grinned sheepishly. "I've always loved a good climb. Haven't I?" His voice wobbled as he asked the question, filling with uncertainty.

He'd been an adventurer before the madness claimed him, scaling mountains the world over, finding rare orchids for his collections.

"Always." Nick smoothed his father's wiry white hair down but it sprang right back up. "Let's find your bed, shall we? Where's Stubbs?"

"Don't know. Maybe still at the Crimson?"

The Crimson? Had his father truly visited such a notorious gaming hell? Didn't seem probable. His many vices had never included gambling, and Nick trusted that Stubbs would never have allowed the duke to enter such a place.

"You didn't really gamble, did you?" asked Nick.

His father cast his gaze to the carpet. "I did." He clutched Nick's hand. "It was you or Sunderland. Had to make a choice, you see?"

The aging duke loved Sunderland House with the desperation of a drowning man clinging to a scrap of driftwood—the house was his last, tenuous link to sanity. Here, in the familiar surroundings of his childhood, with his orchid conservatory and his son to care for him, the duke remained relatively tranquil and his malady harmed no one.

"Easy now." Nick unclenched the duke's gnarled fingers. "We'll speak of it in the morning," he said lightly, steering his father up the stairs.

The duke leaned heavily on Nick's arm as they climbed the stairs. "Lost you to Sir Alfred Tombs. Had the devil's own luck . . ." He yawned. "Daughter's name is Alice. Hear she's . . . pretty at least . . ."

His chin nodded near his chest and Nick propped him up, half carrying him to his chambers.

Sir Alfred—wealthy shipping merchant. Reputation for ruthlessness.

Nick had even met the daughter once at an art exhibition. He remembered her perfectly.

Miss Tombs was pretty, Nick would give her that. On the tall side for a female, with a fine complexion, deep dimples, and sparkling turquoise eyes.

Nick had been contemplating a seductive portrait of a gauze-draped woman when Miss Tombs had suddenly appeared, a vision of virginal white lace and rosy cheeks. Very sweet and wholesome . . . until she opened her mouth.

For some reason, she'd decided to beguile him with a gory description of how the portrait artist had died of a putrid fever. She'd described the entire course of the putrefaction in lurid and gleeful detail, with no agonizing or malodorous aspect spared.

Good God. The ghoulish Miss Tombs was as far from a prospective bride as Nick could imagine.

Not that he ever imagined marriage.

That venerable institution was the snare waiting to trap unsuspecting gentlemen into allowing one lady to ruin them for all others, as it had done to his friends the Duke of Harland and the Duke of Osborne, who were foolishly, irretrievably in love with their wives.

Nick was the last man standing of their disreputable band of ruffians and rogues.

Speaking of ruffians and rogues, where were his so-called servants? Not a one to be found when he needed them.

The duke roused slightly as Nick helped him remove his coat and cravat. "What time is it?"

"Bedtime."

The duke held out his hand to Nick with a befuddled expression. "I think I have a splinter."

Nick plucked a small painted slice of boat from his father's palm. "Good as new. Into bed with you."

Obediently, the duke snuggled under the coverlet. "Nicolas?"

"Yes?"

"I gambled you away."

"So you've said."

"Oh." His father was silent for a moment. "Well, marriage might do you good." He yawned and rubbed his eyes. "You need someone . . . to love. But find someone strong. Not delicate, nor easily crushed."

"Go to sleep now." Nick tucked the covers tighter around his father.

As soon as the duke's breathing grew slow and steady, he left to go find Stubbs. The man had many questions to answer.

You need someone to love.

He tried to shake his father's words away but they stuck like a splinter in his mind.

It wasn't that Nick didn't believe in love. He just didn't believe in tomorrow—or in any kind of permanence.

He kept his amatory liaisons on a surface level, protecting his heart as stringently as he protected against unwanted progeny.

He had no intention of marrying or passing on the suffering of the curse that lurked in his direct line. His sanctimonious curate of a cousin would be delighted to inherit the dukedom and restore the family's reputation when Nick's dark days were done.

"Bargained away like a harem girl," he muttered as he descended the stairs. "I'll never live this down."

It must be one of his father's outlandish imaginings, but the rumor would spread across London like an outbreak of plague and slosh its way across the channel to his mother in her extravagantly expensive apartments in Switzerland.

He'd unravel the tangle in the morning. Right now he had to find Stubbs, before returning to the ballroom and attempting to control the damage.

Give the gentlemen he'd invited enough brandy and actresses and they might forget the duke's announcement.

And even if it did turn out to be true, there was no chance Nick would allow anyone to coerce him into marriage, least of all a grasping merchant and his pretty but decidedly odd daughter.

Nick gripped the smooth wooden staircase balustrade.

They had no idea whom they were dealing with.

Obviously, the Earl of White had no idea whom he was dealing with.

He clearly thought Alice should be overwhelmed with gratitude at the honor he was bestowing by wooing her this fine late spring morning in the small inner courtyard of her father's town house.

They were sitting on a bench next to a flowering hawthorn shrub and Lord White was gazing at her devotedly.

"Miss Tombs, you are a goddess sent from heaven above." He flung a hand heavenward, to make his point. "I adore you most ardently. Your dimples are divine."

Any other young lady of the *ton* would be thrilled. They pined for his pale yellow hair and pale blue eyes, and his languishing, poetic pronouncements.

Silly things.

Fortunately, Alice had always had an uncanny ability for languages. Along with Latin, Greek, French, and the three other foreign tongues she'd mastered, Alice was fluent in Impoverished Rake.

She knew precisely what White's words translated to: *Miss Tombs, my ancestral coffers are running precariously low. Marry me so I may squander your father's vast fortune on gold-embroidered waistcoats and costly courtesans.*

Gracious, how Alice loathed the idle nobility.

Take away their titles and they'd have not one skill with which to earn a living. And if she were poor they would never pay the slightest attention to her dimples.

"Dimples, Lord White, are naught but muscular deformities," Alice said briskly. "Occurring in approximately twenty percent of the population, from my observations."

The earl trailed an elegant, unlined hand through the air. "Pray, do not belittle yourself, Miss Tombs. You are hardly deformed. Your features are fetching beyond compare."

And will fetch forgiveness of my tailor bills, Alice translated.

Lord White must have outrageous tailor bills.

She stared with morbid fascination at his waistcoat. She'd never seen such a shade of chartreuse. And what was embroidered upon the garment? Could those be hounds and . . . *rodents*? The plump creatures had red, beady eyes but the ears were rather long . . .

"I see you are admiring my fox and hare waistcoat." The earl smiled indulgently. "I hope you may have the pleasure of watching me ride to hounds someday at Whitehaven. I'm a crack shot."

Hares? Alice squinted at the waistcoat. The shapes could be construed as rabbitlike, she supposed. Appropriate, really. She felt rather like a hapless woodland creature trapped in the sight of the earl's rifle.

Boldly, Lord White stroked her cheek with one knuckle. "Your skin is as soft as these lily petals." He lifted one of the early-blooming Asiatic lilies he'd plucked from her mother's flowerbeds.

Hadn't even brought his own flowers. Wooing her was an afterthought. He'd assumed she would tumble easily into his arms.

I'll outrun you yet, Alice thought. What she needed to do was turn the tables.

Hunt the hunter.

Her lady's maid, Hodgins, was reading a book on a nearby bench. She must have been instructed to ignore small improprieties in pursuit of the larger goal.

Mama was counting on the earl's proposal.

The wedding invitations had already been mentally composed; the trousseau ordered.

All part of her mother's plans to scale the dizzying heights of London society.

Alice had a plan as well, and it did *not* include marriage to a vain and vapid nobleman. She would marry someday, but not until after she had at least one grand adventure abroad.

"Do stop waving those flowers about, Lord White."

"Oh, that my lips were brushing yours." The earl trailed one of the lilies across his mouth.

"I wouldn't press my lips to that lily if I were you, Lord White. *Lilium asiaticum* are highly poisonous. We wouldn't want you to begin drooling and cast your breakfast all over this blanket, would we?"

He dropped the lily. "I say, you're not like other girls, are you," he said peevishly, scooting farther from her on the bench in a sulk.

No, I'm not. Best do your wooing elsewhere, there's a good earl.

Inconvenient things, suitors.

Stood in the way of one's plans for adventurous voyages to India.

Her younger brother, Fred, who had reluctantly embarked on a Grand Tour of the Continent one year ago, would be home soon. And after he returned, Fred had promised to bring Alice with him on his upcoming voyage to visit potential sites for tea plantations in India.

Papa was a wealthy shipping merchant and wanted Fred to begin assuming responsibilities in the stewardship of his business concerns.

Alice had other plans for India.

When Papa had unexpectedly inherited the baronetcy after the tragic early deaths of his father and elder brother, the family had moved from the provincial Yorkshire town of Pudsey to her grandfather's London town house.

There'd been no love lost between Sir Alfred and his father, who'd been a director of the East India Company, and a notorious voluptuary. Alice's father had immediately discarded or burned most of the late baronet's possessions.

Alice had rescued an entire box of ancient Indian manuscripts from the fire. Teaching herself to read them by studying *A Grammar of the Sanskrita Language*, she'd sent several short translations to Mr. Vidyasagar and Mr. Carey, Sanskrit scholars at Fort William College in Calcutta. The learned scholars had replied with great excitement to say that they believed one of the manuscripts she possessed to be the missing fragment of a larger work entitled *The Kama Sutra of Vātsyāyana*, an ancient Hindu text of great societal significance.

They had invited her to visit the college and bring her chapters of the *Kama Sutra*, along with her translation, and she had enthusiastically agreed.

There was only one slight wrinkle in her plans.

She might have signed her letters and translations as *Fred* Tombs.

It had seemed easier at the time to pretend to be male, to have her scholarship taken seriously.

Interrupting her thoughts, the earl abruptly leaned forward and glued his lips to hers, apparently deciding that where words hadn't produced the desired effect, his kiss would bring her to heel.

Startled by the suddenness of the move, Alice didn't immediately draw away.

She'd never been kissed before, and she'd been thinking quite a lot about kissing lately.

The Sanskrit fragment she'd been translating had proven surprisingly naughty. The *Kama Sutra* described in great detail the sixty-four arts of pleasure.

Sixty-four! Alice was fairly certain she'd translated the number correctly, although it had seemed incredible at first.

The ancient text had given her quite a number of questions about the practical application of its instructions. It described the various types of kissing, all of which were supposed to produce the most rapturous and voluptuous sensations.

Apparently, Lord White had never studied the *Kama Sutra*.

His kiss was rather alarmingly damp. His lips moved over hers with a smacking, rhythmic motion that made her feel seasick.

He smelled of lilies and overpoweringly musky cologne, and his hands were everywhere at once—in her hair, around her waist, stroking her cheek . . . rather like an octopus.

Ugh. This was not making her feel the slightest bit enlightened *or* amorous.

Deciding he had nothing to teach her about the art of kissing, Alice plucked a hairpin from her coiffure and jabbed it into his cheek in a defensive motion her friend Charlene, the Duchess of Harland, had taught her.

"Ouch!" the earl yelped, pulling back. "You needn't poke a gentleman's eye out."

At his exclamation, Hodgins finally lifted her head from her book and glanced their way, frowning as she watched Lord White rub his cheek and pout.

"You brought my retribution upon yourself," Alice said in a vehement whisper. "You shouldn't try to kiss unsuspecting ladies without their consent."

"You'd better not have left a mark." His cheeks were red, his eyes stormy, and his languid, poetic air had vanished.

Alice held her breath, waiting for him to signal to his manservant, who stood a discreet distance away, that he wished to pack up and leave.

To her chagrin, the earl made a visible effort and forced a smile to his lips. "Please forgive me for startling you, Miss Tombs. I was carried away by your beauty. Have you had ample opportunity to prepare yourself now?" He glanced meaningfully at her lips and bent near again.

Drat! This one was remarkably persistent. He must be truly desperate for funds.

Time to utilize the fail-safe method; proven to be effective one hundred percent of the time in dissuading amorously inclined fortune hunters.

"My father thinks very highly of you, Lord White," she said sweetly.

He stopped halfway to his target. "Of course he does."

"Just the other day he was speaking of you." She pretended to have to think about what she'd supposedly overheard. "He said, 'Don't let the earl slip through your fingers, he has a remarkably ancient title.'"

Lord White nodded approvingly. "Sensible fellow, your father."

"And then he said, 'Don't let on about the disaster, though. We mustn't worry him with details of that storm off the Cape of Good Hope.'"

Lord White stared in consternation, his nose

twitching with the scent of scandal. "What's that you say? A storm?"

"Oh, silly me." Alice covered her mouth with her hand. "I wasn't supposed to mention that. I've really no idea what he meant. Of course, he has so many trading ships in his fleet that losing a dozen or more couldn't mean much to him."

The earl gulped. "A dozen, you say?"

"It was nothing, really. Only heavy cargoes of silk and porcelain. I'm sure Papa has simply boat-loads more. Though he was tearing his hair out the other day when that nasty newspaper writer paid us a visit."

The earl's face began to match his title. He scooted back from her on the blanket, rising to his knees.

"Why, my lord, is anything the matter?" Alice asked innocently.

He glanced at his waiting servant, clearing his throat and drawing an ostentatious gold timepiece from his waistcoat pocket. "Oh lud, it completely slipped my mind. I'm late. Ever so late. I must be going. I've an appointment at . . . Tattersall's . . . to see a man about a horse."

Alice hid a smile behind her lacy parasol. "Must you go?"

"I really must. I'm ever so late."

He couldn't return her from the courtyard back to the parlor fast enough.

Hodgins had to run to catch them, and only arrived after Lord White had rudely left Alice without even saying good-bye to her parents, escaping out the front door and fairly leaping into his yellow phaeton.

Alice laughed softly.

Another one down.

Now her third social season was well and truly over. Lord White had been the last prospect standing.

One step closer to her journey to India and to returning her fragment of the *Kama Sutra* to its proper home.

"Oh! There you are." The excitable Lady Tombs entered the parlor, her blue eyes shining and white cap ribbons floating.

"I'm sorry, Mama." Alice tensed her shoulders in anticipation of a sound scolding. "I've no idea why Lord White left in such a—"

"Never mind the earl, my dear." Mama waved the words away. "He was a frivolous fop and you're best rid of him."

Alice stared at her mother suspiciously. "Yesterday you said he was the quintessence of masculine perfection."

"Oh! That was yesterday. This is today. And your father has the most wonderful news. Follow me to the study, if you please."

Alice's senses twitched to high alert like her pet cat's nose twitched when she scented a mouse in the walls.

She and her mother had opposite ideas of what constituted wondrous tidings.

Maybe she had received an unexpected offer of marriage from a mystery gentleman.

Alice smoothed the peony-pink skirts of one of the ridiculously beribboned and frilled gowns her mother forced her to wear.

No impoverished rake would ruin her Eastern adventure.

She jabbed her hairpin back into place.

Whoever he was—she'd make short work of him.

They found Sir Alfred pacing up and down the length of his study, hands clasped behind his back and deep furrows lining his forehead. "Damned good-for-nothing boy," he muttered as he walked. "Ruined. Utterly ruined."

"What's the matter, Papa?" Alice asked, puzzled by the tirade. Hadn't her mother said there was good news?

"We've had a letter from Fred," Mama whispered.

"Oh? What news? When will he arrive?" She was eager to set their plan in motion and obtain permission to accompany Fred to Calcutta. They'd agreed it would be best if Fred suggested the idea.

"What news? I'll tell you what news," Sir Alfred sputtered. "The worst news. Damned empty-pated boy."

"Language, sir," fluttered Lady Tombs, following after her husband with small, worried steps.

"I'll damn him to hell and gone! I'll damn him right out of my will and testament! Marry an opera singer, will he? Throw away everything? If I were there I could have bought her off easily enough, the greedy little trollop. But now the damage is done."

"Oh!" Lady Tombs laid a hand to her high, lacy collar.

"What's this?" Alice clutched the edge of the desk. "Fred is married?"

This was disaster; the end of all her dreams.

How could Fred have been so foolish? Now how would she go to India? And who would deliver the documents and her translations to the college in Calcutta? She couldn't entrust the priceless and fragile palm leaf manuscript of the *Kama Sutra* to the post.

"Never should have sent that fool of a boy to the Continent," her father grumbled. "He was an easy mark for fortune-hunting jezebels. I'm too old for all this traveling. I wanted Fred to assume the mantle. Instead he disgraced us." He jabbed a finger at Alice. "Why couldn't you have been born the heir, eh? You'd have made a damned fine boy, Alice. You've a sensible head on your shoulders."

Why, indeed? Alice thought with familiar frustration. She was the one who loved learning languages and longed to travel to foreign lands. Fred wasn't interested in studies or traveling. It truly wasn't fair.

"Please, sir, I beg you," pleaded Lady Tombs. "Please don't dwell upon it so. There may still be time to have the marriage annulled."

"Not likely," the baronet said, his face flushed with anger. "That doxy will bear him a babe in seven months' time." He stabbed the air with his forefinger. "Mark my words."

"Yet remember that today is also a happy day, my dear husband." Her mother sidled closer. "Our

Alice will be the means to restore us from disgrace."

Oh no. No, no, no.

Now her mother would be even more desperate for Alice to find an aristocrat to wed.

"Tell her the news, dear husband," said Mama. "Such news. Such wonderful news."

Sir Alfred slapped a palm against the desk and Alice jumped. "After I read that idiot boy's letter yesterday I went straight to a gaming house to clear my head."

There was nothing new in that. Her father loved to gamble. And he always won.

He had a ruthless way of making his opponents commit errors.

She couldn't let him do the same to her today.

She squared her shoulders. "Congratulations." She managed a thin smile. "I'm sure you won a great sum of money."

"No." His graying whiskers curved as he smiled grimly. "I won you a marquess."

Alice blinked. "A *what*?"

"Oh happy, happy day!" Mama clasped her hands together. "How good it was of you, sir. Only think what a household you shall have, dear Alice. I always knew such a handsome, clever girl would improve our prospects and make the most advantageous of matches."

"I *was* rather proud of myself," Papa said modestly. "Not every day one wins a marquess."

Alice's mind reeled with shock.

First Fred's defection and now suddenly she had a fiancé?

She wanted to grab the brass paperweight shaped like a raven off the writing desk and heave it through one of the windows. Instead she unclenched her hands from the desk and smoothed her skirts.

She hadn't used every tool in her workshop to unstick Lord White only to be forced to cleave to another conceited, idle aristocrat.

"How exactly does one win a marquess at cards?" she asked.

"Quite easily, as it turns out," her father said. "Found the Duke of Barrington playing whist at the Crimson, won his crumbling old London mansion, and he suggested I take his heir instead. I accepted on your behalf."

At Alice's stricken expression, he frowned. "Well? Aren't you going to thank me? You weren't exactly producing any proposals, my girl. Becoming a bit long in the tooth, I'd say."

Seething, Alice reminded herself that her father probably thought he'd been doing her a favor. "Surely you can't mean the Marquess of Hatherly, Papa," she said through gritted teeth.

"The very gentleman."

Worse and worse.

Alice had met the notorious Lord Hatherly at the Duchess of Osborne's art exhibition last year. He'd more than lived up to his wild reputation, making a splashy entrance with a bosomy woman on each arm, reeking of decadence and power.

He'd commanded the room, insufferably full of himself, certain that every lady in the room would swoon at his feet.

Even more annoyingly, they had.

Lady Melinda had fainted dead away when he spoke to her.

Dizzy-headed thing.

For her part, Alice had made certain to make an impression of a very different sort. She'd given him a lecture on putrid fevers that he wouldn't soon forget.

There was some slight reassurance in the fact that, thanks to her prudence and forethought, she'd already laid the groundwork for ensuring he'd never contemplate marrying her.

"Lord Hatherly is not interested in marriage in the slightest. Everyone knows that," said Alice.

"Then his father shouldn't have bargained him away."

"Isn't the duke mad? Can he be held responsible for his actions?" asked Alice.

"Didn't seem mad," her father replied. "Quite lucid. Entertained me with tales of his orchid-hunting expeditions."

"I'm sure the rumors of insanity have been greatly exaggerated," her mother said. "One day Lord Hatherly will be a duke. *A duke.*" Her mouth trembled with the grandeur of the thought. "What matter a few skeletons in the family closet when you shall be a duchess? We shall assume our proper place in society, no matter what Fred has done, isn't that right, Sir Alfred?"

Sir Alfred's face grew thunderous again. "Damned disgrace of a boy."

Apparently there was no more time for subtle persuasion.

Alice drew herself up to her full height, nearly a head taller than her mother, and spoke in a calm, authoritative voice. "Papa, remember that box of grandfather's Indian books and papers I saved you from burning? I've been corresponding with the Sanskrit scholars at Fort William College and one of the manuscripts could be the missing chapters from an important ancient text. I want to travel to Calcutta with Fred in—"

"Alice Perpetua Felicity Tombs!" said Mama.

Alice flinched. She'd been named for two holy Church of England martyrs. Her mother invoked their long-suffering names only when she was thoroughly fed up with Alice's foibles.

"However could you have fixed upon such a nonsensical scheme?" The ribbons streaming from her mother's white lace cap quivered indignantly. "Have I not taught you your proper place is at the center of the circle of domestic bliss? A female must never stray from hearth and home. Your duty is to marry well. Even doubly so now that Fred has . . . done what he has done."

Oh yes. Alice had been taught her proper place very thoroughly.

Hearth and home. Housekeeping and homilies.

The muscles in Alice's jaw began to ache. She turned to her father. "I'm not asking for a Grand Tour, Papa. Only a very modest and scholarly one. Grant me this one favor and I'll be the most dutiful daughter in the world when I return. I'll marry immediately, and to great advantage."

Her two best friends had found worthy gentlemen to love. Perhaps Alice might find a kind, gentle, scholarly sort of gentleman. Maybe even one who cared for *her,* instead of only her father's fortune.

Papa averted his gaze, rearranging the papers on his desk. "Out of the question."

"But—"

"Beg your pardon, Sir Alfred," interrupted Ellen, one of the upstairs maids, entering the room with saucer eyes and bobbing a quick curtsy. "There's a carriage arrived. Danvers sent me to warn you, sir, as I was closest at hand."

"Well?" Sir Alfred said irritably. "Who is it?"

"It's . . . it's the M-Marquess of Hatherly, if you please, sir."

Sir Alfred frowned. "Are you quite sure?"

"Oh yes. There's no mistaking him, sir. I saw him leave the carriage with my own eyes. So very imposing, he is. And just as handsome as the papers say."

"Do you hear that, Alice?" her father said. "Your intended is quite a handsome fellow."

"Lord Hatherly is here?" Lady Tombs's hand flew to her lace cap. "Oh dear me. I must do something about my appearance. I'm not fit to be seen."

Why must every female flutter so about the man?

Ellen's cheeks were flushed, her bosom heaved, and her eyes had an unhealthy brilliance.

Sure symptoms of a Hatherly sighting.

Alice crossed the room to the maid. "You're not about to swoon, are you?" she asked in a clipped undertone.

"I don't think so, miss. Only those eyes of his. Like twice-polished silver, they are. They quite take one's breath away."

"Calm yourself, please. He's only a man."

"Yes, miss. Only . . ."

"Yes? What is it?"

Ellen twisted her apron in her hands. "You might feel breathless when you see him. Truly you might."

Breathing was essential to life. Alice was never breathless. And wouldn't be until she expired at a ripe old age.

"Inform Danvers I'll be down shortly," Papa said.

"You mean to keep the marquess waiting?" Ellen's eyes widened. "Oh, Sir Alfred, are you sure that's the best—"

A forceful, arrogant blur of black silk and stark white linen strode into the library.

"Oh!" Ellen squeaked, jumping behind Alice and using her as a shield.

Poor Danvers, the butler, followed close behind, breathing heavily.

"His Lordship, the Marquess . . . of . . . Hatherly," Danvers gasped.

Chapter 2

It is notorious that men who have given themselves up to pleasure alone have been ruined
along with their families and relations.

The Kama Sutra of Vātsyāyana

Alice studied the gentleman who made parlor
maids squeak and debutantes swoon, as if he were
a map, plotting out the best route to cross him.

Thick, dark brown hair.

Long, lean nose; long, lean body.

Ruby-red silk waistcoat and indecently fitted
buckskin breeches that sent a clear message: *Here
stands a man who rides hard. Batten the hatches. Lock
up the ladies.*

Alice shivered slightly.

Here stood a gentleman who must have an intimate knowledge of all sixty-four varieties of pleasure. She was quite sure of it.

There was an aura of danger about him—an air
of unpredictability.

The apothecaries of the world would do a brisk

trade if they could distill his decadent allure to sell to the masses.

Only a dab of this, Mr. Smith, and the ladies will swoon at your feet.

Alice stood taller. She might be country bred, but no man, no matter how outrageously good-looking, would make her breathless.

Really, his eyes are an ordinary gray, she reflected. *Mice are gray. Cobwebs. Dirty dishcloths.*

He was perfectly at ease in unfamiliar surroundings.

All that expensive tailoring and aristocratic indolence made the library's new-purchased Aubusson rugs and gilt ormolu clocks look tawdry and pretentious.

"This won't stand, Sir Alfred," Lord Hatherly said with an icy smile. "The duke can't be held responsible for his actions."

Her father crossed his arms, refusing to crumple under the disdainful assault of Lord Hatherly's gaze. "My man of business made some inquiries this morning. We believe the wager to be legal and binding, Lord Hatherly."

A brief flicker of surprise lit Hatherly's eyes. He hadn't expected such resistance.

"You may have one of our other properties." The marquess made an impatient gesture. "You're welcome to the castle in Essex. It's far more profitable and better maintained than Sunderland."

"I'll have Sunderland House or I'll have you for a son-in-law. It's entirely up to you," Papa said belligerently, not yielding an inch.

Mama gave Alice a small push forward. "Here is our daughter, Miss Alice Tombs. Curtsy to His Lordship, Alice."

Alice dropped a grudging curtsy, hoping the marquess remembered the gory details of their last conversation.

"We've met." Hatherly's gaze flicked over her dismissively.

She gave him her best kitten-with-sharp-claws smile. "So your father gambled you away, Lord Hatherly? What must the other gentlemen be saying? How very inconvenient to be society's latest drollery."

"Alice," whispered her mother warningly.

Hatherly's gaze darkened. "I could challenge this in the courts."

"But you won't," said her father with a smug smile. "You don't wish for a protracted public dispute."

Hatherly's wide shoulders went rigid. Slowly, he rotated toward Alice's father. "Do not presume to know what I want, sir."

Her father shrugged. "If you don't wish to marry, Sunderland will be mine. Even if I have to fight you for years. I have unlimited resources, don't forget."

Alice's heart sank into her kid slippers. This was bad.

The only silver lining here was the way Hatherly's cold gaze swept over her with approximately the same amount of interest he might give a moldy carrot.

Excellent. She didn't need him to find her attractive. Quite the opposite. She needed him to find her repellent.

So repellent that he'd be willing to give up his house rather than marry her.

Alice had to make absolutely certain the option of marrying her was inconceivable.

She had more pressing problems. No Fred. No passage to Calcutta. No reuniting the missing chapters of the *Kama Sutra* to make a whole.

An adventureless lifetime stretching before her. Her painstaking translation moldering in a drawer somewhere, unread. Unloved.

She must rid herself of the marquess swiftly and concoct another plan.

But how to send him running?

A man who wore such tight-fitting breeches required something custom-fit, Alice decided.

Hit him where it hurts the most.

"Papa, I simply can't marry Lord Hatherly given his"—she arched her eyebrows delicately and lowered her eyes to his snug breeches—"*condition.*"

"My *what* now?" Hatherly asked with a frown.

"The price you've paid for a lifetime of dissolution and dissipation."

"I've absolutely no idea what you're talking about, Miss Tombs."

"Come, 'tis plain for all to see. The unhealthful sheen upon your brow." Alice warmed to her topic, improvising glibly. "The grayish pallor of your skin." Actually, his skin was a nicely tanned shade, as if he liked to be out of doors in summer in only his shirtsleeves. "How your hands tremor."

He looked down at one of his large hands for a moment in puzzlement.

She shook her head sadly. "It is ever so with gentlemen who overindulge in drink, fatty meats, and other immoderate pleasures of the flesh."

Hatherly stared at her with a gratifyingly dazed expression.

"Stop this nonsense immediately, Alice." Mama stamped her foot and set the perfectly formed clusters of curls about her cheeks shaking.

"What are you implying, Miss Tombs?" Lord Hatherly's deep, bass voice held a jagged edge.

"I'm not implying anything, my lord." She leaned closer to deliver the coup de grâce. "Everyone says you'll never be able to sire an heir. Terribly tragic, I'm sure."

She heaved a dramatic, anguished sigh, as if she were auditioning for the role of Lady Macbeth.

Out, out, damned marquess!

Hatherly stared at her as though she had crawled out from a crack in the wall. No young lady had ever dared impugn his manhood before.

"Alice," her mother wailed. "Such an indelicate topic! Are you just going to stand there, Sir Alfred? You must do something to stop your daughter! She's behaving most impertinently."

Sir Alfred hooked his thumbs into his waistcoat pockets and regarded Alice with an amused smile. "I'm rather enjoying myself, my dear. It's obvious they suit each other perfectly."

"Pardon?" Alice and Hatherly said in unison.

"We don't suit," the marquess growled.

"Not in the slightest," Alice agreed.

What a preposterous notion.

She could never care for an idle nobleman with thoroughly unwholesome appetites, and he could certainly never care for her.

All he cared for was his immediate gratification.

He'd drink himself into an early grave, if he didn't go mad first.

Of course the lady didn't suit him.

Not in temperament—she'd just implied he had brewer's droop, for God's sake—or in appearance. Overly sweet and freshly scrubbed—exactly as he'd remembered—with those deep, symmetrical dimples and glossy, light brown hair clustered in ringlets on either side of her face.

Her dress made his teeth hurt—all strawberry muslin and sugary lace—like a confection placed in a shop window to entice him into ruining his supper.

Fortunately, Nick hated sweets and he never took dessert.

He accepted a glass of sherry from a footman. He needed fortification after the night he'd had. Only a few fitful hours of sleep and then he'd gone to his friend Dalton, Duke of Osborne's house. Dalton had intimate knowledge of every gaming hell in London, and his brother Patrick was a lawyer who had promised to help determine the legalities of his father's wager.

The duke had never gambled before.

Despite his uncle's insistence, Nick had never filed the *writ de lunatico inquirendo* and been appointed his father's committee. He hadn't wanted to drag his father through the lengthy and humiliatingly public process of being found insane.

Where the devil was Stubbs? The caretaker had vanished without a trace. Nick found it difficult to believe that the gentle, caring giant he'd hired to watch over the duke could have led him so very far astray.

Nick swallowed more of Sir Alfred's lamentable sherry. He needed something to alleviate the worst of the pounding in his skull.

Slamming his glass down on a table for emphasis, Nick planted his feet firmly and crossed his arms. This had gone on long enough. "We need privacy, Sir Alfred."

He and the baronet would talk gentleman to gentleman.

There would most likely be fists involved.

Though the baronet didn't appear easy to topple. Brawny arms and bushy whiskers. Looked like he should be throwing logs onto a barge somewhere.

Sir Alfred's calculating smile said he knew he had Nick over a barrel and was enjoying every moment. "Certainly, Lord Hatherly," he said with a jovial chuckle. "Come, my dear, privacy is required." He set a hand under his wife's elbow and nudged her toward the door.

Lady Tombs dug in her heels and turned her head, twining one of the ribbons of her lace cap around a plump finger. "It was gratifying to make your acquaintance, Lord Hatherly," she said in a high, tremulous voice. "I do fervently hope that we shall become far more intimately acquainted in the coming days. Why, as I was saying to Sir Alfred—"

"Come, come, the marquess wants privacy." Sir Alfred propelled her forward.

Miss Tombs shot Nick a pointed barb of a glance and followed after her parents.

Sir Alfred nodded at the footmen and they left the room first. The wife followed after one last bright smile at Nick.

Sir Alfred flashed Nick a conspiratorial grin. "I'll leave the two of you to become better acquainted."

Before Nick could protest, the wily baronet was gone, slamming the door, leaving his daughter behind.

A key turned in the lock.

"Wait," Nick shouted after him. "I meant privacy with *you*. Gentleman to gentleman."

"Father." Miss Tombs pounded on the door. "This isn't funny." There was no answer. "Father?"

She slowly turned around, keeping her back against the door, eyeing him warily. "This is his idea of a little joke, I'm afraid."

Clearly, Nick was being outmaneuvered.

He probably should have eaten some breakfast before he came charging over to the baronet's house. Last night's brandy still sloshed in his belly and it wasn't mixing well with the inferior sherry.

Only one thing to be done.

Drink more.

Nick poured another glass of sherry, willing his hands not to shake again before the damnably perceptive Miss Tombs.

She sashayed to the windows and flung the curtains wide.

He winced in the sudden slash of sunlight.

"Oh, I do hope you didn't overimbibe last night, Lord Hatherly," she said with a sugary smile, her voice dripping with false concern. "I've heard you rarely venture out of your house in the daylight."

Her dimples were truly impressive.

They'd be lethal if she had any idea how to use them.

"Does your father often lock you in libraries with strange gentlemen to become better acquainted, Miss Tombs?"

"Only with gentlemen who were foolish enough to allow themselves to be gambled away."

"The duke didn't know what he was doing."

"That doesn't help our plight, now does it? He mucked everything up."

"I think it was your father that did the mucking."

"Well, the two of them landed us in this steaming mess."

"A poetic turn of phrase, Miss Tombs."

"An appropriate one, Lord Hatherly."

Her eyes sparked with intelligence, wit, and . . . displeasure.

She was as unhappy about the situation as he was. *Intriguing.*

"You don't want to marry me," he stated with surprise.

Marriageable ladies had been heaving themselves at him since he came of age. They were usually willing to overlook the family curse of lunacy in pursuit of the title . . . and the handsome devil that came with it.

"Congratulations." She rolled her eyes. "Give the marquess a prize."

He hadn't noticed before what an unusual shade her eyes were. More intensely green than blue, with flecks of gold around the irises.

"*Why* don't you wish to marry me?" he asked.

"Don't sound so surprised, my lord." She folded her arms over her chest. He couldn't help noticing that the motion mounded her breasts over her bodice enticingly.

She had nice breasts. Generous and lush for such a slender frame.

"It's not the usual response I receive from young ladies."

"I'm supposed to swoon at your feet, is that it?"

"It's been known to happen," he goaded, in order to watch the color heighten in her cheeks.

"Allow me to assure you that I have never swooned, not once in my life, and I don't intend to begin now just because you'll be a duke and you're almost stupidly handsome and your buckskin breeches are tight enough to—" She bit her lower lip, her cheeks flushing, as if she hadn't meant to say all of that out loud.

"Please, by all means, finish your sentence," Nick drawled.

Miss Tombs turned her back on him and gazed out the window.

"My breeches are tight enough to . . ." he prompted, moving closer. "Turn a girl's head? Give a lady ideas?"

She wheeled around, swirling the lace of her hem into motion. "Cause permanent damage."

Nick chuckled appreciatively.

He was beginning to like her unusually bawdy

sense of humor. She certainly talked about a man's
private parts more than your ordinary young miss.

If he had to be locked in a library with a lady, she
might as well make him laugh.

And he might as well make her blush.

He was beginning to enjoy making her blush.

Drawing the edges of his cutaway coat back
even further with his fists, and drawing her gaze
right where he wanted it, he struck a wide-legged
stance.

"You seem to have quite a fascination with
my . . . *anatomy*, Miss Tombs. That's the second time
you've mentioned the subject today."

She jerked her gaze away from his crotch, her
cheeks nearly a match for her dress.

"You're insufferably arrogant. Not all young
ladies are fascinated by your anatomy *or* your title."

"More's the pity. And here I was beginning to
think we might suit after all."

Her eyes widened. "Oh no. We don't suit. Not
at all. A wife would be a dreadful impediment to
your aimless life of debauchery."

"An impediment, Miss Tombs?" His gaze lingered on her cupid's bow of a mouth. Had she ever
been kissed? She set her lips into a thin line and
glared at him. Probably not, he decided. "Or an en-
hancement."

Maybe it was the lingering effects of last night's
brandy, or the two hours of sleep, but a reckless
idea occurred to him.

Reckless, amoral, and probably extremely ill-
advised.

Like all his best ideas.

Maybe the pretty-yet-prickly Miss Tombs *was* the solution.

A temporary engagement could buy Nick the time he needed to find Stubbs and determine the truth of this situation. There had to be a way out of this predicament that allowed Nick to keep both Sunderland *and* his freedom.

Engagements were broken regularly in the *haut ton*. As evidenced by what had happened with his friend James, Duke of Harland. He'd left his pedigreed bride at the altar and married her illegitimate half sister. Now the two ladies were, improbably, the best of friends.

Nick didn't want to hurt Miss Tombs, of course.

He'd end it well before the altar.

The more he thought about it, and the more sherry he drank, the more a temporary engagement seemed like just the thing.

Now . . . to convince Miss Tombs to see things his way.

He'd never had any difficult convincing women to do exactly what he required of them.

He gave her one of his patented slow-burning smiles.

Her eyes narrowed suspiciously. "Why are you smiling at me so wolfishly, Lord Hatherly?"

"Because I remembered that two ladies of your acquaintance married two of my friends. Could this be"—he gazed into her eyes, drawing his words out on a husky whisper—"written in the stars?"

The incredulity on her face was comic. "Written in the stars? Really, Lord Hatherly." She shook her head. "What's gotten into you? I thought you were against this marriage."

This woman might require a bit more convincing.

"Until I spoke with you in seclusion, Miss Tombs. Until those delicious dimples of yours conquered my—"

"Stop right there." She narrowed her eyes further, and her dimples disappeared. "We both know why you came here today, and it was not to pledge devotion to my dimples. I've no idea why you're suddenly so interested in charming me." She tossed her head. "It won't work, you know. I'm thoroughly immune to your charm."

This woman might require a *lot* of convincing.

For the first time in his adult life, Nick actually began to doubt his powers of seduction.

Perish that thought. You're the master of seduction. Hedonistic Hatherly. The Wicked Marquess. One kiss and she's yours.

No, too obvious.

The bigger challenge would be to awaken her sensuality. Make *her* want to kiss *him*.

Instead of moving closer, he walked to a sofa and, ignoring all social protocol, sat in front of a standing lady.

Seduction was nine-tenths anticipation.

He spread his arms across the mahogany edge of one of Sir Alfred's velvet sofas, drawing her eyes to the muscles he kept well-honed with fencing and riding.

She helped herself to a long, lingering look.

The pink flush in her cheeks deepened.

"Why don't you have a seat?" he asked. He patted

the velvet cushion next to him. "We'll talk this through in comfort."

Warily, she seated herself as far from him as possible on the sofa—back straight, hands folded in her lap, ankles crossed—all neatly folded up.

"I'm sure you would prefer a more conventional and accommodating heiress," she said. "What about Lady Melinda? She loves to swoon at your feet." She clenched her hands together. "I'm decidedly peculiar. Everyone says so. You don't want odd, ungracious me thrust upon you."

"Oh, I don't know, Miss Tombs." He settled back against the sofa, shifting his knees wider, increasing the heat in his gaze. "Having you *thrust* upon me could be quite entertaining."

Chapter 3

❦❦

Even young maids should study the *Kama Sutra* along with its arts and sciences before marriage. Some learned men object, and say that females, not being allowed to study any science, should not study the *Kama Sutra*. But this objection does not hold good.

The Kama Sutra of Vātsyāyana

It could be quite educational as well, thought Alice.

Oh, the images his words conjured.

Naughty images . . . wanton imaginings.

Kshiraniraka, or milk and water embrace . . . the woman is sitting on the lap of the man . . .

She'd translated those words from the *Kama Sutra* last night, working by the light of a single candle while the household slept.

They'd only been words upon a page . . . until now.

Now there happened to be an enormous marquess sprawled next to her on a sofa, muscular arms spread wide like an invitation, whispering wickedly of having her thrust upon him.

What, *precisely*, did that mean? It was quite difficult translating a text about a subject of which she had absolutely no firsthand experience.

She couldn't help being curious.

Oh no, Alice. Remember where your curiosity leads? Remember when you were seven and you tasted that orange mushroom with the white spots? Missed the county fair. Sick and miserable for a whole week.

She wasn't seven anymore. And Lord Hatherly was far more appealing than a speckled mushroom . . . and probably far more dangerous to a girl's wellbeing.

It was the way he smiled, as if he had a secret.

As if he *were* the secret.

The answer to all her many questions.

"What are you thinking about, Miss Tombs?" he asked in a deep, sonorous voice that harbored a rumble of amusement.

Alice startled, blushing even harder. "Nothing. Nothing at all." She struggled to calm her rapid breathing.

Regain your composure this instant, Alice Perpetua Felicity Tombs, she admonished sternly. *You don't want to bed him, you want to bedevil him. Inspire him to leave and never come back.*

She was immune to his particular type of decadence.

Well, wasn't she? She risked a sideways glance.

No one should have a jaw so chiseled or eyes so silver. It made her almost angry how handsome he was.

His appearance is the only agreeable thing about him, and he can't take credit for what God bestowed.

Be rid of him quickly and thoroughly.

She must marshal her thoughts to order. Lead the charge.

Hunt the hunter.

"Now then, Dimples," he said. "Why don't you tell me the real reason you don't wish to marry."

Had he called her *Dimples*? He was definitely going down in flames.

She flipped through her mental list of peer-dispersing tactics, hitting upon one that, while not foolproof, could be effective in this situation.

"It's not that I don't wish to marry, Lord Hatherly," she said. "I don't wish to marry *you*. There's a difference. My affections are . . . promised elsewhere."

He raised his eyebrows. "A secret engagement?"

"Papa will cut me off if we marry, but the gentleman cares nothing for my fortune. He's willing to marry me regardless of my prospects."

"What's his name?"

Alice searched her mind. "Darcy." *Oh, that was brilliant.* Use a character from one of her favorite novels. But it had been the first name to come to mind.

"Darcy?"

"*Professor* Darcy. He's handsome and cultured, and a perfect gentleman, though he has no title save that of professor. He wears sensible waistcoats, never red silk or patterned. He smokes a pipe after a meal, and he loves cats. Adores them. He allows my pet cat Kali to climb all over him." *You're rambling, Alice. Wind it up now.* "When we are married we will read together of an evening before the fire."

"What a charming picture—the professor and his young lady. Reading side by side, she, ignoring the foul odor of pipe tobacco, brushes cat hair from his sensible waistcoat. He proclaims that she has bewitched him, body and soul."

Alice jumped. Had he truly seen through her story so easily?

And what was even more surprising, had he read the book?

Hatherly's smile was smug and overly confident. "There's only one problem with your Professor Darcy. He doesn't exist."

"He exists!" Well, he existed in her imagination. He was the kind, scholarly gentleman she dreamt of finding when she returned from India. Though he'd have to be at least a baronet to satisfy Mama.

"Miss Tombs." He shook his head. "What's gotten into you? I know a fake fictitious fiancé when I hear of one. Men like your Professor Darcy simply don't exist, and women's boudoir novels have done womankind a grave disservice by suggesting that they do. You can't have both the sophisticated gentleman of experience and the domesticated, solicitous spouse wrapped in one ardent package."

"Fine. You've caught me out, Lord Hatherly." She infused her voice with the bitterness she felt when she thought of her lost voyage to India. "If I were plain, I wouldn't be expected to fetch such a prize as you, you know. In some cultures I'd be considered downright unsightly. The Aegean countries, for example, would avoid my light greenish-blue eyes for fear they held the curse of the devil."

He laughed. "If you wish to avoid marriage, perhaps you should move to Greece."

"I can easily see how you and my father will benefit from our match. He gains your aristocratic business connections, and you keep Sunderland House. What I fail to see is how I'm to profit by it."

"I should think that's obvious. You'll be the Duchess of Barrington someday. A member of an elite group of the most privileged ladies in England."

"My mother and father are hungry for the title, not I. No one seems to care what I want."

"What *do* you want? Perhaps I can give it to you." His voice dropped so low that her throat buzzed in response. "If you'll allow me to try."

She wanted to follow the plan and board her father's merchant ship bound for Calcutta in July, with the *Kama Sutra* and her grandfather's other manuscripts safe in her trunks.

India! She could already see it in her mind's eye: a riot of orange and red silks, domed temples glinting in the sun, heat shimmering from the streets, the fragrant scent of saffron.

Only she wouldn't be going anywhere. Not with Fred married and staying in France.

She couldn't tell Lord Hatherly about her shattered dreams.

He'd only give that mocking laugh and smile his smug smile.

Brush her dreams aside like castles made of sand instead of a solid bulwark she'd built stone by stone, word by word.

Women were mere amusements to him. He'd

probably never even considered they might want something other than pleasing a man.

His brow wrinkled slightly. "Miss Tombs?"

"You don't wish to marry me, Lord Hatherly," she said. "I'm notoriously peculiar. Have I told you about my devotion to a frugivorous diet? After reading the writings of Mr. Shelley I decided to give up eating—"

"You don't have to do this, you know," he interrupted.

Alice paused in mid-explanation. "What am I doing, pray tell?"

"Putting on an act. Saying outrageous things to make me run away. Why don't you try being yourself for a moment? Tell me the truth," he coaxed. "Why don't you want to marry?"

Had her powers of dissuasion finally failed her?

She'd been so very successful at eliminating suitors, and Lord Hatherly shouldn't be such a difficult case.

It was only that she couldn't think straight when he sat so close. Near enough to smell the sweet sherry on his lips and an underlying aroma of cedar, like the inside of her trousseau trunk.

He hadn't doused himself in musky cologne like Lord White.

Why did he have to be so devastatingly attractive? It muddled a girl's mind.

One of his large hands rested close to her on the sofa.

What depraved things had those hands done recently? The thought started a curious fizzing sensation in her lower belly, like she was a jar of apple cider left in the sun too long.

"I want to know the real Miss Alice Tombs." He caught her hand and lifted her wrist to his ear, as if listening for her pulse. "What has made you so prickly?" His breath tickled the inside of her wrist. "And why don't you wish to marry?"

She wasn't prepared for the jolting sensation that rocked through her body when he flipped her hand over, stroking her palm with one rough-padded fingertip, and kissed her palm.

A crackling. Like sliding her stockinged feet across a carpet. A charge of energy from her fingertips through the ends of her hair.

"You want to know who I am, Lord Hatherly?" She snatched her hand away. "I'm the one lady on this earth who is thoroughly immune to your powers of seduction."

"Oh really?"

"Really." Maybe if she repeated it enough, it might begin to be true. "And there's no use in you seeking to convince me to marry you. I won't wed until after I have at least one exciting adventure abroad."

The truth just slipped out.

She waited for the disbelieving laughter, the cold light of derision in his eyes, but he appeared to be absorbing her confession with gravity.

"Then why haven't you embarked on a tour before now?"

"My mother feels that females should not be allowed to stray from hearth and home. Our place is at the heart of the circle of domestic bliss. Providers, nurturers subjugated by the needs of others. She wants me wed and with child immediately."

"Ah. I see." He cleared his throat. "And you have other plans."

For some reason she felt compelled to tell him the truth. Why? Maybe it was because he hadn't laughed at her or acted shocked.

She nodded. "I do."

"My mother lives abroad—in Switzerland at the moment. My parents' marriage is . . . not a happy one." While his knowing smile never faltered, there was a momentary flicker of emotion in his eyes, but it was gone before Alice could pinpoint what it had been.

Pain? Regret?

Alice didn't know what to say in response. She'd heard the rumors of his father's madness, but the duke rarely left Sunderland House.

Could there be a deeper reason behind Lord Hatherly's dissipated lifestyle? A reason to forget himself in all the wine, women, and wickedness?

"Where do you wish to go?" he asked.

"I will journey to Calcutta in India."

"An unusual choice for a young lady. But your family has ties to the East India Company, is that why?"

"Partially. It's also because I have a talent for languages and among them, Sanskrit. I'm working on a translation of an ancient manuscript I discovered in my late grandfather's personal collection."

"Sanskrit?" He cocked his head.

Alice bristled. "You think me incapable of such a skill?"

"I was merely startled by your choice of languages," he said smoothly, recovering his seductive smile. "I see nothing objectionable about you translating some dried-up, boring old texts."

The *Kama Sutra* was hardly dry and boring, but he could believe what he wanted.

"I know you must think translating texts an unsuitable occupation for a lady."

"But don't you see?" He caught her hand again and stroked a thumb across her knuckles. "This is perfect! If you marry me you may trot across the entire globe and you won't hear the slightest protest. In fact, I would do my utmost to encourage such endeavors." He placed his free hand over his cravat. "I swear it."

She searched his face suspiciously. "You would?"

"Absolutely. I don't want a wife in London. I'd rather have one in India."

She considered that for a moment. It sounded plausible. He was such an unrepentant rake that, if he were forced to marry, he wouldn't want a wife to interfere with his disreputable life.

He waved a careless hand through the air. "Publish dry, scholarly tomes. Found a female colony of bluestockings in the Amazon, for all I care. I can see you are highly intelligent and highly motivated. Go forth, Dimples, go forth and conquer the world!"

This man sitting next to her was conceited, promiscuous, and cared only for his own pleasure, but she sensed he was speaking the truth.

She was even beginning to wonder whether his arrogance masked something more substantial and interesting.

In her years of peer repelling, Alice had learned that a gentleman couldn't feign respect for a lady. Alice always saw through their feeble attempts to placate her, their belittling "aren't you clevers" and their amused smiles when she explained the origin of a word, or made a comparison between cultures.

He might call her *Dimples*, but Lord Hatherly wasn't threatened by her goals, mostly because they were convenient for him, but also because he wasn't threatened by intelligent females.

Which was extremely refreshing, and almost made her want to respect him back.

But of course that was out of the question. The man kept dozens of mistresses. Her friend Charlene had been inside Sunderland House once. She'd said there were scantily clad women and poppy-addled poets around every corner.

Still . . . she'd never considered that a particular type of husband, a disinterested one, wouldn't be a hindrance to her plans at all.

When Hatherly had stormed into the study, she'd seen him as another hurdle to clear—an impediment to her plans.

Could he be a pathway, instead of an obstruction?

Could marrying him actually be the fastest route to making her dreams come true? A respectable matron could choose to voyage. She wouldn't be breaking any major societal rules.

Hatherly lightly stroked her palm. "Marry me and sail off into the sunset."

"You truly wouldn't care what I did, as long as I left you alone?"

A slight smile tilted his lips. "That's about the sum of it."

"You'll continue having affaires."

He shrugged. "I'm a man."

His infidelity shouldn't concern her. It was exactly the manner of marriage preferred by elegant society; a convenient arrangement, nothing more.

They would be separated not only by a lack of affection but by the distance of mountains and oceans.

His fingers continued stroking nonchalantly, as if by accident.

What he proposed was more freedom than she'd ever imagined.

A lifetime of freedom. A married female could come and go as she pleased. Travel unmolested.

Excitement danced between Alice's shoulder blades as she thought about all the adventures she could have. The whole world open to her exploration.

Alice loved Fred dearly, but he was supremely unsuited to traveling. He hadn't wanted to go to the Continent—he'd even begged their father not to send him—and Alice had sat by, holding her tongue, as her brother attempted to refuse the adventures she so desperately craved.

While Fred toured Europe, Alice had been sequestered behind closed doors with Mrs. Grissingham-Porter, the thin-lipped widow charged with the unenviable task of transforming Alice into a fine lady.

The humorless widow had quickly learned that

bookish country mice do not diamonds of the first water make. Nor even of the third or fourth water, whatever that meant.

While being fitted for ridiculously frolicsome bonnets and restrictive kid gloves, Alice couldn't help thinking that if she'd been born male it would have been she on that ship, sailing off for adventure.

The only journey her mother fervently longed for Alice to make was the short distance from the entrance of a church to the altar. It was all she spoke of—finding a titled husband for Alice so their family might raise themselves up from the mire of their origins in trade.

Another thought occurred to her.

Her parents wouldn't be satisfied unless there was a betrothal today. But that didn't mean a wedding must necessarily follow. If she found another way to travel to India, she could always break off an engagement.

Lord Hatherly's father owned at least five houses. She wouldn't feel too badly depriving him of one. It was expedient to go along with the engagement . . . at least for now.

"Well then, sensible Miss Alice Tombs, do we have an agreement?" He traced a line along her palm. "You go your way." His finger stopped moving, pressing the center of her hand. "And I stay right here."

His touch made her shiver with something halfway between fear and desire.

She'd never wanted a man to touch her before.

Never held her breath, waiting for the next playful, teasing swirl of a finger on her palm.

"We'll have a quiet wedding in your parlor," he announced.

"Pardon me." She pulled her hand away and waved it in front of his face. "I haven't said yes yet."

"You will. I'm exactly what you need, Dimples. A title for your parents and nothing more. No demands. No expectations. A one-way ticket to adventure. Think of the lands you'll see. The languages you'll learn."

"It's quite a momentous decision to make. I already sent one suitor away today."

"Really?" His fingers tightened around her hand again. "Who was it?"

"Lord White."

"White?" he exploded. "That frilly fop?"

"I dispatched him with a hairpin."

"A hairpin?"

She nodded. "He attempted to kiss me, and he received a swift jab with a hairpin for his troubles."

Hatherly chuckled. "I wish I could have seen his reaction."

"He was rather put out."

When he smiled a real smile, not a mocking one, Alice noticed his lips were full on top, as well as on bottom, which would have been too pretty on another gentleman, but lent his lean, masculine features a hint of sensual softness.

"I've been meaning to kiss you," Hatherly said. He eyed her coiffure. "Will I receive the same treatment?"

"I suppose . . . in the interests of making an educated decision . . ." She couldn't very well decide to marry the gentleman without sampling his kiss.

What if it were as damp and uninspiring as Lord White's unpleasant embrace?

"It might be prudent, Miss Tombs," he agreed, with a serious expression.

"Very well, Lord Hatherly. You may kiss me now."

He didn't jump right in and start pawing her, as Lord White had done.

The heat in his eyes surrounded her—like entering a warm house on a frozen, snowy night.

Rough, strong fingers caressed her cheek and he dragged a thumb across her lower lip.

He touched her with confidence and self-assurance so profound that every lineament of his body, every brush of his fingers, proclaimed: *Worship me.*

His large hand cupped her chin and tilted her head back.

Still no kiss.

It was the anticipation that made her tingle. The utter certainty that she was in the hands of a master and would soon receive her first lesson in the practical application of the principles of pleasure.

Finally, his lips touched hers softly, only a subtle pressure . . . a whisper.

He stroked the back of her neck with both his large hands, his thumbs tilting her jaw into the embrace. He kissed her neck, her jaw, her dimples. His teeth nipped at her lower lip, asking her lips to . . . open?

Gracious. Well, if that's what rakes expected . . .

She opened for him and his tongue slipped inside her mouth. It felt so foreign to taste him inside her. Ripe, sugary fig flavor of sherry. Warm, firm lips.

She'd read about the pressing kind of kiss . . . when tongues met and conversed . . . but what on earth was she supposed to do with *her* tongue?

He deepened the kiss, angling her head back, his hands bracketing her cheeks, positioning her lips, his tongue stroking hers with sure, commanding movements.

Oh. My. No more time to think. This kiss was becoming serious.

She clasped her arms around his neck, showing him that she approved.

She opened her mouth wider. He entered deeper and made a low moaning sound that traveled through her body and settled somewhere in her belly.

His hands moved to her waist, shaping and squeezing through the layers of lace and muslin, and his thumbs grazed the underside of her breasts.

The warm, bubbly sensation in her chest heightened, made her press against him, wrap her arms tighter, seeking . . . *something*.

When his lips left hers, she made a disappointed noise in the back of her throat. She didn't want the kiss to end. Not when it was becoming so promisingly educational.

He gazed into her eyes, his lips tilted up at one corner. "Well?"

You're hired, Alice thought. "Ah yes . . . that was . . . quite satisfactory. I will marry you, Lord Hatherly," she blurted.

You ninny, she thought. *Don't make him even more conceited.*

Why did he make her so uncharacteristically flustered?

He set her away from him and readjusted his cuffs. "I'll pound on the door until your enterprising father arrives and then we may inform him of the glad tidings." He offered her his arm. She slid her hand over the solid steel muscles beneath the fine fabric of his coat. How did he keep himself so very fit? she wondered. And was he this solid . . . everywhere?

She'd thought of him as a map earlier, and she'd been determined to cross him, outwit him, and rid herself of him swiftly. Now it appeared he could be a map of an entirely different variety.

A new land she would soon have the opportunity to explore. And, if his kiss was any indication, the exploration would be very enlightening, indeed.

This was the perfect convenient arrangement for both of them.

Alice smoothed her skirts and jabbed her hairpins back into place. "Please don't mention my travel plans to Papa."

"It will be our little secret."

"We'll let him think you kissed me into compliance."

"Oh, but I did, Dimples," he said with a thoroughly wicked smile.

"Ha!" Well, it was only partially true. "You may tell yourself so, Lord Hatherly, if that's what you need to believe."

Chapter 4

◎◎

Friends should possess the following qualities: They should tell the truth. They should
not be changed by time. They should not
reveal your secrets.

The Kama Sutra of Vātsyāyana

"*Please, please* tell me you did not agree to marry
Lord Hatherly because of a *kiss*," exclaimed Alice's
dear friend Charlene, Duchess of Harland. "I
thought you were more sensible than that, Alice."

"Must have been one monumental kiss,"
laughed Thea, Duchess of Osborne, her lively blue
eyes dancing with mischief.

The three friends were curled up in comfortable
velvet armchairs in Thea's chambers at Osborne
Court, drinking chocolate and baring their souls.

They gathered as often as possible given Charlene and Thea's many familial and societal obli-
gations, but this time it had been Alice who had
difficulty leaving her house.

Her mother was already frantically planning the
wedding. It was to be a grand pageant designed

to proclaim to the world that their daughter was marrying a marquess, she would be a duchess someday, and the doors that had remained closed to the Tombs family must now miraculously swing open.

"This truly is the most delicious chocolate," Alice said, taking a sip of the richly spiced Duchess Cocoa that Charlene and her husband created. "Has Harland changed the recipe?"

Charlene's blue eyes narrowed. "Do *not* change the subject."

"Details," Thea said, bouncing in her chair. "We want details."

"Well," said Alice, "when Lord Hatherly arrived I could see that he was as displeased about the marriage as I was, perhaps even more so, and then . . . something changed." What had changed? Why had he suddenly become so eager for the betrothal? She'd been so busy kissing the man she'd ceased to wonder about his sudden reversal.

"I meant details about the kiss, you ninny," Thea said.

"Oh. It was . . ." Alice's heart sped, remembering the kiss. "It was like running as fast I could across a field with the wind in my face. It made me feel reckless and . . . alive."

A wrinkle appeared between Charlene's curved brows. She shook her head, and her long, golden curls tumbled over her shoulders. "This isn't good, Alice. Not Hatherly. Anyone save Hatherly. You can't fall in love with an *actual* rake, sweetheart. He'll never love you back. And he's bound to break your heart."

"Who said anything about love?" asked Alice. "We came to a mutually expedient business agreement."

"Even worse," Charlene muttered.

"He wants to keep Sunderland House and I need to be a respectable matron in order to journey to India as planned."

"But what happened to Fred?" Thea asked. "Wasn't he supposed to accompany you to India this summer?"

"Fred married a Parisian opera singer."

"Truly?" Thea blinked. "Stolid, dependable, horseman Fred?"

"Good for Fred," said Charlene. "Marrying for love."

"It may be good for Fred, but it's not good for me," Alice replied.

Thea nodded. "I see exactly why. Fred made an imprudent match and so your mother is even more desperate for you to make a brilliant one. So you're marrying Hatherly to please your parents. It's very noble of you, Alice, but you shouldn't let your parents dictate your life. You have a choice in the matter. Think carefully. You can always run away to India."

"A young, unmarried lady, alone on a merchant ship to India, against the wishes of her parents? I'm not as bold as you, Thea. And honestly, my mother may be silly, flighty, and overpious, but I don't wish to see her humiliated further, now that Fred has disappointed her so keenly."

Alice didn't care about social ranking, but to her mother it meant the fulfillment of a lifelong dream.

Her mother, the small-town girl from Yorkshire, born a vicar's daughter, was now poised to climb the highest rungs of society. Alice didn't want to dash her mother's dream.

"Still, you mustn't marry Hatherly only to please your mother," Thea scolded.

"I'm not. I'm marrying him to please myself."

Both of her friends stared at her from blue-gray eyes gone wide with questions.

Sometimes it still astounded Alice how very alike the two half sisters looked—although once one knew them better it was impossible to mistake one for the other.

Charlene was the fierce, scandalous one; Thea was the passionate, artistic one; and Alice . . . well, she had been the sensible, pragmatic one, until she'd decided to throw caution to the wind and marry Lord Hatherly.

"You *want* to wed him? But . . . but you've been repelling suitors for years now. Why Hatherly?" asked Charlene.

"His kiss couldn't have been *that* monumental," agreed Thea.

"I'm marrying him for two very sensible reasons," Alice explained. "The first is that he doesn't care anything about me and will encourage me to travel. He said he doesn't want a wife in England. He'd rather have one in India."

Charlene snorted. "Sounds like Hatherly."

"Well, I suppose that is convenient," said Thea. "If you won't be able to go with Fred, you'll be free to travel as a married woman."

"And I'll present the translations as Fred's and

say he couldn't come himself because of his new marriage. It may work to my advantage, as Fred won't be there to display his utter lack of knowledge of all things Sanskrit."

"Why should Fred garner all the credit?" Thea asked.

"I don't mind. I want my scholarship to be treated seriously. This is the only way."

Thea's eyes narrowed. "That's not fair."

"What's the other reason?" Charlene asked. "You said there were two."

"Remember how I told you one of the texts I'm translating is rather . . . naughty?"

Thea smirked. "Ah . . . I see where this is going. You've been reading naughty books and now you're curious about lovemaking. And Hatherly is rather undeniably attractive. So it *was* the kiss."

"Thea," Charlene remonstrated. "Alice can't marry Hatherly simply because she's *curious*. He's handsome, and well he knows it. The man mows through paramours like a reaper at harvest time. I don't want you to get cut, Alice."

"I'm more than merely curious, Charlene. I have a scholarly and semantic interest in becoming well-versed in the particulars of physical gratification so that my translation is more nuanced and my technical knowledge more complete. I'm finding that it's no use me attempting to translate experiences I know absolutely nothing about."

Charlene's eyebrows arched. "The particulars of physical gratification?"

"Just how naughty *is* this book of yours?" Thea asked.

If they only knew. The few chapters of the *Kama Sutra* that she possessed were extremely explicit about the principles and postures of lovemaking.

Alice's cheeks heated. "I don't see why I shouldn't think of lovemaking as a foreign language. One which I'll be quite fluent in with the proper teacher, if I set my mind to my studies."

The ability for pleasure must already be living inside her, waiting to be awakened, in the same way the ability to learn new languages flourished so easily. Of course, she would have to discard her maidenly modesty and misgivings.

Alice closed her eyes and touched the center of her palm, recalling the stimulating sensation of Lord Hatherly's caress. She rather thought with Hatherly as her teacher, she could swiftly overcome her trepidation and enter fully into the spirit of libidinous pursuits.

If his fingers brushing her palm set her body tingling in such an interesting manner, one could only begin to imagine what might happen if those same rough-padded fingers were to brush . . . other areas.

"Sweetheart." Charlene's voice intruded into Alice's wayward reverie.

Her eyelids lifted, only to find her two best friends staring at her with concern.

Charlene gripped both of Alice's hands. "Listen to me. I know you are thinking of this as an intellectual exercise, but believe me, the act of love can't be controlled so easily. It's the most intimate conversation two people can have and it sometimes awakens uncontrollable emotions. I'm afraid for your heart, Alice. It's not like you to be so impulsive."

Alice drew her hands away. "I'm not stupid. I know what I'm doing. This is my choice."

"Of course you're not stupid," exclaimed Thea. "You're more intelligent than Charlene and me combined. You are fluent in six languages, for heaven's sakes."

"This manuscript fragment I possess could be very significant if united with the rest of the work housed at Fort Williams College in Calcutta. It's a treatise on pleasure in all its many forms. If published, it could be quite educational for the young ladies of the world."

"Well, you know how I feel about education for females," said Charlene. She and her husband ran a shelter and school in Surrey for vulnerable young girls who had fallen on hard times. "Keeping girls ignorant of the workings of their bodies only leads to bad situations. Ignorance is a weapon men use to maintain their societal superiority."

"This manuscript teaches that females should seek pleasure as well," Alice said. "And it enumerates sixty-four methods for obtaining that pleasure. Not only physical release, but the pleasures experienced through our five senses . . . and our emotions."

Thea's eyes went wide and blue as a summer sky. "I'd like to read this book."

"And you shall. As soon as my missing chapters are reunited with the whole."

"I can't believe I'm saying this," Charlene said

grudgingly, "but maybe marrying Hatherly is an expedient way to achieve your goal."

Thea reached over and touched Alice's cheek. "Never mind that I don't want you to leave for purely selfish reasons, but have you thought that marrying Hatherly means you can't marry anyone else? I had thought . . . well, there was someone else I had thought of for you."

"Someone else?" asked Alice. This was the first she'd heard of such a notion.

"I was waiting to tell you. I know how you feel about matrimony, but now that you're willing to marry, you should think of Patrick."

"Your brother-in-law?" Alice tilted her head. "Somehow I don't think Patrick's looking for a wife. He always has such a sadness hidden in his eyes, even when his lips are smiling."

Thea had told Alice of Patrick's troubled past and all of the loss he'd experienced.

"Yes, but he truly is the most wonderful man," said Thea. "Such a good father to his son, Van. And you make him laugh more than anyone else, Alice."

"I make everyone laugh," Alice replied. "Because I'm so odd."

"Patrick would be better than Hatherly," Charlene mused, sipping the last of her cocoa. "Actually, *anyone* would be better than Hatherly."

"Dalton and Patrick are in the library right now." Thea set down her mug and jumped from her chair. "Let's go and talk to them."

"Thea, I'm not going to marry Patrick." Alice motioned for her friend to resume her seat. "It's not a good, or even a decent, gentleman I require.

At this point what I need the most is the freedom to travel. And the best way to achieve that is by marrying Hatherly. He wants nothing from me save my absence."

"It sounds rather lonely," Thea said. "What happens afterward? After you return from India?"

"I'm willing to relinquish the dream of reading by the fireside with a loving spouse, for a month of instruction in the arts of love from a temporary husband, followed by blessed freedom."

Thea smiled. "It's possible to have both freedom and love, isn't that so, Charlene?"

Charlene nodded. "The right gentleman won't take away your independence, Alice."

"The right gentleman hasn't come along yet," Alice said, with a hint of bitterness. "As Hatherly's wife I will have my language scholarship, my travels, and I will not be married to some vain prig like Lord White who would expect me to fawn all over him and listen to his unpoetic pronouncements all day long. Or, even worse, a gentleman who might be cruel to me." At her friends' worried expressions, Alice smiled bravely. "I know what I'm doing. I'm far too sensible to fall in love with Lord Hatherly."

She'd never felt herself to be even in the slightest danger of falling in love. And she certainly would never be so imprudent as to give her heart to a rake like Hatherly.

"I hope so," Thea said.

Charlene squeezed Alice's hand. "I know you're strong, and I know you have a plan for your life. But please be cautious and careful. Be very, very careful, sweetheart."

"Have you seen this one, Hatherly?" Dalton, Duke of Osborne, asked as Nick strode into his library at Osborne Court. He flourished a roll of newsprint at Nick.

"I've seen them all," Nick said glumly. He flung himself into a chair and held out his hand for a glass of Dalton's excellent Irish whiskey.

The penny paper satirists were having a ball with his forced betrothal to Miss Tombs. Drawings of him in bonnets on an auction block, or him in a bridal gown and veil with Miss Tombs at his side with a drooping moustache and a dress sword.

"All of London's laughing at me," Nick said. "It's not that funny, Patrick."

"It's hilarious," said Dalton's brother Patrick Fellowes, with another snort of laughter and a devilish gleam in his light green eyes. "You look so fetching in a bonnet, Hatherly."

"Doesn't suit me, that bonnet," Nick grumbled. "I'd have preferred a stuffed finch on top instead of a cluster of cherries."

Patrick chuckled. "Cherries are more symbolic."

"Ha ha," Nick said.

He swallowed half the whiskey and felt almost immediately more cheerful. "So what have you two uncovered? Any news of Stubbs? Was he the one who escorted the duke to the Crimson?" He turned to Patrick. "And was the wager even binding?"

"It's a good thing you're already seated," Dalton said. "You may want another drink."

"That bad?"

"Worse. Much worse."

Perfect. More bad news. Nick held out his glass for a refill. "Out with it, then. I'm ready."

Dalton crossed his formidable arms over his chest. "I made the rounds of the hells and spoke with my inside contacts. This isn't the first time His Grace has gambled and lost heavily. As it turns out, for the past two months, he's been gambling frequently."

"Pardon?" Nick exploded. "But I hired Stubbs to watch him . . . oh . . . damn it all! I can't believe Stubbs would do this. I trusted him implicitly."

"I'm afraid Mr. Stubbs has been leading the duke to the lowest gambling hells, encouraging him to be reckless, and pocketing any profits," said Dalton with a pitying look. "Though it was mostly losses from what I gather."

Fury spiked through Nick like the sudden onset of a tropical fever. "I'll murder Stubbs when I find him. How could this happen?"

"There could be someone else behind the scenes," Patrick mused. "Someone who perhaps coerced or hired Mr. Stubbs and wishes to discredit you and the duke. Cause damage to you financially."

"How much damage are we talking?"

"More whiskey?" Dalton said.

Nick groaned and placed his chin on his fist. "Yesterday I received an accounting of my mother's latest bills. Five hundred quid for her milliner. *For bonnets.* Does the woman discard them after one wearing? Three hundred for monogrammed jeweled cravat pins. Some young buck with the initials S.C."

"You may want to ask her to economize," Patrick said.

"You don't know my mother. She's Swiss French. She must have the very best of everything."

"In that case, you may wish to marry Miss Tombs immediately," said Dalton.

Nick's head snapped up.

Had he truly joined the ranks of impoverished peers who required an heiress to bail them out of financial straits?

Though he'd already made up his mind to go through with the marriage.

When he'd left the baronet's house he'd had the sinking feeling that he would never be able to hurt Miss Tombs by breaking an engagement. She'd looked at him with too much trust in her eyes. He simply couldn't bring himself to cause her pain.

He respected her too much.

Besides, he was looking forward to making her blush again. And then watching her board a ship bound for India.

A sudden vision filtered through his mind like a swirl of orange bitters mixing into a glass of whiskey.

Leggy Miss Tombs spread across his bed, long limbs twined with his.

Sliding his toes along a curved instep while tasting soft, full lips.

"Nick?"

"What's that?" Nick glanced at Dalton.

"What were you thinking about?" his friend asked. "You had a silly grin on your face. You looked almost . . . contented."

"Ah, nothing. So who could be behind this? I would suspect my uncle of wanting to discredit the duke, since he's made no secret of the fact he wants his brother declared insane, but this financial loss hurts my uncle as well since his son Barnaby stands to inherit everything in the future. Already paid me a visit, my uncle. Was livid about the marriage. Thinks I'll produce an heir. Which I won't."

"After some investigation on my part, I believe we may rule out your uncle," Patrick said.

Nick tossed back the remainder of his whiskey. "I have to find Stubbs and question the man. I think you're right. I don't think he was working alone. It's just not like him."

"In the meantime," said Dalton, "I'll need you to draw up a list of suspects. Anyone you can think of who would have any reason to hold a grudge against you."

"Ah." Nick scratched his head. "That could be a long list." He wasn't always popular with the gentlemen he stole courtesans away from. Or with creditors. Or . . . It would be a long list.

"About the wager," Patrick said. "I believe that since Sir Alfred is a baronet, and your father a duke, you may be able to involve the Crown if you wished to have the debt of honor nullified. But it will require some petitioning and may be a lengthy process."

Nick sighed. "Sir Alfred was right. I don't want to subject the duke to a long public trial. He's growing more confused every day. He thinks his orchids whisper secrets to him as he tends them."

"Which leaves you only one option." Dalton raised his glass. "To Miss Tombs."

"Do you know she tried to convince her parents I had brewer's droop and couldn't father an heir? She was trying to rid herself of me."

Patrick laughed. "I *do* like Miss Tombs."

"I think Thea was rather hoping *you* might marry the girl, Patrick," Dalton said.

Patrick sputtered over the rim of his whiskey glass. "Excuse me? She's quite odd, isn't she? Always nattering on about some obscure subject."

"She's not odd so much as refreshingly forthright." Why did Nick immediately want to leap to her defense? She'd insulted him, lied to him, and done everything in her power to repel him . . . and somehow ended up completely charming him.

And not just because of her delectable dimples, or her lithe curves.

She'd kept him guessing at every turn with her clever twists of mind and that bawdy sense of humor. And she'd been so very responsive to his kiss. There was fire beneath that prim façade; he'd stake his life on it.

In short—Miss Tombs was his favorite kind of trouble. An intelligent woman who would match him in wits and sensuality . . . and then leave him in peace.

"She only agreed to marry me because she wants to travel to India and restore some ancient manuscript to a library. She speaks six languages, you know. She's been translating a fragment of some dry, dusty book from Sanskrit to English."

"And so the last one falls," Dalton intoned with a knowing smile.

"I haven't fallen," Nick protested. "I'm merely

taking a detour. She'll be gone soon enough. Wed her, bed her, and be rid of her is what I—"

"Ah," Patrick interrupted, making a strange slashing motion with his finger against his throat.

"—agreed to," Nick finished. "I wasn't even planning on going through with the nuptials when I wooed her, until I—"

"You might want to stop talking now, Hatherly," Dalton said in a strained voice.

"Why?"

"Because she's standing right behind you."

Nick jumped out of his chair and dropped his whiskey glass.

Damned if Miss Tombs wasn't standing in the doorway of the library, flanked by Dalton's wife, Thea, and his friend James's wife, Charlene.

All three ladies had thunderclouds in their eyes.

Miss Tombs's face was white, her aquamarine eyes huge, and her full lips compressed into a severe line.

"What are you doing here?" Nick blurted.

"Leaving!" She tossed her head, spun on her heel, and ran away.

"Alice," Nick yelled, racing after her. "Alice, wait!"

Chapter 5

―❧❧―

When she begins coming to see him frequently, he should carry on long conversations with her, for, says Ghotakamukha, "he never succeeds in winning her without a great deal of talking."

The Kama Sutra of Vātsyāyana

Nick caught up with Alice on the front steps, grabbing her by the elbows and whirling her to face him. "Allow me a chance to explain."

She struggled, but he easily held her trapped.

"You kissed me and you weren't even going to marry me." She tried to wrench free. "You're worse than a rake. You're a liar. Charlene was right about you."

"You didn't let me finish my sentence." He stroked a strand of hair away from her accusatory turquoise eyes. "I wasn't planning to go through with the marriage until I—"

"Discovered your coffers needed filling," she interrupted with a sharp shake of her head, flinging the hair back across her brow.

"Please listen for a moment. I was going to say to my friends that I hadn't been planning to go through with it until I realized how much I respect you and your goals. I would be extremely proud to be the man who freed you from the conventions of your sex and sent you wandering freely across the earth. I can't wait to see what you make of that freedom."

She didn't smile, but she relaxed slightly in his arms. "How convenient for you to have my father's money and no wife to worry you."

"It is convenient, I won't deny it. We suit each other perfectly because our goals go hand in hand. We both want freedom. You want the freedom to travel and I want my elderly father to remain in the comfortable and familiar surroundings of Sunderland House."

"You want to keep the house for your father's sake?"

"It would kill him to leave Sunderland and his orchid conservatory. I honestly believe that."

She regarded him for a moment with a perplexed expression. "Why didn't you tell me earlier?"

"Because everyone always assumes the worst about me, and since I usually live up to their expectations, I would hate to disabuse a young lady from thinking me anything other than the sinful sensualist she longs for me to be."

Since they were on the topic of sin, he pulled her tighter, enjoying the feeling of her lissome form in his arms.

"I'm not sure I can trust you, Lord Hatherly. I can't read your eyes. Sometimes I think you're laughing at me as though I were an amusement fashioned specifically for your enjoyment."

"You're not?"

"You know what I mean."

He dropped his teasing manner. "You can trust me in this, Alice. May I call you Alice?" he belatedly remembered to ask.

No more formality. Not when she had, apparently unconsciously, nestled closer, and slid her hands inside his coat for warmth.

"It's better than Dimples, I suppose."

"You don't like Dimples?" He stroked a hand down her back. "But it fits you so well."

She fit him so well.

Her soft curves pressed against him, making him eager to taste her lips again.

It was a chilly evening and she was only wearing a thin, muslin gown.

He wrapped his arms around her. "Of course you're free to back out of our arrangement. I wouldn't blame you. Maybe you'll even find your Professor Darcy and have those quiet nights by the fire."

"I never truly believed that fantasy. Marriage was always an abstract principle to me—something to consider only after my travels."

"There's something else you should know about me, Alice."

"Is there?" She tilted him a saucy smile. "I've done my research in the past few days. I'd say I know quite a lot about you."

"Is that so?"

"I know that your full name is Nicolas Philip Arthur Hatherly. I know you fence at Angelo's, have a fondness for steak and kidney pie, and never gamble. You ride fast horses and squire scandalous ladies to the opera, with a preference for buxom brunettes. Your favorite jewelers is—"

"Not the ordinary details, clever Alice." Nick drew circles on her lower back. "If we're truly thinking of marriage I want to be completely honest with you about the fact that I will never sire an heir. I may go mad someday, and I've no intention of passing on the curse. My cousin will inherit the dukedom after I'm gone, and during my lifetime I will always take the necessary precautions to ensure I never produce issue. So if you want to have a child, you shouldn't marry me."

"I hadn't considered offspring," she said softly, her eyes clouding over. "They were always something that came with the marriage. An eventuality, but a distant one. I always had more pressing things to think about. I think . . . I think maybe if I wanted a child I would have known that by now."

He soothed her back with both hands, warming her cold flesh. "I'll give you time to think it over. As much time as you need. Your father can't force you to marry me. We could find a way out of this if we worked together."

She smiled. "Why, Lord Hatherly, what's gotten into you? Are you trying to repel me?"

There were those deep indentations, appearing on either side of her curving lips. Nick realized he'd been waiting for her dimples to reappear like a child promised a pudding.

"My mother is already planning the wedding," she said. "It's to be a grand affair."

"I'd rather have a small, private ceremony."

"As would I, but this means so much to Mama. She'll want the world to know we've arrived into the upper echelons. And Papa will want to parade you before his investors."

"I've no doubt." Nick wondered how his life had changed so much in the space of a few days. Here he was discussing what type of wedding to have with the young, innocent lady in his arms.

He had to keep his arms around her because the night air held a frigid chill.

It wasn't because he never wanted to stop holding her. Or because she really was ridiculously pretty. The kind of pretty that made him feel like a fish out of water, flopping about waiting to be clubbed over the head and served on a platter with a sprig of parsley in his gaping mouth.

Or because she possessed a radiant, inner beauty and intelligence that glowed from her wide-set aquamarine eyes.

"I'm not sure if you're aware, Lord Hatherly, but Papa only inherited the title four years ago and it was a shock to everyone. At first he didn't even want to move to London, but Mama needled him until he agreed."

"I didn't know that."

"I've been miserable here. I loathe balls. I could see that all the gentlemen only wanted my father's fortune, and they weren't really asking *me* to dance.

I was even invited to your friend the Duke of Harland's house as one of his four potential brides. He overlooked my inferior bloodlines in favor of my father's shipping lines."

He'd heard that she'd been there, of course. All of London had followed Harland's bride hunt with bated breath.

"Of course I swiftly repelled him," Alice said, with a note of pride.

"You've been avoiding marriage for years. A gentleman has to admire your resourcefulness."

"I *was* rather successful. I had dozens of dissuasive tactics at my disposal. More than the many suitors after Papa's vast fortune."

"Your dimples may have had something to do with their advances," he teased.

"I doubt that. During my years in society, I've had plenty of time to think about what I want and don't want. You may think I'm being forced into this marriage of convenience, but I've decided to choose you, Lord Hatherly, because you are perfect for my purposes."

"You mean your travel plans."

She nodded. "My brother Fred and I had planned to voyage to Calcutta on a merchant ship in my father's fleet, which departs in two months. I will be on that ship, even if Fred will not be, and I shall be a respectable matron. Perhaps I'll even hire a respectable spinster as my companion."

"You shall?" Nick tried to catch up.

"Yes. Which means that after we marry, you will have exactly one month to fulfill your end of our bargain."

"One month." *Stop repeating everything she says, you fool.*

"If you choose to accept my terms, which I will now enumerate, we may wed. If not, I will find another gentleman."

Now who had whom over a barrel?

She would always surprise him—that much was abundantly clear. "What are your terms?" If she eventually ever wanted a babe, the bargain was over and he'd have to find another way to keep Sunderland.

"I require a month of instruction in . . ." She swallowed, her throat working nervously. She raised her head and stared him straight in the eye. ". . . in the art of . . . sexual congress."

Nick's jaw dropped. She hadn't said what he thought she'd said, had she? "Er . . . we will have to consummate the marriage at least once, to be sure."

"Not once, Lord Hatherly. On multiple occasions. I wish to learn the finer principles of physical gratification, and I hear you are the gentleman for the job. Though I may not be buxom or brunette enough for your preferences."

He couldn't help giving a surprised snort of laughter.

She drew her shoulders back, which pressed her bosom against his chest in a most distracting manner. "Do you think that's funny, Lord Hatherly? Why should it be? Men are never laughed at for seeking *experience*."

"I was merely startled by your forthrightness. I think it's an admirable goal. Extremely admirable."

"I thought you might approve."

"I approve, Dimples. I approve."

His kiss must have awakened her latent sensuality more thoroughly than he'd at first assumed. Why should he be surprised? The lady was eager for love lessons and he would be more than happy to oblige.

He touched his lips to her cheek, his body tensing with desire. If they weren't on the front steps of Osborne Court, in full view of passersby and servants, he would definitely be giving her a lesson right here and now.

Drawing a thick, glossy curl back from her cheek, he murmured in her ear, loving the way she shivered and pressed closer. "And slender ladies with light brown hair might be my new preference."

"I chose you for your wicked reputation," she stated primly. "And I expect you to deliver thorough instruction in the methods of pleasure."

"Have no fear, I'll *rise* to the challenge."

"I expect you to hold nothing back."

"I'll be more than happy to teach you everything I know." He couldn't resist sliding his hands lower and squeezing her bum. "And I'll hold *everything*."

"Lord Hatherly," she squeaked, twisting and dislodging his hands. "We are not married yet."

"I forgot."

"Please do be forewarned that while our persons may be engaged in . . . fleshly pursuits, we must both be careful to refrain from falling in love with one another, as that would be a serious breach of our business agreement."

"My thoughts exactly," Nick said, wondering how he could maneuver his hands back to her luscious bum. It had been surprisingly full. He liked a generous arse.

Hold a moment. What had she just said? Shouldn't *he* be the one warning *her* not to fall in love with him? What did she think him, some panting schoolboy who would fall in love with her if she let him between her long legs?

This conversation had somehow veered into completely uncharted territory.

Innocent young misses demanding sexual education. Setting conditions for physical relationships with no emotional entanglements.

"Haven't you ever thought of finding a love match like your friends Osborne and Harland?" she asked with a curious tilt of her chin.

"Never," he scoffed. "I'll never let one lady rule my affections. Where's the fun in that? How do you think I got my shocking reputation? You want the best instructor . . . Dimples, I'm the best."

"Your arrogance knows no bounds. Precisely why I chose you for this assignment."

Now it was an *assignment*?

"You're the unrepentant rake who doesn't believe in the existence of love."

"Not true, Dimples." He smiled lazily. "Sometimes I fall in love six times before breakfast. I worship every woman I bed and I adore them until the moment they leave."

"Well, that's certainly honest."

He never allowed himself to become too close to a woman. If the relationship had an expiration date, they never had the chance to leave him, as his mother had left his father after he went mad.

Each liaison remained a shining memory, perfect and pristine without the mess of emotions, the inevitable sordidness of the shine growing tarnished, like a coin passed through too many palms.

"Oh, one more term, Lord Hatherly."

"What's that, Dimples?" So far he liked her terms. A lot.

"I want all your attention during my brief sojourn in your home. I will not share you with courtesans. You will not bed me one night and then go off to the opera. While I reside under your roof you will be faithful to me."

"How many females do you think I keep?" he teased.

"Enough to satisfy your depraved needs."

"Ah. Yes. My depraved needs."

He wrapped a hand around her neck, keeping the pressure light—the suggestion of a lover's control.

He slid his other hand along the small of her back. Soft, feminine curves yielded to his taut frame. A slight thrust of his pelvis, and their bodies met in a new way.

Her breath caught and she wriggled, almost imperceptibly, a small shift in the angle of her hips. The suggestion that she already instinctively knew how to seek her pleasure with his body had him hard in an instant.

Oh, he was going to enjoy having Alice in his bed for a month of tutelage.

Maybe they'd never even leave the bed. He could have all their meals sent to his chambers.

"H-have your man of business draw up an agreement detailing the terms of our arrangement," Alice said breathily. "I trust you have one who is discreet?"

He nuzzled her neck and nipped at her earlobe. "The most discreet in London."

Patrick served as his solicitor on occasion. He had a strange history—he'd been stolen as a child and raised in America, but now he was restored to his rightful place as brother to a duke. He could probably have given up his profession as a lawyer, and he had, to a certain extent, but he still helped Nick with any contracts he needed, as well as other, more clandestine activities.

"Wouldn't you rather have a special license?" He kissed the hollow in the center of her neck, inhaling the fresh, bright scent of her, like a crushed leaf from a lemon tree. "You could be in my bed within the week. To begin your lessons."

She placed a hand on his cheek, stilling his movements. "My mother wants a society wedding. She's foolish sometimes, she flutters and flaps so, but she means well. She only tried to stop me from traveling because she truly feels the place of a female is by the hearth and home. Her father was a vicar with a meager living and she cared for him until his death. And then she married my father—a wealthy merchant. Now she wants what she never had—a place in the upper tiers of society."

She had a glib and persuasive way with words. Now he was even feeling twinges of sympathy for the matchmaking Lady Tombs, something he'd never thought possible.

"We'll have to wait at least three Sundays for the banns to be read," Alice continued. "But this isn't a love match. You don't need to court me or take me riding in Hyde Park. Although if we are seen in public together you will have to act besotted. Mama will be so gratified."

He lifted his head. "Right. Act infatuated with you, if seen in public, and show up at the church."

"Do you think you can manage it, Lord Hatherly?"

"I'm the gentleman you require, Dimples." He lifted her hand and touched his lips to her smooth skin. "You can count on me."

Chapter 6

❦❦❦

For it is a universal rule that however bashful
or angry a woman may be, she never disre-
gards a man's kneeling at her feet.

The Kama Sutra of Vātsyāyana

One month later . . .

Hatherly was late.

Beyond late.

Maybe he wasn't even coming.

Alice ripped a pearl off her wedding dress and
pressed the hard little globe between her thumb
and forefinger.

She sat in the front pew, back straight, cheeks
flaming with humiliation.

Her parents flanked her. Grim Papa. Nervously
fluttering Mama.

She imagined Mama was wishing she'd agreed
to a small, private ceremony, as the whispers
behind them grew louder.

She was marrying in all the pomp and circumstance her father's fortune was expected to supply. No expense had been spared.

The church was filled with hothouse roses. The distinguished priest had officiated at the ceremonies of no fewer than three dukes.

Why wasn't Hatherly here yet? He'd promised her, over and over, that he'd be here, and she'd believed him.

Despite her telling him he didn't need to woo her, he'd visited several times, under heavy supervision from Mama, of course, and she'd thought they'd . . . well, she'd rather thought they had been on their way to becoming if not friends, at least allies.

They'd spent hours picking apart the frivolous fops of the *ton*, Hatherly performing a deadly impression of Lord White, and Alice amusing him with her caricatures of the many simpering society misses she'd encountered in her days of self-imposed wallflower-dom.

Had he only been amusing himself at her expense?

What if, she thought with a lurching feeling in her stomach, what if he'd planned this entire episode as one of his infamous entertainments?

Enter the virgin sacrifice, trussed in pink silk and crusted with pearls, like some slab of underdone beef to be devoured by the gossips.

Admit the aristocratic audience, riveted by the possibility of scandal looming larger with every passing second.

Supply one very dour-faced priest who glanced

up from his prayer book every few moments and skewered her with a disapproving glare, as if the lack of groom were somehow her fault.

Cue solemn, melancholy music from sonorous organ pipes.

Send a weak ray of sunshine wavering through the stained glass windows, striking Our Lord as he suffered upon his cross.

Teach Sir Alfred a lesson in suffering. Teach him that upstart merchants should never aspire to marry their daughters into the true nobility.

"He's not coming, Mama," Alice whispered.

"He'll be here any moment now, I'm quite sure," her mother said with false cheer.

"He'd damned well better be," her father muttered. "Or he'll wish he'd never been born. I won't just confiscate his bloody house. I'll strip him of *everything*."

"Lower your voice, sir." Mama glanced around fearfully lest anyone hear her husband curse.

Her father's whiskers quivered with fury. "He won't have two brass farthings to rub together when I'm through with him."

Alice felt like a wilted cabbage under the weight of all these petticoats and pearls.

It was unseasonably hot for June. The air was stifling and wet with the threat of rain.

Heat brought out the worst of London. The refuse in the gutters became ripe and rotten. Coal smoke stuck to her skin and the insides of her nose.

She wished she were back in Pudsey, reading under the shade of her favorite oak tree, with her pet cat Kali curled up next to her.

She wished she were anywhere except here, in this church, having her hopes crushed.

She glanced back at Charlene and Thea who sat three rows away. The sympathy in their eyes nearly made her break down in tears. But she wouldn't cry.

Not for a man.

And most definitely not for an arrogant aristocrat who played cruel jokes on trusting young ladies.

Alice squared her shoulders. "We should leave now. I don't want to stay any longer."

Though she didn't relish the thought of walking back through the audience past all the people her mother had invited.

"Have patience, dear," said Mama. "He will come. He *must* come."

"What's this? Not at the church? Wake up, man!"

Loud, insistent voice in his ear. Heavy hands shaking his shoulder.

"Go 'way," Nick muttered, slapping the hand away.

"Wake up, you reprobate."

His dream's long limbs and teasing dimples fled and were replaced by the decidedly less attractive vision of Captain Lear's darkly whiskered visage looming over the bed.

"It's your *wedding* day, for Christ's sake," said Lear. "Thought you'd be at the church by now. Was going to raid your wine cellar while you were out."

"My wedding day," Nick repeated groggily. Of course it wasn't his wedding day. He was never going to marry. The words made no sense.

And then they did.

Awful, stomach-churning, death-knell-ringing sense.

He bolted upright. "What time is it?"

"Half nine."

"Damn it, man! Why didn't you wake me earlier?" Nick leapt out of bed, stubbing his toe on the bedpost. "Bollocks!" He gripped the bedpost as pain momentarily hobbled him. "Berthold was supposed to wake me at seven."

Nick and Patrick had been out late last night, not carousing, as one might suppose a bachelor with one night of freedom left might do, but following a lead on someone who might have led them to news of the missing Mr. Stubbs.

They'd made little headway in that regard. The man had vanished. Probably on a ship bound for America by now.

"Alice is going to kill me. One assignment. I had one assignment. Drag my sorry arse to the damned church. I told her she could count on me. I promised her I'd be there."

"Well, I hope so, since you're the bridegroom."

Marry Alice. Keep roof over father's head. Send Alice to India. Resume life of dissipation.

He'd had weeks to think about the terms of their agreement.

Weeks to imagine Alice's tutelage in vivid, glorious detail.

Which must be the reason he'd stayed celibate throughout their engagement, though there had been plenty of prodding by his more unscrupulous friends to enjoy his last days of bachelorhood.

Her mother had kept Alice occupied with a whirlwind of fittings, social calls, and whatever else ladies did to prepare for weddings, but Nick had visited her several times, thinking to steal a few more heated, lingering kisses.

Unfortunately, her parents had never left them unsupervised again.

Probably too worried he'd ravish the lady.

Which, given the opportunity, he would have seriously considered, as every time he saw her, it struck him anew what an unusual and arresting combination of beauty and brains she possessed.

The papers were fascinated by the wedding, and wagers were flying fast and furious in the clubs as to how long the marriage would remain amicable.

What they didn't know was that the union would remain more than amicable, because it required only a temporary exchange of affections.

Every gentleman who'd ever attended one of his disreputable entertainments would be there to smirk as he tied the noose.

To hell with them. This was the perfect, expedient union.

Or it would be if he made it to the church in time.

Nick searched the room, flinging clothing left and right. "Don't stand there laughing, you hairy arse."

"You're buggered any way you look at it," Lear said cheerfully.

"This is bad. Very bad. Help me find my coat."

"I'm not a valet," Lear said.

"Neither is Berthold." He was a former champion prizefighter and a middling valet, but Nick kept him on because Berthold wouldn't have been able to find other employment.

"If I don't make it to this wedding you can kiss my business good-bye," Nick reminded Lear. "No more Portuguese red or oak-barrel Jamaican rum for me. So you'd best find my boots. And find Berthold, too. He ought to be able to help."

That lit a fire under Lear. "Right. I saw old Bert sleeping in the hallway."

He strode to the door. "Berthold," he bellowed.

Nick's purported valet stumbled into the room, rubbing his eyes. "You needn't shout."

"Pull yourself together, man," Lear barked. "We must assemble this miscreant of a marquess into a respectable member of society, fit to wed an innocent heiress before God and the jaded eyes of the *ton*."

Berthold's bleary eyes widened. "What time is it?"

"Nearly too late," said Nick irritably. "Where's my best beaver topper?" He hadn't seen his best hat for days.

Berthold started guiltily. "May have been sold to pay the butcher's bill."

"Christ," roared Nick. "I have to reach that church before we all starve." He threw a shirt over his head and buttoned the neck.

"Here, have mine." Lear handed over his sleek top hat.

As Lear and Berthold helped him struggle into his tight-fitting tailcoat, Nick's mind raced across town, picturing Alice standing at the altar all alone, wearing something frothy, with diamonds in her light brown hair and tears sparkling in those big turquoise eyes.

Some other fellow in the congregation might see all that divine beauty and volunteer to wed her then and there.

Panic flared like brandy touched by a flame.

He shoved a hand through his hair and grimaced at his disheveled reflection in the glass. "Good enough," he announced.

"Wait," cried Berthold. "I've got to shave you."

"No time. Saddle Anvil."

Berthold hastened from the room.

"Looks like rain," smirked Lear. "You'll be soaked."

"But I'll be there," Nick said grimly. "I promised Alice I'd be there. Damn it, Lear. What's wrong with me? I had one assignment, and I'm already mucking it up."

Within minutes, he was swinging onto the broad back of his favorite black stallion.

Anvil pawed the gravel, eager to be given his lead.

He understood the need for urgency. He had a taste for fine oats and expensive fillies and wouldn't take kindly to being thrown into inferior lodgings.

"Trample anyone who stands in our way," Nick instructed. "There's a young lady counting on us."

Grumbling of thunder outside the church.

Sunlight darkening to gloom.

Wind keening to the coming rain.

Murmurs growing louder; a gathering summer storm of scandal.

Alice ripped off another pearl. She had quite a pile gathered in the folds of her gown. Before long her wedding gown would be entirely denuded of ornamentation.

This was growing ridiculous.

Heavy rain began pounding the roof and splattering against the windows.

"Mama, please. We mustn't—"

"Wait." Her mother twisted toward the entrance. "I heard a noise." She clasped her hands. "It must be Lord Hatherly. It simply must."

"It was only thunder, Mama."

But as she opened her mouth to argue for their departure, the wooden doors of the church gusted open and Hatherly appeared, dark as a storm cloud against the gray stone backdrop.

"Oh! Thank the dear Lord. We are saved. He is here," exclaimed Lady Tombs. She rose to her feet, pulling Alice along with her.

The pile of pearls she'd amassed in her skirts skittered across the marble floor, making their escape.

Alice nearly ran after them.

She wasn't feeling at all thankful.

She'd already given up on him in her mind.

The entire church fell silent. Even the organist ceased playing.

His eyes met Alice's, glinting like rain on wrought iron.

He handed his water-soaked beaver hat and black cloak to a footman and walked purposefully down the aisle, his shoes leaving wet footprints on the red carpet.

He shook his collar-length brown hair, shedding water in a wide arc, showering the gaping wedding guests.

She shivered as if the drops had hit her own skin.

As he strode toward her his gaze never wavered. In his eyes she read an apology.

And a promise of moonlit kisses . . . and long, sultry summer nights.

He flung himself onto one knee in front of her and grabbed her hand. "Do forgive me, my love," he said loudly. He flipped a lock of wet hair away from his eyes. "My carriage wheel flew off halfway to the church. Nearly lost the coachman."

Mama clutched the lace at her throat.

"After I made certain the fellow would live, I rode the rest of the way," Lord Hatherly continued. "I rode as hard and as fast as I could."

Such a deliberate emphasis he placed on *hard* and *fast*.

Several members of the congregation gasped, hanging on his every word.

Some were probably hoping for a scandalous last-second jilting.

Alice contemplated fulfilling their every fantasy by snatching up a piece of religious statuary and smacking the marquess across his aristocratically hewn jaw before making her escape.

She could clearly imagine the fun the newspaper editors would have tomorrow: *Bride Bludgeons Bridegroom with Blessed Saint and Bolts.*

Of course, she'd do nothing of the sort. She needed him too much. The plan was already set in motion. The scholars in Calcutta were waiting for her to arrive with the lost chapters of the *Kama Sutra*. Well, they were waiting for *Fred* to arrive, but they'd have to make do with her.

"Lord Hatherly, please stand up," she hissed. "You're making a scene."

"Not until you forgive me, my darling," he said loudly.

He was a consummate performer; she'd allow him that. It almost made her giggle, the sight of the arrogant Lord Hatherly down on his knees, playing the attentive, besotted bridegroom of her mother's dreams, the assembled witnesses hanging on his every word.

He winked at her and her anger dissolved.

He was here now, and everything could go on as planned.

She could make him pay for his tardiness later.

"Well then . . . I forgive you," she proclaimed loudly.

A sigh rippled across the room. Her friend Thea caught her eye and gave her a brief, encouraging nod.

As he rose, he took the opportunity to whisper in her ear. "I'll make it up to you. Tonight. When we begin our lessons."

Alice felt her cheeks heating.

She'd been thinking about those lessons. Preparing for them. She'd nearly translated the whole of the *Kama Sutra* chapters. But there were still some words and phrases whose meaning eluded her.

All would be revealed tonight.

Sir Alfred nodded to the priest, who moved to his post and opened his Book of Common Prayer.

"Shall we begin?" The priest's flat blue eyes pierced through Alice, daring her to lose her nerve. "Dearly beloved, we are gathered together here in the sight of God, and in the face of this congregation, to join together this Man and this Woman in holy Matrimony . . ." droned the priest in his dry, raspy voice.

Hatherly's rain-soaked pantaloons were practically painted onto his powerful, thickly muscled thighs, Alice noticed.

He caught the direction of her gaze and gave her another intimate wink.

She swiftly tore her gaze away and stared at the stained glass window.

The priest droned on about the holy estate of matrimony, enjoining Hatherly to love her, comfort her, and forsake all others.

Ha, Alice thought. *Not much chance of that*.

"I will," Hatherly lied blithely.

He didn't seem at all concerned that the entire ceremony was a lie and that they barely knew each other in any meaningful way.

With a sudden rush of confusion, Alice wondered whether holy matrimony was truly only ink blotted on a registry. Or should a wedding *mean* something more? Would she come to regret tying her fortunes to his, despite the freedom being a married woman with a disinterested and otherwise occupied husband could afford her?

"Miss Tombs?" The priest's voice rattled through her mind.

Alice snapped back to the room. "Pardon?"

"Wilt thou have this man to thy wedded husband, to live together after God's ordinance in the holy estate of Matrimony? Wilt thou obey him, and serve him, love, honor, and keep him . . ."

Obey him? *Serve* him?

The priest stared at her expectantly.

Hatherly tapped one foot on the marble floor, crushing one of her runaway pearls.

She couldn't promise to *obey* and *serve* him.

What if he decided to interpret those words literally and keep her in England as his scullery maid?

"Having second thoughts, Dimples?" Hatherly whispered in her ear.

"You know I won't obey you, right?" she whispered back.

"You'll obey me in bed," was the extremely inappropriate response he delivered with a smoldering look that made her cheeks too warm, as if she'd fallen asleep next to a burning candle.

"And I won't serve you, either," she whispered.

"I'll serve *you*, young lady," he responded with a devilish grin. "You'll receive just what you deserve tonight."

The priest glared so ferociously that Alice nearly giggled. "The Lord might smite you for that, Lord Hatherly."

How did he overcome her resistance and dissolve her fear with only a few playful words? Her body had gone boneless with longing, and her thoughts had flown ahead to the wedding night.

Alice darted a backward glance at her best friends. Charlene was frowning, probably thinking about her warning to Alice.

Be very, very careful, sweetheart.

"Ahem." The priest cleared his throat. "May we continue?"

"Remember," Hatherly whispered. "My solicitor

is finalizing the contract you asked me to prepare. You'll go your way and I'll stay right here."

She'd completely forgotten the contract. The set of rules and parameters for their convenient arrangement. If both of them followed the rules, everything would go as planned.

Hatherly pressed her hand. "Take a deep breath," he said. "And trust me."

The sound of excited whispers swept through the room. Every second of delay meant the tantalizing possibility of scandal.

"Miss Tombs?" the priest asked again.

Alice inhaled deeply. "I will."

Chapter 7

A wise man having a regard for his reputation
should not think of seducing a woman who
is apprehensive, timid, not to be trusted, well
guarded, or possessed of a mother-in-law.

The Kama Sutra of Vātsyāyana

Of course Alice hadn't expected showers of rose
petals and a doting husband to carry her across the
threshold.

This wasn't a romance, after all. This was an adventure story. In one month's time she'd be boarding a ship for the East.

But no bridegroom at all?

Hatherly had refused to attend the traditional
wedding feast her mother had proposed. And directly after the ceremony he'd instructed her parents to deliver her to Sunderland House with no
delay, prompting titters and scandalized gasps
from the assembled guests.

Alice's lady's maid had gone back to their home
to fetch Alice's cat and a change of clothing.

Hatherly had given a commanding performance

as a bridegroom so eager for his wedding night that he would suffer no delay, leaping astride his huge black stallion and setting off at a breakneck pace.

So where *was* he? Surely his mount had conveyed him to Sunderland more swiftly than her father's carriage.

A frisson of anticipation swept her frame when she thought of his whispered promises in the church. She had to admit she was impatient for the sun to fade and the moon to rise.

Alice stared up at the massive mansion with its tortured gargoyles and spindly turrets, black against the gray sky, so unlike the usual blank stone faces of London town houses. She'd learned that the estate had been constructed by the eccentric first Duke of Barrington, and was quite unique among London's grand houses for its size and its sprawling gardens and lawn.

"It's very . . . fanciful," Alice's mother said doubtfully, in her high, tremulous voice.

"It's a bloody lunatic's nightmare," her father replied. "Knock it all down, I say. Build something more modern. What a waste of a prime location. Right near Green Park. Perhaps I should have accepted the house after all."

"Oh no," Mama stated with conviction. "The marquess was a much better investment."

The sun broke from behind the gray clouds and Alice shaded her face with one hand, raising her head to study her new home. "I think it's a fascinating mélange of building styles," she said brightly.

The sunshine illuminated every architectural

vagary—here a narrow battlement; there a soaring turret aiming for the heavens.

The effect reminded her of a description she'd read of the ruined Sun Temple in Kashmir. How the Karkota Dynasty architect had used influences from China and Rome to create something new, and wholly unique, carved from stone and cleverly constructed to dance with the sun's rays, using light as much as limestone to create a place of worship.

Fitting, as this house would be the place where she completed her translation of the *Kama Sutra* fragment she possessed, in precise and correct detail—once all the mysteries of carnal pleasure were revealed to her and she could find the right way of expressing the sensations the ancient sage had meant to evoke.

Most of her possessions had been sent ahead, but Alice hadn't been willing to entrust the *Kama Sutra* to a footman. She carried it in a small valise.

Hodgins carried Kali in a wicker basket, and the maid stared at Sunderland House with a mistrustful expression. A yowl from Kali reminded Alice that her poor cat didn't like being shut up in the darkness for too long.

"Hush," Hodgins whispered sternly, addressing the basket.

Alice cracked the lid of the basket. "What have we agreed to, Kali?" she whispered. "I'm having some misgivings."

Kali glanced up at her with wide, doleful yellow eyes, as if to say she had grave misgivings about baskets, and there had better be a bowl of milk in it for her.

Alice hadn't had a chance to tell him she was bringing a cat with her. Not that she would have accepted any objections.

"There doesn't appear to be anyone waiting to greet us." Mama shook her head disapprovingly. "I must say I expected more from a duke."

He is a *mad* duke, Alice wanted to remind her mother, but refrained.

"Well we can't leave the girl here at the front door." Sir Alfred marched to the door and pounded the heavy black iron knocker against the plate.

There was no response.

Her father pounded harder, going quite red in the face.

Finally the door creaked open a few inches.

"Yes?" a quavering voice said.

"I say, inform His Lordship that his bride and her family are here."

There was a pause. Alice couldn't see the butler since the door was only cracked open.

There was the sound of more voices from inside the house.

"He hasn't got a bride," came the answer.

Alice stepped forward and her father moved away. "Yes, he has."

The door opened wider.

The tall, thin butler was wearing a white, curling wig that sat slightly askew on his head, as if he'd donned it only a moment ago. "No, he hasn't."

Alice placed her hand on her hip. She was tired,

hungry, and she longed to be rid of all these heavy pearls. "Look here," she said sternly. "I'm Lady Hatherly. We were married not one hour ago. Now go and fetch my lord husband."

The butler's jaw dropped and his lips flapped open, giving him the appearance of an astonished codfish.

He twisted away from the doorway and Alice heard more urgent whispered conversation with someone she couldn't see.

The butler turned back to Alice. "My friend Mr. March says you're mad."

"I'm not mad. I'm Lady Hatherly."

"No you're not."

Alice was beginning to be quite irritated with this conversation. She was about to grasp hold of the door and fling it open when a loud, rumbling roar emerged from inside the house.

"Wh-what was that?" squeaked Hodgins.

It had sounded rather like a . . .

"Lion," shouted the butler, dancing about on his long, thin legs like a praying mantis. "Lion on the loose!"

The door crashed open and the butler ran down the steps, shortly followed by an enormous golden blur.

Her parents and maid leapt out of the way and Alice gaped at the giant beast streaking across the drive. Surely it must be a large dog. Lord Hatherly couldn't keep lions in his house, could he?

Sir Alfred caught hold of his quivering wife.

The normally unflappable Hodgins promptly

dropped the basket on its side and Kali was off like a shot, racing across the garden lawn after the lion.

"Kali—no!" Alice called.

Kali had been a fearless huntress back in Pudsey, bringing Alice a daily offering from the fields. A severed robin's head. A poor, stiff little mouse.

She'd named her cat after a Hindu goddess of war.

Kali wasn't dainty and refined . . . and she wasn't afraid of anything.

And neither was Alice.

Setting down her valise and lifting her skirts, she plunged down the steps after her very brave and very foolish cat.

"Alice—no!" her mother yelled.

But there was nothing for it but to join the chase.

Nick swore under his breath as he chased his escaped lioness, Gertrude. She was being chased by a small streak of gray-and-brown striped fur, and the streak of fur was in turn being pursued by his very disheveled and cross-looking bride.

He drew alongside Alice. "Fall back," he shouted. "Gertrude's not dangerous but I want to secure her as a precaution."

The only response was a narrowing of turquoise eyes as she increased her pace despite the silk skirts wrapped around her long limbs.

Nick sighed and burst past her. "Gertrude," he yelled. "Stop, girl."

Gertrude skidded to a halt, glancing behind warily at the hissing gray-and-brown cat.

"Easy now," he said to Gertrude.

She plopped down on the lawn, lowering her head. She was a very old, very decrepit lioness.

He clipped the chain he held to her collar and fixed it to a nearby fence post.

The ferocious ball of fur, which he could now see was a small, tiger-striped cat, hissed and spat at Gertrude until Alice scooped it into her arms.

"Kali," Alice scolded, stroking her cat under the chin and breathing heavily. "You naughty thing. You can't go chasing after lions. They're much bigger than you. Why, you could have been eaten."

At least she wasn't screaming hysterically, as most females would have done at the sight of Gertrude.

Perhaps she'd adapt to life at Sunderland, after all.

She glanced at Nick from beneath her lashes. Her bonnet had fallen down her back and was dangling by its ribbons, and most of her hair had escaped its pins and was tumbling over her shoulders.

Her chest heaved from the exertion of running, and her pelisse had come undone, revealing plump breasts straining over the narrow, pearl-dotted bodice of her wedding gown.

Kali settled against her mistress's chest, the excitement of the chase forgotten in the quest for more chin scratches.

Nick couldn't help wishing he could nestle between her breasts as well.

He raised his eyes, not wanting to be caught staring at her bosom, although it was truly magnificent and would deserve his full attention later.

"You keep a menagerie, Lord Hatherly?"

"Of only one beast."

Gertrude flicked her tail, and Kali raised her head and growled.

"Your cat is terrorizing my lioness," Nick said.

"Your lioness terrorized my maid." Alice glanced toward the gate where her lady's maid had exited, probably never to be seen again.

"Gertrude's harmless. She wouldn't hurt a fly. She's had all her teeth filed down by her previous owner and her claws removed. Barbaric really."

Nick patted Gertrude's head. "All she wants to do is sun herself and eat apples from our trees."

"She won't harm Kali?"

"I promise."

Alice set Kali down and the cat hissed at the lion. Gertrude cowered away from the ferocious little beast.

Kali advanced and sniffed Gertrude's enormous paw. Gertrude regarded Kali with a funny expression, almost a smile.

The cat decided she wasn't a threat, and promptly curled up next to Gertrude.

"Oh, so now you're best friends, are you?" Alice asked.

"I told you there was nothing to worry about."

"But how can you be certain? She's a wild beast."

"Have you ever visited Tombwell's Menagerie? They were pitting her against dogs who savaged her cruelly. They took away her claws and she only has a few teeth left, and no fight to speak of. You saw how terrified she was of Kali."

Alice smiled. "Kali's very brave."

And so was his new bride.

A brave, independent lady who went chasing after lions and who would chase her dreams to India.

A fellow had to admire that much spirit in a woman.

It almost made him sorry that she couldn't have found a more worthy opponent with which to spar.

Instead she'd pledged herself to him. A man who would most likely go insane one day and forget not only their wedding ceremony but her name . . . her very existence. His father rarely remembered he was married. His forgetfulness and delusions were periodic, but this latest bout had lasted so long that Nick feared he would never regain his grasp on reality.

"Your parents are distraught," Nick commented. "We should rejoin them."

Sir Alfred was fanning his wife with her bonnet.

Alice lifted Kali from the ground and they walked together back to her parents.

"This won't do, Hatherly," Sir Alfred sputtered as they approached. "I won't have my daughter's life endangered. If I had my hunting guns I'd shoot that lion dead."

"Is it gone?" Lady Tombs asked, her shoulders trembling.

"All's clear, my dear," said the baronet.

Lady Tombs raised her head. "Alice. My dear child. You cannot live with a lion."

"Lioness, Mother. And she's harmless. Old and feeble with all her teeth and claws filed to bluntness. Why, she was frightened of little Kali." Alice placed her cat back in its basket and fastened the lid more securely.

Sir Alfred cleared his throat. "Is that true, Hatherly?"

"All true. I rescued her from a traveling menagerie. She's very old, and very feeble. I can't believe she escaped from her enclosure. I'll make sure it's repaired today."

"See that you do," grumbled Sir Alfred.

"Oh," moaned Lady Tombs. "My nerves. I'm all aquiver."

"Lady Tombs," Nick said smoothly, "a small brandy, perhaps? It would have a calming effect."

She drew herself up regally. "I never imbibe spirits, my lord, and neither does Alice."

March, Nick's footman, emerged from the house. "Oh, you're still here?" He glared at Alice and her parents.

"Found them skulking about the door," March whispered to Nick, his mouth turned down. "Highly suspicious. We must be vigilant, what with Mr. Stubbs turning traitor, and all." He waved in Alice's direction. "Says she's your wife, but I know you haven't got a wife."

"I *am* his wife," Alice said.

He had a wife.

It was still an entirely foreign concept to Nick.

A *temporary* wife, he reminded himself.

"That's enough, March," Nick warned. "Go back inside."

He didn't mind March's incivility—the man had been born with enough disadvantages to give him the right to grouse—but Lady Tombs was about to have an attack of nerves on his front steps.

"My heavens," Lady Tombs sputtered. "That is the rudest servant I've ever had the misfortune of coming in contact with."

"My sincere apologies," Nick said. "We don't often entertain polite company."

And he wasn't about to entertain them further.

When Nick invited guests to Sunderland they always arrived after dark and left before the dawn. They saw only what he wanted them to see—the spectacle, the illusions.

His new in-laws would have to become accustomed to the idea that he didn't follow society's rules.

Before Nick could send them away, the duke hobbled through the doorway with Berthold lumbering close behind. "Hello there, who's this?" He eyed Lady Tombs. "Madam, you are a vision most welcome. An angel come to earth."

Lady Tombs, somewhat mollified by this turn of events, smiled at Nick's father. "Your Grace?"

"Yes, 'tis I." The duke attempted a sweeping bow and had to clutch Berthold's arm for support. "Barrington, at your pleasure, madam. And you are . . ." He lifted his brows.

"Lady Agatha Tombs. The new Lady Hatherly's mother. So very pleased to make your acquaintance, Your Grace. I was so very disappointed you were unable to attend the wedding. It was a most elegant affair. The very height of elegance! There are hundreds of pearls embroidered upon Lady

Hatherly's gown. Everyone pronounced the gown a triumph."

Pearls sewn along the bodice and tiny pearl buttons marching down the back.

Nick had been imagining unfastening them for the last two hours.

Which was not an appropriate thought to have while standing in skin-tight pantaloons in front of the lady's easily perturbed mother.

Though the father would no doubt approve, since he'd made abundantly clear in the settlement that the marriage must be legitimized before he handed over a farthing. Sir Alfred was a businessman first and foremost. And he wanted to secure his investment.

"Oh come now, you can't be her mother," the duke chided. "You must be her elder sister. Your satin curls have the very same luster and your cheeks the very same blush." He reached for her hand and kissed the air above her gloved knuckles. "Beautiful, beautiful Agatha. Lovely lady. You remind me of my *cher amie* Marie Antoinette."

Sir Alfred frowned. "Your Grace, we really must be going now."

"Fie, Duke, how you flatter me," Lady Tombs said with a delighted little giggle.

The duke grinned with a hint of his former debonair charm. "I'll flatter you more if you come with me to my orchid conservatory where we may converse in private. The blooms have a delightful scent and their forms are quite . . . suggestive." He waggled his eyebrows.

Lady Tombs gulped. "Er . . ."

She had the dazed look of a lady who'd been insulted by a footman and propositioned by a mad duke in the space of two minutes.

"Now see here," Sir Alfred said. "This is my wife, Your Grace."

Alice flung Nick a panicked look.

"Come dear," said Sir Alfred stormily. "I shall convey you home if there is to be no breakfast."

"No breakfast," Nick said firmly.

He'd agreed to the public ceremony but he'd refused to host or attend a wedding breakfast.

"Be good, dear," Lady Tombs said in a tremulous voice, darting Nick a half-terrified look, as if she'd only now realized she must relinquish her beloved daughter to the likes of him.

Alice kissed her mother on the cheek and smiled at her father. "You needn't worry about me. I'll be fine. Come, Mama, don't trouble yourself so." Alice helped her mother tie the feathered and beribboned millinery back on her head.

"Your daughter will be quite safe with me," Nick vowed.

At least she'd be safe from lions.

He couldn't pledge her safety from marquesses.

She looked entirely too delectable with her light brown hair tumbling about her shoulders and her bodice askew.

When Sir Alfred and his wife were situated in their carriage, Nick turned to the duke.

"Well, Barrington, scared away another one."

"I can't think what I said to distress her." The

duke stared forlornly at the feathers bobbing in the carriage window. "Beautiful, beautiful Agatha." He sighed and waved his handkerchief as the carriage rolled away. "I only wanted to show her my blooms."

Nick laughed. "The ones from Captain Lear?"

"I helped plant them," Berthold said with great pride. "I mustn't water them too much or they'll die."

The duke cheered, nodding vigorously. "Lear brought one species I haven't been able to identify yet. We'll have to see if it will flower. Ten of the plants died but two will survive, I think. I predict the petals will be ghostly white and elongated with long trailing tails. Wait until I show Pemberton!"

That might be difficult.

His father's explorer friend Sir Pemberton had died five years ago after being thrown from his carriage by balking horses.

Alice saw Nick's long face and immediately smiled at the duke and took his arm. "You may show *me* your orchids, Your Grace."

She was adept at taking charge of difficult situations. He'd notice that about her immediately.

"Splendid my dear," the duke said. "And who are you?"

As Alice led his father into the house, and listened patiently to his meanderings, Nick hoped she wouldn't run screaming when she encountered the madhouse of his life.

Her shoulders were held high but her neck drooped from the weight of all the pearls sewn into the heavy silk of her gown.

She should remove the gown as soon as possible.

He would remove it for her.

If there was one thing Nick was good at, it was divesting beautiful women of troublesome articles of clothing.

Chapter 8

Vātsyāyana says that the man should begin to win her over, and to create confidence in her, but should abstain at first from carnal pleasures. Women being of a tender nature, want tender beginnings.

The Kama Sutra of Vātsyāyana

Alice followed the duke and the hulking man-servant with the pockmarked cheeks and kind blue eyes, whom Hatherly had called Berthold, down a long, cavernous entrance hall, through heavy wood-paneled doors, and up a flight of stairs.

Hatherly walked beside her, a huge, looming presence carrying her small valise.

The Mad Duke didn't seem too terribly mad. He had a courtly manner and a bewildered air. Every now and then he glanced up as if he heard voices calling from afar.

He had thick white hair that was probably meant to be tamed into submission but stuck up every which way, and his nose was very grand,

and made grander by the frailty and thinness of his frame.

Kali yowled when Alice accidentally jostled the wicker basket against the stair railing. "Hush my sweet," Alice whispered. "We're nearly there."

"Is that a cat I hear, my dear?" The duke called over his shoulder.

"Yes. And she doesn't like being cooped up in baskets."

The duke stumbled at the top of the stairs, and Hatherly passed Alice and threw an arm around the duke's shoulders, propping him up against his broad chest to help him walk.

"Go with Berthold now," Hatherly said gently, giving his father's shoulders a squeeze.

Berthold and the duke disappeared down a branching corridor.

The short footman who had been so rude to Alice and her parents earlier popped his head out of a nearby doorway. "She won't be staying long, will she?" he asked Hatherly, wrinkling his snub nose. "I don't trust the look of her, or that furry rodent in the basket. If she'd only mind her own business, our world could go on as before."

"I don't think your footman likes me very much," Alice whispered to Hatherly.

"Go on with you," Hatherly said to his servant. "Go about your duties."

The servant made a disgusted noise and slammed the door.

"Don't mind March," said Hatherly, offering her his arm. "He's sometimes a bit too loyal."

"I can see that. I think he believes I mean to

have my devious way with you and your household."

Hatherly flexed his arm beneath her hand, and muscles played enticingly under his coat. "I mean to have my devious way with you tonight, Dimples."

Tonight, tonight, her slippers pattered as they traversed the narrow corridor carpeted in a deep, rich purple color.

"You were kind to my father," said Hatherly. "His company can be trying at times."

"I do want to see his orchid collection. I heard about his conservatory from Charlene—from the Duchess of Harland."

Charlene had become rather intimately acquainted with the duke's orchid conservatory when she'd held a romantic tryst there with her future husband, the Duke of Harland.

If Alice remembered the story correctly, he'd thrown her over his shoulder like a sack of flour and carried her to the conservatory.

She wondered if Hatherly was the throw-a- - lady-over-his-shoulder kind. She rather thought he might be, and she rather thought she might enjoy it.

"Here we are," he said, pausing in front of an open door halfway down the corridor. "We have adjoining chambers."

He pushed the door open, indicating Alice should enter the room first.

Once inside, she turned in a slow circle. "This is for me?"

"All for you."

She hadn't expected much after the oppressive atmosphere of the entrance hall, but the large chamber was light-filled and airy, with a matched set of elegant pale pine furniture upholstered in rose-colored satin.

Domed, mullioned windows set at intervals along the walls commanded a pleasing view of the pink and white flowering apple trees in the gardens below.

Alice ran to the bookshelves, trailing her fingers along cracked leather spines. So many more books than she'd sent over.

"Why, this is the English translation of the *Bhagavad Gita* by Charles Wilkins! Where did you find this? It's quite rare."

Hatherly made a disparaging noise in the back of his throat. "I found some foreign books on the duke's shelves. He traveled to India and Nepal more than once collecting orchids."

She flew to the desk. Such a vast expanse of a desk, with rows of shining new quills, several pots of ink, stacks of parchment—everything she needed.

She'd never had a study of her own.

Stolen moments with Fred's schoolbooks . . . nights hunched over a desk studying by candlelight, hiding her studiousness from her disapproving mother.

This room was spacious, airy, stocked with the tools she required for her scholarship, and the perfect haven in which to finish her work.

"My lord, I don't know what to say." She hugged her arms around her chest. "I simply love it."

He cleared his throat. "I'm glad you approve." He sounded embarrassed to have been caught making her happy.

Kali yowled piteously and Alice undid the latch of her basket. Kali hopped out, landing on all fours on the fine woolen rug.

"Poor little beastie." Alice bent down and scratched Kali's chin. "I forgot all about you. Just see." She lifted her and walked to the window. "See all those birds in the trees? You're going to have quite a feast."

Kali's tail switched back and forth as she surveyed her new kingdom.

"What does your cat eat?" Hatherly asked.

"The bird population in your gardens will be sadly decimated, but I usually feed her kippers and a bowl of milk. She's a very spoiled cat." She kissed Kali's head. "Aren't you, my darling?"

"I'll have some kippers sent."

Alice set her down, and Kali bolted away to sniff the corners of the large room.

Alice shook out her skirts, remembering that she was still in her wedding finery. "What time will we dine this evening?"

"We're not formal here. We dine when we please. The duke mostly takes his meals in his chambers. But we may dine with him tonight if you wish."

"I would enjoy speaking more with your father."

"You may revise that sentiment, I'm afraid. He harms no one, but his delusions can be troubling. He likes you immensely. Has a weakness for beautiful women, my father." His gaze traveled across her body. "As do I."

The fizzing feeling began in her belly again. She'd been imagining her wedding night for a month now. It couldn't possibly live up to her imaginings . . . could it?

"I'll leave you to settle in," Hatherly said. He turned to leave and Alice had the sudden thought that if he left her here all alone, she wouldn't be able to undo the complicated buttons along the back of the wedding gown.

"My lord," she called to his retreating back.

"Call me Nick. I've already told you we don't stand on formality in this house."

"Please send a maid to assist me since my Hodgins appears to have deserted me in the lion's den."

"I have no live-in maids. The hired ones only come on certain days."

Alice tucked her chin. "No maids today? Well, send the housekeeper then."

"No housekeeper."

"That can't be true."

"I have difficulty keeping housekeepers. As fast as I engage one, they find a reason to flee."

"Perhaps Gertrude has something to do with that."

"Maybe."

"There are other reasons for servants to run screaming from the premises?"

Lord Hatherly shrugged. "Might be."

"Well." Alice drew herself up, ready to shoulder new burdens. "I may have to institute a few improvements during my time at Sunderland."

Lord Hatherly's gray eyes darkened. "No changes. The household functions perfectly well."

"With no housekeeper and only intermittent

maid service?" Alice sniffed. "Mama would be scandalized."

He gave her a seductive smile. "I'd be happy to assist with your toilette, Lady Hatherly."

Closing the distance between them in two long strides, he placed his large hands on her shoulders. "Turn around."

Alice's heart raced as he nudged her shoulders until she followed his instructions.

He untied her bonnet and laid it aside. The pelisse quickly followed.

Then he began plucking hairpins and strands of pearls from her disheveled coiffure.

Could the removal of hairpins make one's knees buckle? Seemed a commonplace enough procedure. One Hodgins had performed hundreds of times.

But there was nothing commonplace about Alice's reaction to his strong, sure movements in searching for the pins, freeing them gently without once pinching her scalp.

"Hold still," he commanded. "One's caught."

She held her breath as he yanked on the pin. This was the most intimate contact she'd ever had with a gentleman. Somehow more intimate even than his kiss in her father's study.

No gentleman had ever seen her with her hair completely unbound before.

When every pin was gone, he gathered up her hair and slid it all over one shoulder, exposing her back. "Now, the gown," he whispered in her ear.

Alice spun around. "I can't allow you to remove my gown in broad daylight."

She'd never contemplated exposing herself in such a way.

She'd imagined candlelight. Moonlight.

"I'll find a way," she said. "I'll manage."

"Really?" Hatherly folded his arms. "Show me."

"Pardon?"

"Show me that you can undo the top button."

Alice twisted this way and that, reaching back and finally managing to undo the top pearl button. "There," she said, a bit breathlessly, only because she'd been exerting herself.

Certainly not because he was standing so close, watching her disrobe.

His eyes glinted. "Now the next one."

"My lord, I'm not going to shed my gown in front of you."

"Because you can't," he said smugly.

"Because it's not proper. Not in the daylight." She wanted to have her questions answered, but only in the proper, dimly lit setting.

"No, it's because there's not even a slight chance you can reach those middle buttons."

He was right, of course. With no maid, she'd never manage. She shrugged, feigning nonchalance. "I'll rip my bodice if I must."

"And ruin your lovely wedding gown?"

He was so close now she could feel the heat from his body warming her. Solid arms circled her, reaching around to work the delicate mother-of-pearl buttons loose. The gown went slack. How was he doing that without even looking at his fingers?

"I'm London's foremost authority on unbuttoning," Hatherly said with a wicked gleam in his silver eyes, as if he'd heard her unspoken question.

Alice's cheeks flushed and her heart thumped an erratic cadence.

Was his heart pounding as well?

Following an urge, she pressed her palm against his chest.

A heartbeat, fast and strong, detectable even through layers of linen.

He stilled, fingers tangled in the back of her gown, brushing the small of her back.

She met his silvery eyes.

I don't have to wait until tonight.

Here is the moonlight.

Here the answer.

And then his lips claimed hers.

Chapter 9

❦❦

Kissing is of four kinds: moderate, contracted, pressed, and soft, according to the different parts of the body which are kissed, for different kinds of kisses are appropriate for different parts of the body.

The Kama Sutra of Vātsyāyana

Nick kissed her carelessly, as he would any winsome, half-clothed woman in his arms, forgetting for a moment that she was his bride, and a virgin, and required special handling.

Special care.

Her lips were so smooth—like fine, aged rum, sliding against him, her tongue, when he discovered it, surprisingly responsive to his movements.

He kissed her casually.

At first.

Content to learn the melody of her sighs. The supple ridge of her spine.

She had full hips and a rounded, high-sprung arse made to fit his palms.

When he pulled her closer, firm breasts molded against him and soft arms twined around his neck.

He kissed her with no deeper design . . . no danger of being carried away . . . until something changed.

Intensified.

He couldn't have articulated why suddenly the walls of the room expanded outward with a whoosh and a roaring began in his eardrums.

He'd gone a whole month without a woman; that must explain this lifting sensation in his abdomen. The dizzying rush of pleasure.

The same golden haze of oblivion he found after pounding a glass of strong whiskey.

He crushed her full lips beneath his, intoxicated on the woman-sweet scent of her, overwhelmed by the desire to claim his bride.

He tilted her head back roughly, deepening the kiss, opening her for him, his tongue mimicking the act of love.

She moaned, deep in her throat, and the sound nearly drove him past reason.

Heeding only the heat crackling between them, he slid the pearl-studded sleeve of her gown off one shoulder, exposing one of her rosy nipples.

She broke the kiss, the startled expression in her aquamarine eyes stopping him cold.

Nick lurched back to reality. What was he doing?

This was his wife, an innocent lady. He wanted to make the experience memorable for her. Not some sordid, hasty coupling mere hours after the wedding.

He'd planned to seduce her slowly, prolonging the pleasure for both of them.

He could wait a few more hours.

Taking a full breath to steady his racing pulse, Nick replaced her sleeve.

"I think that ought to do it," he said gruffly. "The gown, that is. I believe it's . . . unbuttoned."

The gown's undone. And so are you. Unraveled by a kiss. Unacceptable.

"I rather think it is." She gave a short laugh. "I never cared for this gown. My mother chose it for me."

She plucked at a pearl stitched to her skirts. "Reminds me of a speckled mushroom our cook warned us of back in Pudsey. She called it a Panther Cap but the true name is *Amanita pantherina*. If you accidentally ingest one, you will hallucinate for—"

"The gown's lovely," Nick said. "And so are you."

She was nervous. Actually, it was rather touching how nervous she was, twisting the silk of her loosened gown, tugging at the pearls and speaking all in a rush about poisonous mushrooms and hallucinations.

It confirmed what he already knew—she was an innocent; a bookish lady who had no idea how close he'd been to spreading her across the nearby bed and having his way with her.

Despite her request for love lessons, she required a leisurely seduction, which wasn't a problem, because he was the master of control and finesse.

Plenty of time for sun-soaked morning and afternoon dalliances after she shed her inhibitions.

Virgins required velvety darkness and gentle kisses.

Her jittery fingers worried a pearl loose, and it rolled into a dusty corner of the chamber, her cat giving chase.

It occurred to Nick that he might find her pearl years later.

When the lady was long gone.

A luminescent memory . . . pearls glowing in a dark corner like her skin would glow in his mind.

You should leave now. Thoughts like that will get you into trouble.

"I'll leave you now, Alice. I'll return in a few hours."

"But aren't you . . . that is to say . . ." Eyelashes flicked toward his waist. "I believe you are in a state of . . ." She licked her lips. ". . . *tumescence.*"

Her gaze caressed him, her voice a husky whisper inviting him to open a few buttons and satisfy her curiosity.

It seemed his new wife was determined to progress to the bedding as swiftly as possible.

"My cock is stiff," he said, not mincing words, "because I'm thinking about all the things I'll do to you tonight."

She pursed her lips and her dimples reappeared to flirt with his heart.

"Cock." She enunciated the "ck" with a crisp emphasis. "Is that what you call it? As in a male domestic fowl." She tilted her head. "I think I can surmise why. I have observed cocks on a farm in Pudsey become excited and aggressive when my brother set them to fighting. They swelled all red about the wattles and head."

Nick nearly choked. "Strike that lesson from memory. I never should have used that crude word with you."

"I do have married friends, you know. If you give the duchesses a few glasses of wine they wax positively bawdy."

"Then nothing I do or say will shock you?"

"I didn't say that," Alice amended hastily. "I'm quite certain I shall be shocked several times this evening."

"And awed. Shocked and awed."

"Really?"

He shrugged. "What can I say? I'm the best there is, Dimples. That's why you chose me, remember?"

She tipped her head down, perusing his bulge again. "I'm curious . . . how long does this state of swelling last? And how does it begin? Do you require physical stimulation, or would the mere sight of an ankle suffice? Mama always told me the sight of a lady's ankle could drive a gentleman to commit unseemly acts of lust."

Nick guffawed. "Ankles aren't really my choice of incitements. Now your cupid's bow lips, on the other hand." Drawing a thumb across her lower lip, he watched her eyes haze over and her breathing quicken. "One touch and I'm drowning in desire."

"Oh." She exhaled, her warm breath heating his thumb where it rested in the center of her lower lip. "I think . . . I think I like your lips, as well."

She lifted her hand to his mouth, stroking a finger across his upper lip. "I've never seen a gentleman with such a pronounced curvature *here*."

This questing conversation had to end, or the consummation would happen here and now, with no more preamble than this.

Nick grabbed her by the waist, spun her around, and swatted her bum. "No more lessons just now, Dimples."

She smiled at him over her shoulder. "But I have so many questions, my lord."

"I've already bade you call me Nick." He grasped her hips and pulled her flush against his cock. "Don't disobey me again."

She rested her back against his chest, and her rounded bum fit him so perfectly it made his heart gallop and his mouth dry.

"I think I made it quite clear that I wouldn't be obeying you, *Lord Hatherly*."

"You'll call me Nick tonight," he whispered, low and hot in her ear. "You'll *moan* my name. Again and again."

He was always in control in the bedchamber. He decided when the bedding would occur. Better to let her imagination run free for now. He wanted her to be as ready as he was to engage in, what had she so quaintly termed it? "The art of sexual congress."

And so, even though his fingers wanted to slide inside her gaping gown and tease her rosebud nipples until her cheeks flushed a matching pink, he made his escape.

He left swiftly, without a backward glance to see what the inquisitive temptress he'd married was doing now, and he didn't stop walking until he reached Gertrude's enclosure, against the far wall of the gardens.

Pigeon, his gardener, was there already, working on repairing the hole.

"How did she escape?" Nick asked.

"Gnawed her way through the wood with those gummy stumps of 'ers. Think she was hungry. I'll increase her feed portion."

Wordlessly, Nick fell into rhythm with Pigeon, hoisting boards and nailing them into place.

The sudden squall was completely gone and the day had turned fine. As they worked, Nick shed his coat and rolled up his shirtsleeves.

"Pretty bride you have there. Caught a glimpse of her as she arrived. Why aren't you inside, you know . . ." Pigeon hammered a nail into wood with a suggestive chuckle.

"She's an innocent, Pigeon. I have to take things slowly. Don't want to frighten her."

Innocent, curious Alice required candlelight, rose petals, and French champagne.

She deserved proper wooing.

He didn't want to think too much about how good it had felt when she thanked him with a wide, delighted smile for preparing her study. Or how patiently she'd listened to the duke's mumblings.

Nick worked faster, grazing the edge of his thumb with the heavy hammer. The pain cleared some of the haze from his brain.

He couldn't run about *liking* his wife. What good

would that do him when she left? This was a fascination forged from desire.

Keep everything surface and superficial.

A nice, mutually pleasurable melding of bodies, followed by her father settling all his debts. Adhere to the terms of the agreement, and life would return to normalcy in four short weeks.

Alice sank into a chair, her knees suddenly too wobbly to support her anymore.

"Nick," she spoke aloud, tasting the short, punchy name on her tongue.

He'd told her she would moan his name tonight. But a nick was what happened when you sliced your finger while peeling potatoes. Her mother had insisted upon Alice learning the rudiments of cookery, in order to ascertain the quality of her cook's meals.

Alice knew what a nick was.

It was a warning. *Stop now . . . or you might draw blood.*

Charlene had warned her of the danger.

He did make Alice breathless; she was woman enough to admit it. But that wouldn't matter in the slightest when there were oceans between them. They had only a few weeks in the same house, after all. She wouldn't be foolish enough to let him hurt her.

Alice wriggled out of her wedding gown and kicked it aside.

Kali kneaded her paws on the discarded dress, sniffing at a pearl hopefully to see if it could be eaten.

Her trunks were in the corner. Bypassing the frilled gowns her mother had insisted on purchasing, Alice found one of the sensible traveling costumes she would wear on her voyage to India.

Such a waste, all these delicate, hand-embroidered confections.

She wouldn't need them where she was going. On her travels she would wear only serviceable cottons and linens in practical hues that wouldn't show dust or attract attention.

Shaking one of the gowns, Alice noted with satisfaction that the dove gray muslin hadn't even wrinkled after being folded at the bottom of the trunk for days.

She didn't need a maid to help her fasten this gown because it had only three concealed hooks in front. Very sensible for ocean crossings.

Kali rubbed against Alice's ankle.

Sinking to the floor, she scooped Kali into her arms, cradling the cat's warm, squirming body against her chest. She scratched her belly, and Kali flopped back with her legs spread wide in a most unladylike manner.

Kali's ears perked up and her body stiffened. She jumped out of Alice's arms and ran to the glass-paned balcony doors.

Kali growled, low in her throat, scenting something interesting on the air.

"If I open the balcony doors, you mustn't leap off. We're several floors up, you know."

Kali quirked her head. She was quite a clever cat and nearly always followed instructions.

Alice tried the doors. They finally creaked open after she threw her shoulder against them. Obviously, they hadn't been opened in quite some time and there was a shameful amount of dust and cobwebs coating them.

Kali swept past her feet and perched on the edge of the balcony balustrade, staring down at the gardens.

Alice stepped outside.

The air smelled of apple blossoms and the clean fresh scent of the world after a good, cleansing rain.

Nick was helping his gardener repair Gertrude's enclosure. As Alice watched, he stripped off his coat, tugged off his cravat, and opened the buttons at the top of his white linen shirt, exposing a triangle of tanned skin.

Next he rolled up his sleeves.

She probably shouldn't be watching him like this. Suppose he glanced up and noticed her staring. But she couldn't seem to look away.

Especially when he began working, lifting heavy boards and using a hammer and nails to fix them into place.

Sinuous muscles rippled in his forearms and his large, strong hands moved with swift skill.

The noonday sun and the hard labor soon dampened his shirt until it clung to his broad back and chest.

Tonight she would have his hard, muscular frame pressed upon her bosom.

He would touch her. *Here.*

She slid her hand beneath her bodice and lightly squeezed one of her breasts as she watched him lift another board and hold it with one arm as he hammered, swift and sure.

She snatched her hand away from her bosom and ducked back inside, resting against the wall, shaken by how deeply the mere sight of him affected her.

She was panting, her chest heaving up and down in the same way it would if she had been running.

There was no question as to whether she found him attractive. She'd never felt this way before, not even close. She wanted him to touch her. Wanted his hands all over her body.

This wasn't mere intellectual curiosity. It was too strong and elemental and it captured her too completely. It was frightening how this longing changed her into someone she barely recognized.

Could she control her emotions? Would her desire for him end when she needed it to end?

Her friends had tried to warn her. Yet ladies of the *ton* made loveless, expedient matches every day.

But did those ladies receive such thrilling kisses? Did their expedient matches include this odd wobbly feeling at the backs of their knees? Like sealing wax melting over parchment.

And that's quite enough of that, you silly thing. You're as bad as Lady Melinda swooning at his feet. Do at least try to keep your head on your shoulders.

Kali raced across the room to the door and scratched with her front paws, mewling loudly.

"I can't let you explore yet, my sweetling, until I know you'll be safe. There are wild beasts out there."

Some of them were lions.

And some of them wore tight breeches and had an arrogant gleam in their silvery eyes.

Chapter 10

━━━━━━━━━◍◍━━━━━━━━━

They should then carry on an amusing conversation on various subjects, and may also talk suggestively of things which would be considered as coarse, or not to be mentioned generally in society.

The Kama Sutra of Vātsyāyana

"Alice?"

"Pardon?" Nick must have asked her a question. Alice had been thinking about his hands.

About how they made his wineglass look like a child's cup. And how, even though his entire frame was constructed on such a massive scale, he moved with a lethal grace.

They were seated in the formal dining room, Nick at one end of the table and Alice at the other. The duke was sitting next to Nick, with Berthold positioned behind him.

"I asked how do you find the meal?" Nick called down the long table.

"It's very rich," Alice replied.

And very unhealthful.

Veal in cream sauce. Rare beef dripping with blood that had fair turned her stomach to even see it. Nary an enticing vegetable in sight.

Only an enticing marquess.

She probably shouldn't think about those skillful hands of his.

Holding a hammer. Holding her in place for his kiss.

It made her own hand tremble as she lifted her fork.

"You're not eating your beef, my dear," said the duke. "Don't you like it?"

"I never eat beef, Your Grace," Alice replied.

"Never?" asked Nick.

"I believe it to be insalubrious."

"I suppose I should have asked for your preferences to give to Cook." Nick studied her plate. "You're not fond of potatoes either?"

She didn't want to appear ungrateful, but the potatoes were smothered in such a large amount of butter and congealed beef drippings that she could scarcely force herself to take one bite. "I prefer more colorful vegetables. I am a devotee of Mr. Shelley's writings on the subject of a frugivorous diet."

"Frugivor-what, my dear?" asked the duke, stopping with his fork half raised.

"The theory that man is by nature more fitted to a purely vegetable diet."

Nick scoffed, helping himself to a large slice of pink beef. "All those sensitive poetic types think they can live on air and kisses."

"Surely you must have a kitchen garden?" Alice

persisted. "You have heard of green vegetables? Leafy, healthful things. Grow in the earth. Broccoli. Spinach. That sort of thing."

Nick laughed. "I think we could find you a few green leafy things to chew on."

"Don't like vegetables," March interjected from his post by the door. "Don't trust 'em."

Alice stared at the man. Footmen were never supposed to interrupt repasts.

"I don't much care for vegetables, either," said the duke.

His skin did have an unhealthy pallor. Alice would have to do something about that. Before she left for India she would make it her mission to introduce a more healthy diet to the household.

"The populace of England has a horror of uncooked vegetables," she said. "Yet a diet must be sufficiently varied with vegetables, fruits, and nuts. Mr. Shelley has published quite a revelatory treatise on the subject, if you would care to read it, Your Grace."

"Grow in the dirt, they do, vegetables," grumbled March. "With grubs and other nasty things."

"Precisely why we wash them," said Alice.

"I don't like washing. Don't trust it," replied March.

Alice narrowed her eyes. "I can see that." The footman needed a good dousing.

"Well la-di-da," he replied, sticking his nose in the air. "Ain't we fine."

"Mr. March, this is my wife you're talking to," said Nick. He smiled at her, a private smile . . . a promise, and Alice's irritation with his unconventional serving staff vanished.

"Said you'd never marry," March grumbled. "Wives are too much trouble, you said. She'll try to change things around here, just you wait."

He all but stuck his tongue out. What a churlish little fellow.

"Are you married, my boy?" the duke asked Nick with a puzzled expression in his watery gray eyes. "Can that be true? Why, you're only fifteen!"

Alice blinked. "I think you are mistak—"

"Actually," the tall, spindly butler with the long, grave face who seemingly doubled as a footman, said, "he's thirty years, two months, twenty days and twelve hours old."

"Thank you, Bill," said Nick gravely.

"Madam, I must protest," the duke said, setting down his fork with a bang against the table. "The marriage must be annulled. You are robbing the cradle. You are . . ." his voice trailed into silence as he gazed at her raptly ". . . as comely as a cymbidium blooming upon a craggy mountaintop. Just like your mother. Beautiful Agatha. I hope she will dine with us tomorrow."

"Why, thank you," Alice said. "A cymbidium is a genus of—?"

"Orchid," Hatherly finished. "And we'd better not encourage the topic or we'll all be trapped here for hours."

"It's quite rude to interrupt a lady when she is speaking," the duke scolded. "Didn't you learn anything at your expensive boarding school, you young rascal? Do forgive my son, dear lady." The duke inclined his head. "He's still growing."

Alice very much doubted that. If he grew any wider in the shoulders he wouldn't be able to fit through doorways. She nodded politely. "Of course."

"As I was saying, the *Cymbidium* is a hardy genus of orchids in the family of . . . in the family of . . ."

"I've heard of your celebrated collection," Alice interrupted, seeing that the duke was flustered by his inability to remember his botany.

"Beautiful lady," said the duke, staring at her dreamily. "You remind me of a young Marie Antoinette. She had such melting eyes and rosebud lips. Her dimple was in her chin, though. Such a charming dimple. Ah . . ."

He plucked a handkerchief from his sleeve and touched it to his nose. "I was a great favorite of hers at the court of Versailles. I once had the distinct honor of presenting her with a rare black orchid for her conservatory. She wanted to run away with me. She was madly in love with me. It's the nose, you see. She did admire a stately nose. But, alas, she is gone. Too soon. Too soon."

He blew the stately article in question noisily into his handkerchief.

"Ah . . . it is quite an impressive nose," said Alice.

"Thank you, my dear. It's all in the stories a nose has to tell." He placed a finger on the bump in the bridge of his nose. "Now, this particular bump was received during my first voyage to South America, when our ship encountered the dread pirate—"

Nick clanged his fork against his wineglass. "I'd like to propose a toast."

The duke's eyes lit. "Oh, I love toasts." He raised his glass. "What are we toasting, my boy? Wait a moment. Are you old enough to be drinking? Seems to me that young lads in my day were only allowed a thimbleful of claret. And here you've had at least three glasses."

"Four." He rose and held his glass toward Alice. "To my wife, the Lady Hatherly, health, wealth, and a westerly wind."

"Wind?" scoffed the duke. "One mustn't wish for one's wife to pass wind. Manners, my boy. Manners."

Alice suppressed a giggle, and March and Berthold grinned widely, but Bill's face remained impassive.

Nick frowned. "I said an *easterly wind*. To fill her sails. On her voyage. She won't be staying with us for long."

"Oh?" the duke said. "Where are you going, my dear?"

"To India," Alice replied.

"Bully!" cried March. "Hear that Bill? She's leaving soon."

Alice chose to ignore him. Really, if she responded to every outlandish or discourteous pronouncement this evening, she'd say something she might regret.

"India, my dear? Why, how smashing," said the duke. "Do say hello to the Sultan of Mysore. Do you know they call him the Tiger? But he's a dear old fellow upon better acquaintance. Are you planning to visit his palace?"

Alice knew the sultan had died twenty years

ago, in the act of fighting off her countrymen. "I wasn't planning on it, no."

"You simply must visit him. I'm a great favorite of his. He's a devoted admirer of my nose. 'Such a nose,' he said to me one day, as we walked in his lovely gardens, 'such a nose denotes vast wisdom. *You* should be King of England, Barry old boy . . .'"

He continued on with his story, barely stopping to breathe.

Alice was beginning to see why Nick had interrupted his father before.

He broke into the monologue when the duke finally paused. "She won't be visiting any sultans, Barrington. She's a studious lady who plans to visit libraries."

"Oh?" The duke's impressively unruly white eyebrows climbed. "Are you one of those . . . What do they call them? Something to do with stockings."

"I rather think her stockings are blue," Nick drawled.

"But you must have some *real* adventures, dear lady," said the duke. "You can't spend all your time in musty old libraries."

"I'll have you know I've done dozens of exciting things already. I fell into a river once. And I drank brandy." She'd had a sip from the Duke of Harland's flask.

And I kissed your sinful son today.

"Do you indulge in a nip every now and then, m'dear? How nice to find a lady who's willing to admit such a thing. March, my boy, bring the lady some of my special supply of ouzo from the Greek isles. What did you say was your name, madam? Have I told you that you remind me very strongly of a young Marie Antoinette? She had such melting eyes and rosebud lips . . ."

Thankfully, March arrived with the requested bottle before the duke had a chance to expound upon the splendors of his nose again. The footman poured clear liquid into small, thin glasses and passed them around the table.

"Drink it straight down, my dear," urged the duke. "I find it takes the bite from the air on these chilly winter evenings."

"I believe it's summer, Your Grace," Alice said respectfully. "Although it's always winter in some places. The Northern Pole, for example."

"Well said, my dear. Drink it down now. It's bound to improve your outlook on my son."

"I don't suppose I might have some water as well?" asked Alice.

"Water?" sputtered Nick. "My friend Captain Lear risked life and limb to bring us this bottle. It's precious. Every last drop. Watering it would be a crime."

Though she rarely indulged in spirits, as the duke had said, a few sips could only improve this meal. And might give her courage for what lay ahead. After the meal.

In Nick's bedchamber.

Alice lifted her glass and gave her father-in-law a cheeky smile. "To your nose, Duke."

He chortled. "To your beauty, my dear."

The clear liquid burned going down, but it left a very pleasant licorice aftertaste, like the herbal drops Alice's nurse used to give her when she had a head cold.

"She's not a classic beauty, if you ask me," mumbled March.

"I did *not* ask you," the duke replied. He yawned mightily. "I can't seem to stay awake these days. I do apologize, my dear. I fear I must leave you."

"It's nothing, please don't apologize." Alice could see the duke was not only befuddled, but exhausted as well. He'd barely eaten anything, and what he had eaten was laden with sugars and animal fat. She'd have to have a talk with Nick about the duke's diet.

"Excuse me," Nick said to Alice as he rose from his seat. He laid his hands on his father's shoulders. "Shall we go upstairs?"

The concern and tenderness in Nick's eyes as he helped his father pulled at Alice's heart.

The duke nodded sleepily. "I can't . . . keep my eyes open. Until tomorrow, my dear." The duke performed a wobbly bow, propped up on one side by Nick, and on the other by his towering attendant, Berthold. "I hope to have the pleasure of your company for a turn about my orchid conservatory."

Alice rose and took his thin, knotty hand in hers. "It would be my pleasure, Your Grace."

The duke squeezed her hand. "You know the orchids talk to me. They don't talk to everyone. But I have a feeling they may be persuaded to converse with you."

"Ah . . . that would be quite an honor, Your Grace."

"Noon tomorrow?" the duke asked eagerly.

"Noon it is," Alice replied.

Berthold helped the duke from the room. March and Bill followed, leaving Alice and Nick alone.

Nick took the seat next to her. "Much better. This table is far too long for ease of conversation. Thank you for being so patient with the duke."

"I like his adventure stories, be they ever so exaggerated."

He smiled, but sadness lingered in his eyes. "Most of his adventures happened only in his imagination. Not all . . . but most."

"Does he truly believe the orchids speak?"

"He's utterly convinced. Sometimes he brings a quill and parchment to record their speech. It's mostly harmless. But if he weren't wealthy, and he didn't have me to care for him, it would be enough of an affliction to ensure he would be shut away in a private madhouse where he would suffer the worst ill treatment."

A shadow passed across his face and was gone as swiftly as it came. "He still fancies himself quite the debonair lady's gentleman, though."

Alice smiled, remembering his courtly compliments. "I'm sure he was quite devastating in his day."

"Favors me in that regard," Nick said with a teasing grin, his careless charm restored.

Grabbing her wine, Alice gulped down half a glass. When Nick summoned the charm, a lady needed liquid courage.

One wouldn't think the combination of the sharp, herbal liqueur and the wine would be pleasing, but as the wine dissolved on her tongue there was a pleasant burst of sun-dried plums that mellowed the lingering fire of the anise-flavored spirits.

"I'll taste the wine later," Nick said in a low, intimate voice, "On your lips."

There he went, setting her senses aflame again.

Charlene's words echoed in her mind: *The act of love is the most intimate conversation two people can have . . .*

She must remain composed. Distant. Detached.

She must observe her body's responses from a remove. Separate her mind, heart, and body and keep them compartmentalized.

Which would be no easy task, as her body and mind were ready and eager for more kisses.

She'd tried to banish her nerves, but the moment he looked at her with that hungry expression, her trepidation rushed back tenfold.

She must stall a moment more. Keep him talking of other subjects. Seek the composure required to view this evening's activities from a scholarly perspective.

"My lord, I'm worried about the duke's diet," she said. "He ate hardly any of his meal and what he did ingest was either animal flesh or smothered in butter."

Nick shrugged. "My cook is French."

"When I asked about your kitchen garden I was not being facetious. It's a well-known medical certainty that the nourishment one ingests plays a role in one's physical and even mental health. I wonder if the duke is truly deranged? Or could his malady be the result of a lifetime of unsalutary eating?"

Nick's eyes lost their teasing light. "My father is mad. And no amount of vegetables will improve his condition." He rose from the table and held out his hand. "If you don't believe me, let me show you."

His strong grip crushed her hand as he pulled her from her seat and led her down a long, dark hallway, following a glimmer of moonlight into a spacious, open, window-lined gallery, which opened out onto the shadowy gardens.

He took a flickering lantern from a hook near the door and held it aloft.

The halo of light illuminated rows of paintings, somber with blood red and inky black.

"This is why you shouldn't become too fond of the duke, Alice."

Chapter 11

When a man and a woman embrace each other while the woman is sitting on the lap of the man . . . then it is called an embrace like a "mixture of milk and water."

The Kama Sutra of Vātsyāyana

Or too fond of me, Nick added silently.

"I am descended from a long line of madmen, Alice." He strode across the cavernous room, lantern held aloft, stopping to point out the more notorious of his ancestors.

He paused before a forbidding portrait of a man with black eyes and black hair. "Edgar Hatherly, the ninth Marquess of Hatherly, until he was created Duke of Barrington by Queen Anne in the early 1700s. Poor old Edgar was convinced he could fly. Built this house and then died by flinging himself from a tower with a pair of feathered wings strapped to his shoulders."

"Gracious." Alice shivered as she studied the portrait. "He does have rather a maniacal gleam in his eyes."

"Exactly." Nick drew her by the hand to another

painting. "My great-great-grandfather, Warren Hatherly, whose elder brother died in infancy. He believed he was being persecuted by miniature men with green skin who probed his brain with common household implements at night in order to steal his thoughts."

"An inventive fellow, your great-great-grand-father."

"A madman," Nick corrected. "He published a letter to Parliament warning about an invasion of the tiny green men who wished to take control of first Parliament, and then the world. Very embarrassing for the family, I'm told."

Alice nodded. "I imagine so."

He walked past several portraits, marching swiftly, avoiding her eyes, and stopped in front of a painting of a woman wearing red silk skirts stretched stiffly to either side with the aid of panniers. "The third duke's sister, Lady Grace, wife of the Earl of Langdon."

Alice lifted a hand to trace the lines of Lady Grace's cheek. "She's beautiful—such silver eyes, and such a feline face. Staring straight ahead. Such an impression of strength."

"She accused the earl of poisoning her and ran away one night, never to be seen again."

"The family curse strikes females as well?"

"There's no discernible pattern. Sometimes it skips a generation. There've been several sober, sane Hatherlys." They walked farther down the row. "Virgil Hatherly, brother of the fourth duke. Entered the clergy and denounced his brother from the pulpit every day."

The man in the portrait was thin and ascetic, but his eyes were no less filled with demons and shadows. Nick lowered the lantern. He'd made his point.

Alice continued walking down the line. "Is this the duke?"

Nick nodded. He hated to look at his father's image because it made him too sad.

His father had been so hale and robust, the battle lance of his nose balanced by the strength of his shoulders and his proud, upright carriage.

The artist who had painted his father had been more creative than most. The duke held an orchid, its pale white flowers glowing eerily near his heart.

Reluctantly, he joined Alice, illuminating his father's portrait. "He thought he could avoid going insane by strenuous mental exercises. He memorized thousands of plant species and became an expert botanist and celebrated orchid collector."

Alice placed a gentle hand on his arm. "How wonderful that he achieved so much."

"And yet he couldn't stave off the inevitable," Nick said bitterly. "He was attempting to extract a serum from a species of orchid in Nepal that he believed to be a lunacy preventative. But nothing helped in the end. The madness took him on the voyage back from Nepal. As it will most likely claim me."

"I'm so sorry." She touched the back of his hand, and a lump rose in his throat.

"My mother left for the Continent soon after. Their marriage couldn't survive his descent into madness." He laughed. "I tried to stop everything from falling apart but it was useless. I couldn't fix my mother's broken heart or stop her from leaving."

The soft light in Alice's eyes was worse than any harsh derision.

Excellent work, Nick.

Bring her here to warn her about the dangers of caring for a lunatic and then lapse into some self-pitying monologue that has obviously achieved the exact opposite effect.

Moonlight splashed across Nick's face, caressing his angular jaw, and gleaming on dark hair and white linen.

His voice rasped lower than any voice Alice had ever heard. Gruff and rough-edged.

This darkness was so contrary to the teasing, lighthearted man she'd come to know over the last month.

Always joking, always making risqué innuendos.

He was giving her a warning.

Making certain that she knew he could never allow himself to grow close to anyone. Not when he thought he would go mad. Not when he believed that anyone he loved would leave him.

Seeing this raw, real side of him confused her.

She searched the wall. "Where's your painting?"

"I refused to sit. I told you, Alice, the line ends with me. I'll never sire an heir. I'm the last of my cursed line."

"Have you ever considered the possibility that maybe you won't go mad? That maybe there's no chasm of lunacy waiting to swallow you?"

"No."

"How would you live your life if you knew you had ten more years? Or twenty, even?"

"I never consider my future because I can feel that I will go insane." He placed his fist on his flat stomach. "*Here.* In my gut." He stared at his father's portrait. "There have been . . . signs."

"What signs?"

"Sometimes the world seems as though it's closing in on me. My vision blurs."

"Have you ever been examined by an eye doctor? You may need spectacles."

"Rakes don't wear spectacles," he scoffed.

"Maybe you're not a rake," she rejoined. Which would be quite problematic. She was counting on him to be a rake. A conceited rake whose single purpose in life was the pursuit of pleasure.

"Don't go thinking I'm more than I appear, Alice. What you see is what I am." He spread his arms wide. "Descendant of madmen. Idle aristocrat. Pleasure-obsessed rake."

Alice couldn't accept his word anymore. He spoke with too much feeling, and too much pain.

"You're also your father's refuge. His anchor. You don't let him drift too far into the deep."

"He harms no one so I keep him here with me. He'd never gambled before now. Dalton believes there was someone behind the scenes besides the duke's hired caretaker, Mr. Stubbs. Someone who wishes my family ill. Every day, my friends and I search for news of Stubbs in pubs, coach passenger lists, and on ship registries. If I find Stubbs, he'll lead me to my true enemy."

Alice saw the steely resolve in his eyes. "I don't like the idea of someone holding a grudge against you."

He smiled. "Says the lady whose father practically blackmailed me into marriage."

"Says the lady who requires nightly instruction in the particulars of pleasure, or have you forgotten our arrangement?" she teased.

She needed to turn the conversation back to her love lessons, because she didn't like the rush of emotion stirring in her heart.

She heard the suffering in his words, but she didn't want to understand the reasons for his darkness and his pain.

It made her feel too sympathetic.

Too vulnerable.

She had to regain control over her emotions.

Follow the plan.

She glanced at the large, thronelike chair she'd noticed earlier. It was time to turn imaginings into reality. "Sit," she urged.

When he wavered she pushed against his chest. "*Sit*, Lord Hatherly."

He settled into the chair looking like some medieval painting of a mountain king. All he needed were wolves at his feet and a fur strapped across his chest.

She'd twisted her hair into a simple knot. All it took was one yank to release the curls. The swift hiss of his breath informed her that he liked her hair unbound.

Kshiraniraka, or milk and water embrace . . . the woman is sitting on the lap of the man . . .

The wine coursing through her body was making her feel quite reckless.

But how was this going to work? He was so very large, and she had long skirts. She'd have to hike them to her hips.

She reached for the hem of her skirts, hefted them into the crook of one arm, and climbed onto his lap. Recalling the description in the *Kama Sutra*, she situated her limbs to either side of his enormous torso.

"Good God." He looked stunned. "Dimples, what do you think you're doing?"

"Wind your arms around me and clasp me to your chest," she instructed.

Was this right? It felt rather ridiculous. But she bravely continued since there was no use stopping now, not until they achieved the correct position.

"I think if you . . ." She adjusted herself on top of him, squirming to find a comfortable seat.

He caught hold of her waist with his hands. "I wouldn't wriggle quite so much," he said with a grimace.

"Are you in pain? Am I hurting you?"

"You could say that."

She was doing this all wrong. Perhaps if there were fewer impediments.

She tugged on Nick's cravat, attempting to loosen the knot.

He emitted a strangled laugh. "You are the most surprising woman I've ever met." His laughter died and his hands tightened around her waist. "And the most arousing."

If someone painted their portrait right now, what a scandalous painting it would be.

The way his large hands wrapped nearly all the way around her waist made shivers run up and down her spine.

His hands rearranged her to suit his needs with unspoken commands.

Hips here.

Arms around my neck.

Lift your bum.

She liked being rearranged. Disarrayed.

Deranged.

"This gown's too rough. You should wear silks," he rasped.

"It's a sensible gown."

He tugged her bodice lower. "I crave the silk of your skin." He lifted her hand and placed it in the center of her chest. "Feel what I crave."

She'd never laid a hand directly across her breastbone before.

Such a serviceable bone.

Protecting her heart.

It made her think about how easily a heart could be pierced.

By a dagger.

A sliver of bone.

By silver eyes filled with longing and buried pain.

She shouldn't allow herself to think such thoughts, but recklessness was building inside her.

One more hard tug from Nick and her bodice slipped down, exposing her to his gaze.

"Touch yourself there," he commanded.

She knew what he meant. He wanted her to touch her breasts. As she had this morning while she watched him working in the garden.

She couldn't bring herself to obey. It was too much. She wasn't bold enough.

He lowered his head and blew cool air on her naked flesh.

The tips of her breasts tightened and throbbed.

"Alice." He caught her gaze. "Touch yourself for me. Make me an offering."

Slowly, with trembling fingers, she slid her hand from her breastbone to cover one of her breasts.

"The other one, as well."

She cupped both her breasts with her hands and closed her eyes.

"Good girl."

He rewarded her for obeying him with a long, lingering kiss, his tongue stroking inside her mouth while his hands held her captive against his arousal.

Every time he shifted beneath her, he rubbed against the center of her body through her linens, sending waves of pleasure along her inner thighs.

Only leaving her lips to kiss his way along her neck, he murmured encouragement as she arched into the embrace.

"I want to be bad," she heard herself whisper.

"With all the mad dukes watching?"

"Let them watch."

Who knew good, sensible girls would burn the hottest?

The heat emanating from her was enough to

burn all the canvases to ash and rid him of his cursed legacy forever.

He filled his hands with her breasts, shaping the peaks, tugging and teasing.

The lantern had long since burned out and the room was lit only by moonlight. He couldn't see her eyes in the darkness, but he knew their color. The clarity and depth of the turquoise, like the heart of a candle flame. Like a rare orchid blooming in the night.

He lifted his hands and she exhaled through her nose, a disappointed little sound that made him smile.

"I'm only finding the wine," he reassured her.

There was always a bottle of wine here, next to this chair. For the nights he couldn't sleep. The nights he came here to sit and stare into the maw of madness.

The stopper came away easily with a soft sucking noise.

Imported Portuguese wine with a rich, ripe berry flavor and hints of tobacco and chocolate.

He kissed her with wine pooled inside his mouth and she gulped greedily, kissing him hard and fast.

"More," she demanded.

Another deep draw of wine transferred into her lips.

She purred like a cat. "It's delicious, Nick."

He lifted her skirts higher, pressing upward with his cock against the layers of buckskin and linen separating them.

Just some woman, he reminded himself.

Some beautiful fever dream of a woman.

Like all the women he'd had. All of them saying his name in the same purring, pleasure-soaked way.

She was no different. Merely one of many in a long line.

Stretching along his past like the portraits lining the gallery.

The history of lovers gone.

Courtesans. Opera singers.

And now Alice.

Innocent, intelligent, inquisitive Alice.

Gown around her waist.

Breasts spilling over her stays. Nipples red as wine in the moonlight.

When his lips sought her breast she held still, surprised, as he sucked gently and rhythmically, flicking her nipple with the tip of his tongue.

Some women were able to climax simply from a lover playing with their breasts.

Her nipples were sensitive; that was obvious from the way her belly trembled against him and she made small, tentative thrusting motions with her hips, rocking against his erection.

He moved to her other breast, lavishing the same attention and care. She rocked faster, instinctively seeking her release.

She was close now.

He could feel it.

This was the moment he lived for. When he knew he could make a woman shatter to pieces in his arms.

Such power.

This he knew. This he owned. This pleasure. This drunken abandon.

In a practiced movement, he hiked her skirts, separated the folds of her drawers, and sought the pearl awaiting him there . . .

"Oh . . ." Alice jerked against him, trying to escape but he tightened his elbow around her waist and held fast.

One firm sweep of his forefinger against her clitoris while his lips resumed suckling her nipple and she came—only a small crisis, but he'd work her up to the big, earth-shattering ones soon.

"You touched me," she said in a stunned voice. *"There."*

"Shh." He kissed his way from her dimple to her lips. He didn't like it when women talked too much during sex. Easy enough to keep them sighing instead. "Let's get you to a bed."

"Mmm." Her head dropped to his shoulder and she fell against him, still riding the pleasure.

"That was very educational," she murmured.

"I'm glad you approve, Dimples."

"Oh, I approve," she said, her voice a satin whisper, sliding over his skin, making him want to slide into her.

Heat and tightness and . . . Alice.

Innocent.

Not yet.

Not here, out in the open where anyone could stumble upon them. He wanted to seduce her in a leisurely manner. He was determined to make this night memorable and special for her.

The loud sound of fists pounding on wood startled Nick.

"Hatherly!" a faint, deep voice shouted. "I know you're in there."

Lear.

Nick would murder him with his bare hands.

"A visitor this late in the evening?" Alice asked. "One of your friends?"

Nick lifted her off his lap and lowered her to the floor. "My so-called friend Captain Lear. I'll tell him to leave."

"Does your butler ever do any . . . butling?"

"Bill? Only when he feels like it. I have to answer the door, Alice. It could be important."

Her eyes told him he'd better be quick about it.

Nick stood and adjusted his waistcoat. "Don't move. This won't take a moment."

More shouting and pounding.

"Go," she said, giving him a little push. "Before he breaks the door down."

Nick walked swiftly to the entranceway, eager to return to his bride.

When he opened the door Lear immediately strode into the room, bringing a cold gust of air with him.

"What the hell do you want, Lear? It's midnight. Are you drunk?"

Lear shook his head with a sober expression in his black eyes. "I have a delivery for you."

Nick stilled. "The one I told you about? But it's not scheduled for weeks."

"Had a message from Hawkins. Thought it would be the one you told me about, but it was something else entirely. I waited outside. Hawkins brought her out the back entrance. She's in my carriage."

"*She?*"

"It's a girl. A lady, I think. Not sure. She hasn't spoken much."

"A female?" Nick exploded. "You know I never harbor females. Not in a houseful of men. We'll have to find someplace else for her."

"No time. Had to take her tonight. And haven't you got a wife now? There's at least one female in your house."

"My wife will be leaving in a matter of weeks."

Lear looked puzzled. "She's leaving?"

Nick sighed. "It's a long story."

"Might I inquire what's happening here?" a soft, clear voice asked.

Alice stood in the doorway to the inner rooms, her hair still loose and tumbled, turquoise eyes glinting in the shadows.

Lear gazed at Alice with appreciation filling his eyes. "That your wife?"

Nick inclined his head.

"Christ." Lear whistled admiringly. "You're in a whole world of trouble, mate."

Chapter 12

In the event of any misconduct on the part
of her husband, she should not blame him
excessively, though she be a little displeased.

The Kama Sutra of Vātsyāyana

"It's not what you think," Nick said.

"Oh?" Alice was in no mood for lies. Not after
she'd trusted him so fully.

Tonight, in the gallery, she'd touched herself for
him. Exposed and wanton. Trusting him.

And now this sordid scene of . . . what was this
exactly?

She'd heard the dark-haired man tell Nick that
he had a female in his carriage. He'd also said that
the female was to come and live here.

Nick opened his mouth but she cut him off. "You
know what I think this is, Nick? This is one of your
mistresses refusing to go quietly off to pasture.
She's demanding to come back and live here. Well,
that's not acceptable." She folded her arms across
her chest. "Recall the terms of our agreement."

"You've got it all wrong," Nick said, shaking his
head.

"Lady Hatherly?" The man at the door swept her a dashing bow. "Captain Lear, at your service."

He was younger than Nick and nearly as handsome, with collar-length raven-black hair. Was that a gold hoop glinting in his ear? Trust Nick to have outrageous friends.

"Have you told her?" he asked Nick.

"Told me what?" asked Alice.

Nick sighed. "No, I haven't told her."

"I'll go and fetch the delivery, shall I? While you explain to your bride what's happening in this unusual household." Captain Lear spun in a flapping of black cloak and a flash of polished black boots, and left.

The delivery? Oh, this just got more and more damning. Women were not *deliveries*.

Alice tapped her slipper against the entrance hall's marble floor. "I'm waiting."

"It's difficult to explain." Nick shoved a hand through his thick, dark brown hair. "I take people in sometimes. My servants. . . . they're not really servants. More like . . . wards. It started with Berthold. Found him unconscious outside a public house. Left for dead. Prizefighter who fought one too many fights. He had a head wound. Could barely speak."

"What are you telling me, Nick? That your servants are former prizefighters? And what's that got to do with a girl arriving in the dead of night?"

"If you'll allow me to elaborate—"

"You'll excuse me if I doubt whether you could offer me a satisfactory explanation."

"There is an explanation, if you'll be quiet for a moment—"

"I will *not* be quiet. And I won't have you referring to girls as *deliveries*."

"Alice, for the love of God, will you—"

"I think they dosed her with laudanum." Captain Lear reappeared with a slight, cloak-wrapped figure on his arm. The girl wove unsteadily on her feet, her face obscured by a hood.

When she saw Nick she emitted a squeak and broke away from Lear, running straight into Alice's arms. She wrapped her arms around Alice's waist and buried her head in her neck.

"Don't let them hurt me," she said.

"Are you injured?" Alice asked her.

The girl nodded.

"Right then." Alice could learn the particulars later. This girl was terrified and injured in some way.

Alice was sometimes squeamish when it came to injuries. She didn't like the sight of blood. But this situation clearly required her to overcome her fear and help this poor girl, whoever she was.

"Right then," she repeated. "You lot stop standing about. She'll need fresh linens and hot water. Bring some brandy as well, I'm sure you have plenty on hand, and something nourishing to eat, such as beef broth. Can you manage that?"

Nick stood frozen for a moment, as if he wasn't accustomed to taking orders, but then he gave a brief nod. "Of course. We'll arrange everything."

"And if she's severely injured or ill we will need a physician," added Alice.

"I know just the fellow," Nick said.

Alice squeezed the girl's shoulders. "Come with me, love."

Light purple eyes, swimming with tears, stared at Alice. "Where are we going?"

"Somewhere safe. Will you allow Lord Hatherly to carry you upstairs?" Alice asked.

She shrank closer to Alice, her eyes huge. "No, no, no," she muttered.

"I'll help you then." Alice steered the girl toward the inner door.

"Take her to the guest chamber one door down from your study," Nick called over his shoulder as he and Lear left for the kitchens.

"What's all the shouting about?" March appeared in the doorway, rubbing his eyes, his nightcap askew on his head.

"Nothing," Alice said. "Go back to sleep."

"Who's she?" March asked.

"I've no idea. What's your name, love?" Alice asked as they passed March and began to climb the stairs.

There was a pause as the girl fought back tears. "Jane."

Climbing the stairs was slow going. Jane was so weak that they had to stop every second step.

What had befallen her? Alice wondered.

When they finally reached the guest chamber, Alice's arm ached from holding Jane upright. She swiftly unlatched the door and guided Jane to a bed.

She untied Jane's bonnet and slipped it from her head, stopping in dismay when she saw the short tufts of dark hair and the white stretches of scalp visible on her head.

"Who did this to you?" she whispered, clenching her jaw.

Jane lifted her hand to her head. "I—I don't know." Her eyes grew wide and panicked. "I can't . . . remember. My head feels so queer."

They'd mentioned laudanum. It would account for her stumbling speech and confusion.

"Never mind," Alice said soothingly, loosening Jane's cloak. "We'll sort everything out tomorrow. Right now you should rest."

Jane nodded. "I'm very tired."

Alice turned down the covers and helped Jane climb into bed. "Where are you injured? Do you think you have any broken bones?" She felt her ribs and arms.

"No broken bones. Only these." She held out her wrists. "On my ankles as well."

Alice held a candle close and flinched when she saw the raw red marks around her wrists.

"What are these marks from?" Tears sprang to Alice's eyes.

Chains would leave such marks. Or thick ropes.

There was a knock at the door, and Jane cowered into a corner of the bed. "Don't let them find me. I won't go back. I'll never go back to the Yellow House."

"No one's forcing you to go anywhere," Alice said firmly.

She opened the door only wide enough to slip through.

Nick and Lear stood outside with everything she'd asked for. "She's very frightened right now, especially of men. I don't think you should enter the room."

Nick nodded. "I'm sorry to foist her on you."

"Her name's Jane," said Alice. "And I must go back and wash her wounds."

Nick's jaw tightened. "Wounds?"

"Her wrists and ankles. I think she's been chained."

Nick and Lear exchanged a tense look.

Alice hoisted the heavy pot of boiling water, and Nick held the door while she entered the room. "It's only me with some hot water," she called to Jane. "I'll make you some chamomile tea."

She went back for the linens.

"Will you be all right?" Nick asked, his eyes heavy with concern.

Captain Lear turned away, pretending a sudden interest in the wall.

"I'll be fine."

He touched her cheek. "Alice, I know you have questions."

His touch made her long to curl up in his arms.

She wanted to twine her arms around him and kiss him. She wanted to be back in his arms in the gallery, feeling him solid and strong beneath her.

"Thank you," Nick whispered. He smoothed her hair away from her cheek. "I promise I'll explain everything tomorrow. Lear and I must go out now."

Where did he have to go so late at night? And why were he and Lear both so very grim?

"I'll have March leave a tray with some food outside the door." He turned to leave.

Alice wanted to shout at him, beg him to stay, but Jane was frightened of men, and Alice was scared of needing Nick too much.

"Bring us Jane's cloak," Lear said.

"Why?" Alice asked, perplexed.

"I'll tell you later," Nick said impatiently. "We have to go now."

Alice went back inside the room and gathered Jane's torn cloak and handed it to Nick.

Lear touched the brim of his hat. "My lady. I hope to speak with you again under less troubling circumstances."

She nodded and reentered the room.

Thankfully, a fire had already been laid in the grate and all she had to do was light it.

With great care she washed Jane's wrists and patted them dry with a clean towel.

She opened a jar of the herbal salve Nick had brought. It smelled of lavender and comfrey. A comforting, calming odor with only a slight medicinal bite.

She smeared some over Jane's wrists. After the first flinch, Jane remained motionless, allowing Alice to cleanse and dress her wounds.

She was wearing a dirty, torn gown that probably used to be fine.

Alice helped her disrobe and used hot water to wash away the worst of the dirt from her skin.

"I'll return in a moment," she said. "I want to fetch one of my nightdresses."

Jane nodded dully.

Alice closed the door behind her and walked swiftly to her room, choosing a soft, flannel nightdress and a pair of woolen stockings. Jane might catch a chill. She was blue about the lips.

When she returned, Alice helped Jane into the flannel nightdress. Nothing much could be done with her short hair. Still, Alice ran a brush across her head softly.

"Never mind," Alice told her. "Your hair will grow back. I've never seen eyes such a lavender shade. Have you ever picked lavender from a field? We have fields of lavender near our house in Pudsey. Lying in those fields was my favorite thing to do. It smelled like heaven . . ."

As she talked of any simple topic that came to mind, Jane visibly relaxed against the pillows.

Nick had said he took people in sometimes. Obviously, this woman was in terrible need.

She'd met with some manner of dreadful fate.

How did Nick know her? Was she under his protection, somehow? Had one of his disreputable friends harmed her in some way?

The thought made her stomach roil. She knew Nick had unsavory friends—the debauched lords who attended his scandalous entertainments. Could one of them be involved?

"Where did you come from tonight?" Alice asked.

Jane shrank back into the bedclothes. "Won't go back. Don't make me go to the Yellow House."

She twisted the covers in her fists.

Whatever this Yellow House was, it must be an awful place.

Jane raised her eyes and Alice nearly took a step backward, there was so much suffering there.

"They will come for me," Jane whispered. "They will find me."

"Who? Who will find you? Tell me whom you are running from. Who did this to you? Was it a gentleman?"

"Can't tell you. So . . . tired." Jane's head fell back against the pillows as she slipped into a deep sleep.

Alice's head throbbed from the wine she'd had earlier and spun with questions.

This was not exactly how she'd pictured her wedding night ending.

It seemed that life with Nick was going to be far more complicated than she ever could have imagined.

She only hoped he had a reasonable explanation for Jane's predicament. And that he'd had nothing to do with her suffering.

She didn't want to think this way, but perhaps it was a good thing they hadn't consummated the marriage yet.

There were some things a lady simply couldn't forgive.

Nick and Lear moved swiftly in the darkness.

The squat silhouette of the Yellow House loomed to the west. Any charm its ivy-covered brick façade possessed was lost in the darkness. It was a heavy, oppressive lump of a building at night.

A scream pierced the air, chilling Nick's blood.

Alice had handled the situation so well, calm and collected, not flying into a rage or shutting down with fear. Not many ladies would have accepted a strange girl with sunken cheekbones, a shorn head, and a haunted look in her eyes, with barely any questions asked.

"Where should we plant the cloak?" he asked Lear.

Lear pointed away from Yellow House, across the open fields to a barely discernible ribbon of darkness. "Along Regent's Canal. Leads straight south to the Thames at Limehouse. We drop her cloak at the edge and make it appear that she lost it while climbing down into the canal."

Bodies were found floating in the Thames nearly every day.

One would be identified as hers if they were lucky.

"I'm sorry, Nick, I know you didn't want to involve your wife. But what was I to do? Hawkins said the girl was too delicate—said she would die if we left her there."

"You did the right thing."

"Did you at least have a bit of fun before I ruined everything?" Lear asked.

"Was about to when you pounded on the door. Thank you very much."

Lear chuckled. "Sorry, old boy, you know I had to bring the delivery to you. Nowhere else she would have been safe."

"I know. But she can't stay. I never harbor females. Not in a house full of disreputable ruffians."

"You have a respectable wife now."

"She's leaving, Lear. She's off to India on a grand adventure. She has no more desire to stay here with me than I have for her to stay."

Were those words still true?

He'd wanted her to leave, so he could resume his hedonistic life. But his mind shied away from thinking of the actual day of her departure.

Watching her slim back walk away, climb into a carriage, board a ship.

"That's what you tell yourself, eh?" Lear asked.

"It's the truth."

"I saw the way you looked at her. There's something between you. Even I could see it, and I'm notoriously thickheaded when it comes to romantic matters."

"Why are wives so much more complicated than mistresses?" Nick asked.

Lear laughed. "Like I said, you're in trouble, my friend. But you don't know how much trouble yet."

Nick sobered as they neared the bank of the canal. "We must find the truth about Jane, Lear. If she's someone of consequence . . . if her presence puts Alice in any kind of danger, I'll find somewhere else for her immediately."

"Maybe she could go to the charity house the Duchess of Harland runs for young females in distress."

"Maybe." Nick lifted his head toward the pearl-streaked sky. "It's nearing dawn. We should finish this swiftly."

He needed to return home. There was a lady waiting for him with accusatory eyes and twenty questions.

He hadn't liked the hurt in Alice's eyes, the mistrust.

As soon as he knew the particulars of Jane's situation, he would offer Alice a full explanation.

He never wanted her to think ill of him.

Chapter 13

Everything is therefore in the power of destiny,
who is the lord of gain and loss, of success and
defeat, of pleasure and pain.

The Kama Sutra of Vātsyāyana

A knock sounded on the door, rousing Alice
from a fitful sleep that had been interrupted often
to help Jane, who'd mumbled about the Yellow
House all night in her sleep.

Expecting Nick, Alice was disappointed to find
March waiting outside the door.

"You're to go to the library," he said without preamble.

"Why?"

"Because the doctor is waiting for you." He
shook his head. "You're quite slow, you know."

Perhaps Nick had summoned a physician to examine Jane. "Where's Lord Hatherly?"

March tugged at his earlobe. "Not home yet.
Went out with the cap'n last night and never came
home."

"Never came home?" Alice exclaimed.

"Come *on*, hurry up. Daft girl," he grumbled as he started down the corridor. "Don't know why 'e wants her 'ere."

"You needn't be so rude. I don't think—"

"Then you really shouldn't speak."

Indignant, Alice was about to make a cutting retort when she remembered what Nick had said last night: *They're not really servants.*

Apparently not. No one would pay wages for such insulting behavior.

She intended to find out more about what he'd meant as soon as she saw him. She had so many questions. About Jane, and his servants, and . . . everything.

Kali raced down the hallway and rubbed up against March's ankles. The manservant made a face. "Oh, it's you, you rodent of an unusual size."

Alice paused outside the door of the library. "Will you carry Kali outside for some exercise?" Now that Gertrude's enclosure had been repaired, Kali could go explore.

March lifted Kali and held her at arm's length, scrunching up his already deeply wrinkled face. "Maybe it'll run away," he said hopefully.

Kali purred, oblivious to his insults.

"She won't run away. She always comes back to me." Alice scratched under Kali's chin. "Have fun exploring, Queen Kali."

The grumpy March carried Kali away, muttering all the while about daft ladies and their precious royal rodents.

Alice entered the library.

A tall, well-built gentleman with dark hair, dark eyes, and light brown skin was waiting by the fireplace. Young—maybe the same age as she.

"Lady Hatherly?" he asked.

"Yes."

"I'm Dr. Forster." He paused. "You're expecting me?"

"Actually, I'm not. Are you here for an . . . examination?" Jane had arrived in such mysterious circumstances that Alice didn't know how much she could divulge to a stranger.

"I'm the Duke's personal physician. When you and I are finished, I'll go and visit him."

He spoke with slightly accented English. An Indian accent, if Alice wasn't mistaken.

"Finished with what?" she asked.

"Lord Hatherly led me to understand that you might require assistance in translating a Sanskrit manuscript. I'm no Sanskrit scholar, but I do read the language and would be happy to help, if I'm able. I apologize if my visit is a surprise. Is Lord Hatherly here?"

"He's out this morning." Nick had asked someone to help her with the translation? When had he done it? And why? "Please have a seat, Doctor." They sat in comfortable chairs arranged before the fireplace. "What part of India are you from? I will voyage to Calcutta soon."

"Then you travel to my home city. How do you happen to be in possession of ancient Indian manuscripts?"

"My grandfather was a director in the East

India Company and a collector of literature." She wouldn't reveal that his collection had been of a decidedly salacious nature.

A momentary disquiet crossed Dr. Forster's face, but he quickly regained his smile. "So your grandfather acquired the manuscripts directly from India."

She nodded. "And I will return them there. I'll donate them to the Fort William College library for use by the Asiatic Society."

"Won't Lord Hatherly have something to say about all this voyaging when you are newlyweds?"

"He wants me to travel." One month of marriage and then the freedom for both of them to pursue their disparate interests.

"He's a good man, Lord Hatherly."

"He is?" Alice replied. "I mean, yes, of course he is."

"He funds my research into the causes and treatment of mental derangement, especially milder cases, such as the duke's, which I believe to be entirely curable."

This was news to Alice. "You believe the duke may be cured?"

"I believe that Lord Hatherly's care and attention to his father's needs, and the wide berth he gives him in which to roam, are the best possible methods for attempting a cure."

"You mean that locking up lunatics is harmful for them?"

"If the case is mild, locking away someone with a nervous or mental complaint and treating them with contempt and callousness can only exacerbate the malady, and in some instances may even hasten an untimely demise."

"How fascinating."

"The methods of care Lord Hatherly employs are quite novel," the doctor continued, "and I believe they deserve serious study. Encouraging the Duke to continue cultivating his orchids has had an extremely therapeutic effect."

"I'm to visit his orchid conservatory today."

"You'll be amazed. I've never seen a more beautiful collection."

Alice smiled at his enthusiasm. "I'm curious, doctor, whether you know anything about Lord Hatherly's servants?"

Dr. Forster ducked his head. "I'll leave that subject for your husband to explain. You know, I've been attempting to convince him to write about his father's case. Perhaps even publish a case study."

Interesting how he'd changed the subject so swiftly when she mentioned Nick's servants.

"But I'm sure you would rather speak of Sanskrit manuscripts than case studies, Lady Hatherly. What are you working on?"

"I've been translating a fragment from a temple text on the subject of love and desire."

"The *Ananga-Ranga*?"

Alice stared in surprise. "You've heard of the *Ananga-Ranga*? Well, this may be of some interest to you, then. The fragment I possess is believed by a scholar in Calcutta to be from *The Kama Sutra of Vātsyāyana*, referenced so frequently in other works, but much more uncommon."

"Extraordinary," exclaimed Dr. Forster. "I've heard of this elusive *Kama Sutra.*"

Should she go and fetch the manuscript? But the subject matter . . .

"If you know of the work, then you know of its sometimes prurient subject matter," she said carefully.

"I'm a physician, Lady Hatherly. My trade lies within the intricate workings of the minds and bodies of men. You needn't feel embarrassed. I would dearly love to see the manuscript. Perhaps another day."

"Perhaps."

"It would be my pleasure, Lady Hatherly. And I mean that in an entirely professional way," he said with a quick grin. "I'd better, because Lord Hatherly is not a man I would wish to anger. I did bring a Sanskrit grammar." He drew a small book from inside his coat. "Why don't we study this today?"

Alice returned his smile. "That would be wonderful."

It had been kind of Nick to ask the doctor to assist her. Of course, hastening her translation assured her timely departure, which must have been his reasoning when he asked Dr. Forster to help.

Not because Nick was kind, or thoughtful, or any of the things he simply couldn't be if she were to keep her heart an impenetrable fortress.

Nick arrived home dirty from the muddy banks of the canal and tired as hell.

All he wanted was a hot bath, a comfortable bed, and a bottle of brandy.

But when he headed to the library in search of the brandy, the sound of ringing, clear tones reciting words in a foreign tongue stopped him outside the room.

He couldn't understand a word, of course, but the sound of her voice . . . listening to those dulcet tones was like sinking into a steaming bath and feeling the ache in his muscles ease and his joints loosen.

He hazarded a glance inside the room. He should walk on, find his bed, and sleep away this foolish feeling that he wanted to come home to the sound of her voice every day, but instead his legs carried him closer.

Standing outside the open library door, out of her line of sight, he watched her poring over a book. Light brown head and dark black head bent together in concentration.

Forster pointed something out with his finger and Alice nibbled on her lip as she focused her attention on the words, attempting the sentence.

She stumbled over a few of the words but Forster seemed to think she sounded good. He praised her liberally.

Watching anyone do a difficult task with skill and ease was a pleasure. She obviously took great pride in her ability with foreign tongues.

He enjoyed the thought of Alice marching about the globe acquiring languages in the same way other ladies acquired new bonnets.

Alice glanced up at Forster with a fetching tilt of her head, to see if she'd understood the words correctly, and Nick thought he caught an admiring gleam in her eyes.

That's when it struck him that Forster was too handsome.

Why hadn't Nick noticed it before?

He'd known the doctor for years and greatly admired his research into cures for lunacy, but he'd never before noticed quite how much masculine beauty he possessed.

Fine black eyes, tousled hair, pouting lips . . . he was a maiden's fantasy.

And now he was touching Alice's hand, guiding her fingers along a line of text.

A rush of jealousy grabbed hold of Nick's heart.

You're tired. You're imagining things.

And even if you're not, you've no right to jealousy. She's not yours. She never was, and she never will be. Walk away. Find your bed.

He strode into the library, all thoughts of sleep forgotten in this unfamiliar rush of possessiveness.

Forster in his fresh linen and gleaming boots made Nick feel a mud-spattered brute.

"Lord Hatherly," Forster said enthusiastically. "You have an extraordinarily clever wife." His dark eyes shone with approval.

Nick didn't like how shiny the man's eyes were.

Alice smiled at Forster, and Nick had the entirely irrational thought that he should be the only person in the world to see her dimples.

Nick must have betrayed something of the direction of his thoughts on his face, because Forster pulled his timepiece from his waistcoat pocket. "I say, is that the time? I should be examining His Grace. It was a great pleasure, Lady Hatherly. I wish you the best of luck with your translation, and your travels."

Forster bowed over her hand. Did he kiss it? Not quite. But too close for Nick's tastes.

What's wrong with you? He can kiss her hand. Why should you care?

"I'll walk you to the door." Nick tried not to growl, and failed.

"That won't be necessary." Forster took his leave swiftly.

Good man. Sensible man.

When he was gone, Nick turned to Alice, who looked fresh and pretty this morning in another simple gray gown with her hair pulled back in a loose knot.

He fought the desire to wrap his arms around her. She smelled so clean and wholesome. Like lavender and old parchment; a faintly rustling odor like the sound of a field of herbs ruffled by wind, or pages turning.

Then he noticed the warning blue light flashing in the depths of her eyes.

"Well?" She arched her eyebrows. "Do you have something you'd like to say to me?"

"Um . . . good morning?" His brain wasn't working correctly. He was too exhausted.

Wrong answer.

Her lips clamped together. "I mean do you want to tell me where you've been all night?"

"I do want to tell you. But I can't. Not yet." He

didn't have all the details. Jane could be nobility. She could have a powerful, ruthless husband who would stop at nothing to regain control over her.

If that turned out to be the case, then the less Alice knew about Jane, the better.

Nick had witnessed too many lost souls committed to private asylums against their will. Left to die, lonely and chained.

Husbands who locked away their wives because it was more convenient than obtaining a divorce.

It made him so furious. And some of his emotion showed on his face.

Alice obviously interpreted his expression in the wrong way.

Red spots appeared high on her cheekbones.

Nick reached for her shoulders and drew her closer. "Alice, I'm so very tired. Can we speak of this in a few hours, after I've had some sleep?" He kissed her cheek. "I'll explain everything later today. Trust me."

"You keep asking me to trust you, Nick, but you won't trust *me*. I'm your wife. I think I have a right to know where you've been all night. And what is the Yellow House? A brothel?"

"It's not a brothel." Nick battled for control.

She had helped care for Jane last night, and she did have a right to know more details, but he didn't have those details yet to give.

Her fists curled tight at her sides. "If one of your friends has harmed her in some way and you're keeping it quiet . . ."

He swiped a hand across his face, tension boiling in his blood. "Is that what you think of me? You truly think I could have something to do with her suffering? God, Alice. I'm a rake, not a monster."

Doubt flooded her eyes. "But what am I to think? When gentlemen use young girls as playthings there are tragic outcomes. Charlene has told me all about the horrors. She has a sanctuary for girls like Jane, who've been mistreated by men. Used. Abandoned."

He rotated his shoulder, easing the tightness of his muscles. "The Yellow House is not a brothel. None of my friends have anything to do with her misery. I'll explain more when I know more. You'll have to trust me, Alice."

"I'm to help without asking questions, is that it?"

He could barely form coherent sentences, he was so exhausted. This wasn't the state in which to hold a conversation with an accusatory Alice. "No, that's not what I said."

"I understand that perhaps your methods of communication are somewhat less, well, communicative than mine, but you cannot shut me out. There is a girl upstairs with haunted violet eyes and red marks that will soon be scars around her wrists. I want to know why."

"I don't possess all of the particulars of Jane's situation yet. Until I do, I don't want to put you in danger by divulging too much."

"Don't protect me and don't patronize me, Nick. I have a right to know what's happened to her."

Nick wasn't accustomed to having to answer for himself.

He was good in bed—not good with serious conversations.

But he could see that Alice was shaking with hurt and anger and it tore at his heart to be the cause.

He'd give her a brief explanation. But then he was going to bed.

"The Yellow House is a lunatic asylum, Alice," he said wearily. "Lear rescued Jane from almost certain death. I spent the night wading through a muddy canal, planting false evidence of her death by suicide."

He gave a short, humorless bark of laughter. "Hardly a sybaritic night on the town. Now if you'll excuse me." He made a curt bow. "I'm in desperate need of a bath and a bed."

He spun on his heel and left her standing there.

Because she made him weak with wanting.

He longed to bury his head against her fragrant skin and sleep upon her soft breasts. Beg her forgiveness, tell her he'd never keep secrets from her again.

But she'd immediately assumed the worst about him.

Well, what did you expect, Nick? She didn't marry you because of your fine, upstanding moral character.

He'd never cared before what anyone thought of him.

And he couldn't afford to start now.

Chapter 14

It is the opinion of ancient authors that a marriage solemnly contracted in the presence of fire cannot afterwards be set aside.

The Kama Sutra of Vātsyāyana

Nick and his friend had rescued Jane from a madhouse?

Alice searched her mind, hunting for clues, and found them.

Jane's shorn hair.

Nick's personal connection to lunatics.

Something he'd said last night when he'd been speaking of the duke: *It would be enough to shut him away in a private madhouse where he would be made to suffer ill treatment.*

You misjudged him, Alice.

Her emotions had been stretched thin and had frayed, like an old rope bridge across a river with one too many foot passengers.

Hurt and anger kept the ropes stretched taut, kept her from falling into the waters below and drowning in the dangerous current of an entirely different emotion.

Admiration. Understanding.

Respect.

She'd thought him an idle aristocrat and an arrogant rake. She'd thought there would be no danger of losing her head . . . or her heart.

Had she made a serious error?

First the tour of the portrait gallery, the anguish in his voice as he spoke of his father's lunacy and his mother's desertion, and now this.

Rescuing women from madhouses.

Drat! It was quite irritating, if one thought about it hard enough.

Couldn't he just fulfill his end of the bargain and be the selfish, pleasure-obsessed rake she'd contracted to marry?

How could she give her body to him tonight, share in the intimate conversation that Charlene had warned her about, knowing that he was so much more than he appeared to be?

This changed everything. Granted him a dangerous power over her. She couldn't guarantee she'd be able to protect her heart anymore.

A clock chimed from somewhere deep within the house.

Noon. She'd promised the duke she would come for a tour of his orchid conservatory.

Still worrying over her new, precarious situation, she grabbed a cloak and bonnet from their hooks in the hall closet and left the house, following the winding pathway that led to the domed glass and wood conservatory.

The air was humid and fragrant inside the structure, and vines and plants twined over all available surfaces.

Berthold met her at the door and bowed, his pockmarked face lit by a smile. "Thank you, milady. His Grace will be happy you came."

Alice stared with delight at the lush, green bursting of life, her heart lifting.

"Do I hear a beautiful lady?" The duke's unruly white head appeared over a row of glossy green leaves.

"It's Lady Hatherly, Your Grace," Berthold called, humor sparking in his eyes. "Your son's *wife*."

The duke cleared his throat. "Oh yes, ahem . . . well, she's welcome. Come here, my dear, come and see my newest treasure."

Alice approached, crossing the wooden bridge spanning a small pool of water. Hearing the sound of flapping wings, she glanced toward the ceiling. A brilliant flash of blue and red caught her eye. A popinjay flew from one branch to the next, calling a warning.

She'd better not let Kali explore the duke's conservatory. She might come home with red and blue feathers stuck in her whiskers.

"Smell those white blooms, my dear," called the duke.

"These?" Alice trailed her fingers along the frilly petals of a cluster of white blooms like stars in a dark green sky.

"Yes, the oncidiums."

Alice bent forward and the delicate aroma of spiced vanilla rose to meet her.

"Aren't they delicious?" the duke asked. "You may break off a stalk from time to time if you would like to scent your chambers. I've plenty to go around. Though you must only pluck those, not any others. I have some very rare blooms here."

He seemed so much more lively today and less confused. Almost sane, in fact.

Perhaps it was as Dr. Forster had said: tending orchids was an effective treatment for the duke's lunacy, even if he did continue to believe the flowers spoke to him.

She joined him where he stood clipping at some brown stalks shooting from a tangled mass of moss and roots.

"He was with me, you know. On my last voyage," the duke said suddenly.

"Who was with you?"

"Nicolas. My son. Perhaps you've met him?"

"She's married to him," Berthold interjected.

The duke blinked. "Are you, my dear?"

She was. For better or for worse.

Alice nodded.

"Then perhaps he's told you that he was with me on that fateful voyage, when my orchids began speaking to me, revealing all the secrets of life."

Nick had spoken of his father's last voyage in the portrait gallery. But Alice didn't remember him mentioning that he'd been with his father on board the ship. How difficult the journey must have been for Nick. How helpless he must have felt, watching the madness overcome the duke.

"Bend down, my dear." The duke gestured for

her to lower her head. "Bend down and listen. Tell me what you hear."

Alice placed her ear above a pink-tinged orchid bloom with four delicately pointed petals.

She heard water dripping.

The duke breathing.

She heard her own thoughts, tangled like tree roots.

You've made a mistake.

You should run away . . . before it's too late.

"What do you hear, my dear?" the duke asked eagerly. "Are they chattering away? Have they revealed their secrets?"

"I think perhaps they are sleeping."

"Oh." The duke's gray eyes saddened. "I thought they might confide in you."

There was a commotion at the door, and Alice rose to her feet.

"Mama?" To Alice's surprise, her mother stood in the doorway, flanked by a surly Mr. March.

"Found this female skulking about the shrubbery, I did," March announced to Berthold "Highly suspicious behavior."

"This is my *mother*, Mr. March," Alice scolded, walking swiftly back over the bridge.

"So you say. So you say. Why was she lurking about, then? Answer me that."

"Lurking?" Mama declared incredulously. "You impudent fellow. I knocked upon the front door." She drew her arm from his grasp and shook out her skirts.

"It was a lurking sort of knock." March jabbed

a finger at Mama. "Who hired you, eh? Same one as hired Stubbs? I know there's something shady going on around here. Someone what wants to harm 'Is Lordship."

"Alice," appealed Mama. "Please do something about your footman."

"March must have thought you were someone else," Alice said. "Isn't that right, March?"

March trained his gaze on Alice. "You're still 'ere, are you? Thought he would 'ave got rid of you by now. Like the others."

"You'd better leave now, March," said Alice. She'd have to speak with Nick about the footman. Truly, his incivility was becoming a nuisance.

March made his grumbling exit.

Mama shook out her skirts. "I do hope all of your new servants are not so ill-behaved."

Alice smiled at Berthold. "Not all of them."

"Do I hear a beautiful lady?" The duke's head appeared again above his plants.

Alice's mother startled. "Oh, is that you, Your Grace?"

"Yes, 'tis I, my angelic Agatha." He hastened across the bridge, his footsteps sprightly and sure. "I knew you would come," he declared. He caught Mama's hand and pressed fervent kisses along her gloves.

Alice thought her mother would snatch her hand away, but she only batted her eyelashes and giggled. "Your Grace. You mustn't."

"Oh, but I must."

Alice watched in disbelief as her mother and

the old gallant flirted. Berthold caught her eye and grinned.

"Come with me, fair Agatha, and I will show you things you've only dared to dream of before now." The duke tucked her mother's hand into his arm.

"Mama," Alice interrupted. "Why have you come?"

Her mother glanced from the duke back to Alice. "I came to take you shopping, Alice."

"But you will return, won't you, divine Agatha?" the duke asked. "Come back to see your Barrington?"

"Of course, my duke, I will return."

"Adieu." He waved a handkerchief he plucked from somewhere. "Adieu, fair Agatha."

"Mother," Alice remonstrated, tugging on her hand to pull her out of the conservatory.

Her mother giggled like a schoolgirl as they made their way outside.

"I do like the duke, Alice. If his son possesses half his charm, my goodness, you're in trouble. You know your father never looks at me that way anymore." She said this wistfully, glancing back at the conservatory door.

Alice realized it was true. She never saw her father speak tenderly with her mother, or pay her any compliments. It must hurt her.

Alice looked at her mother in a new way. Was she . . . lonely? Feeling unattractive?

"Where is Lord Hatherly?" her mother asked.

"Asleep." Alice sighed as they walked down the path. "I think I've made a dreadful error, Mama. I may have married in too much haste."

"Oh, my darling." Her mother stopped walking

and clutched Alice's arm. "Did he . . . last night . . . did he hurt you?"

Alice shook her head. "No, he didn't hurt me. Didn't have a chance to. He never even came home last night."

Mama's squeezed Alice's arm almost painfully. "Never came home? On his wedding night? Oh, this won't do. This won't do at all." Her mother shook Alice by the shoulders. "We must do something, Alice. But what's to be done? Oh, what's to be done? This is a disaster!"

"Calm yourself, Mama." Alice loosened her mother's grip on her shoulders. "I only need some time to think things over. I could come home with you for the day."

Run away, her heart urged. *Before it's too late.*

"Oh no, dear, you couldn't do that. Why, I have plans to convert your room into a nursery, for when Fred brings his bride to see us with the babe. Your father is still blustering and posturing, but he'll come round. I know he will."

Alice had longed to escape her parents' house for so long, but she didn't know how she felt about her chamber being put to use so swiftly.

"You're only upset, Alice; you'll think differently tomorrow. You can't back out now; you can't give up. A marriage is not something to throw away lightly. I know this wasn't a love match but perhaps . . . with time, you'll learn to care for one another."

Exactly what she could never do. Care for Nick. But speaking with her mother wasn't helping matters. "Don't worry, Mama, I'm sorry I troubled you. Everything is fine."

"It's not fine. It's a disaster." Mama kneaded her hands together, staring up at the stern stone battlements atop Sunderland House. "Lord Hatherly must be accustomed to much more sophisticated ladies. Perhaps you're simply too innocent for his jaded tastes? Oh dear. What's to be done?"

"He wasn't out last night with courtesans if that's what you—"

"I have it!" Mama interrupted. "My sister-in-law will know what to do. Come, dear, we haven't a moment to lose." She pulled Alice with her and headed for the drive and her waiting carriage.

Alice knew it was useless to reason with Mama when she fixed upon an idea.

"You mean Aunt Sarah?" Alice had never been allowed to visit her Scandalous Aunt Sarah, as her mother usually referred to her.

"I don't like asking for help from such an impious woman, but these are desperate times. This marriage must be legitimized, and quickly."

Alice couldn't very well say no to a visit with Scandalous Aunt Sarah, since she'd always wanted to meet her.

Jane had been slumbering peacefully when Alice left her this morning, and Nick would no doubt sleep the day away.

Leaving the house would give her time to think about what she truly wanted.

Mama wanted her to consummate the marriage so there could be no danger of an annulment.

But what did Alice want?

Everything had become so much more complicated than she'd anticipated.

The duke's orchids may not have whispered any secrets to her, but they had made her listen to her own heart.

Acknowledge her own secrets. The tendril of caring taking root in her heart, threatening to bloom despite her resolution to maintain a scholarly detachment.

She must find a way to control her emotions . . . or she must find a way out of this marriage.

Chapter 15

> She walks with swanlike gait, and her voice
> is low and musical as the note of the Kokila
> bird.

The Kama Sutra of Vātsyāyana

Scandalous Aunt Sarah lived in opulent apartments, bequeathed to her by one of her lovers, on the entire upper floor of a lavish building overlooking Hyde Park.

She'd had many lovers, Aunt Sarah. And not one husband. She was the family disgrace.

Despite her emotional turmoil, Alice was excited to finally meet her aunt.

Her apartments were everything Alice had imagined. Red silk and black lacquered furniture from the Orient. Low divans piled with velvet cushions. Stalks of jasmine flowers in vases on every table, their sweet, heady fragrance scenting the room.

Aunt Sarah lounged on one of the low divans, swathed from her turban to her toes in white silk trimmed with dyed-red feathers. Miniature white poodles nestled on either side of her.

Alice noted a generous display of bosom and ruby rings on every finger.

An inordinately handsome young footman in close-fitting livery of white satin trimmed in red stood at attention near the door.

"Do come in, Agatha," said Aunt Sarah. "When my butler brought your card I thought there must be some mistake."

Mama pursed her lips, eyeing her sister-in-law and the gorgeous footman with distaste. "You know I would never visit, Sarah, if it weren't a matter of great importance."

"I'm well aware of that. Since you haven't visited me in . . . oh . . . *ever*."

Her mother approached. "We need your help. There's been a . . . situation." She bent closer. "Hatherly never came home. *On his wedding night*."

Aunt Sarah laughed. "My, that is a situation. And so you thought you'd come here, for a little amorous advice?"

"It's not for me," Lady Tombs said. "It's for Alice."

"Come here, girl," Aunt Sarah commanded, waving her bejeweled hand.

Alice approached.

"Let me have a look at you." Her aunt caught hold of her chin and turned her face to the window. "Fortunately you have your father's chin." She glanced at Mama's soft, wobbling chin. "And the family dimples, I see. Altogether charming. You, my dear, are *not* the problem."

"I know that, Sarah," Mama said disapprovingly. "It's not her face . . . it's her mannerisms. She's a very nervous girl, always saying whatever comes into that changeable mind of hers. Always putting her foot squarely in her mouth. She's never been successful at attracting a gentleman's lasting attentions."

Because I hadn't wanted to attract them, Alice thought.

"So that's why you had to win her a husband at cards," Aunt Sarah said.

Mama nodded. "Now she must win him"—she lowered her voice, glancing at the footman—"*in the bedchamber. To legitimize the union.*"

This marriage meant everything to her mother. She longed for her elevated place in society.

Aunt Sarah sat up. "I accept! Antonio," she called, and the footman was at her side instantly, helping her rise. The poodles were dislodged with little yelps of displeasure.

"Lavinia," Aunt Sarah shouted, and a pretty maid in a crisp white pinafore appeared at the door.

"Sit down, Agatha," Aunt Sarah said, placing a hand on Mama's shoulders and giving her a push.

Alice's mother fell onto a divan with a grunt of surprise.

"Lavinia will rub your hands with a softening oil while you wait for us; it's delightful," Aunt Sarah said. "Come, Alice."

Alice followed her whirlwind of an aunt outside, leaving her mother sputtering in the center of a pile of cushions.

"Are you as foolish as your mother?" Aunt Sarah asked, as the footman handed them into a gleaming white carriage.

"I don't think so."

"Then we shall suit each other famously. Now then." Aunt Sarah settled back against the cushions. "You must mount that steed. Hoist that lance."

"Er . . ." Was her aunt speaking of a jousting tournament?

"What we need is the proper armor."

"Chain mail?" Alice asked helpfully.

"Chain mail? I was thinking lace . . . with a few wisps of silk."

Wispy was right.

Practically nonexistent.

She might as well appear in her altogether.

Alice was blushing merely looking at the scandalous garments the ginger-haired shopgirl laid upon the counters. If one could call them garments.

Alice rather thought more fabric was required to deserve the designation.

"I could never wear something like this." If there was even a slight draft, she'd catch pneumonia and die. "I only wear linen or flannel nightdresses, to protect against drafts."

"Very prudent, I'm sure," Aunt Sarah said with a twinkle in her lively brown eyes. "However, for tonight something a little less sensible and a lot more seductive is required."

The shopgirl surveyed Alice from head to toe. "You would look well in scarlet, milady. It'd bring out the roses in your cheeks." She held out a corset fashioned from thin red silk. "This one's direct from Paris. We only had it in yesterday. They call it the Gay Lady."

Alice frowned. Her garments didn't have *names*.

She preferred sensible cotton, linen, or muslin, fashioned for ease of movement.

"It won't cover very much of me," Alice said.

"That's the point, milady, if I may be so bold as to say so."

"Suppose I catch a chill?"

"You won't." The shopgirl winked. "Not in this. You'll have plenty of company to keep you warm, I'll wager."

The shopgirl and Aunt Sarah exchanged amused glances.

"See how even the lacing is the finest of silks? Have a feel, milady," the girl urged.

Alice had never in her life pictured herself wearing something so utterly sinful, and yet . . . She slid her forefinger along the folds of the fabric.

Smoother than flesh.

Smoother than rose petals.

As soft as Kali's fur after she'd grudgingly had a bath and dried herself in the sun.

A silk that made even a sensible girl think purely decadent thoughts.

The shopgirl, sensing victory, rubbed a scrap of the silk between her fingers. "Your husband will never have felt anything so soft." She drew a pair of thin pink silk stockings from a box. "It's to be worn with these." Next she unwrapped scarlet and white lace garters. "And these. Trimmed with real Swiss lace, they are."

Garments such as these could make a lady feel more confident. More in control.

The silk between her fingers whispered of midnight seductions.

Of strong hands deftly untying lacings.

She pictured the silk crumpled next to his bed.

Then she pictured herself naked . . . in his bed. All her many questions about to be answered.

His strong hands on her body.

Shaping her waist. Tangling in her hair. Pulling her close . . .

She wanted to experience lovemaking with Nick, but would she be able to protect her heart?

Aunt Sarah drew near and the potent scent of jasmine enveloped Alice. "What's the matter? This is perfect for your purposes."

"I'm worried," Alice whispered.

Aunt Sarah made a motion with her hand and the shopgirl busied herself folding fabrics a short distance away.

"What are you worried about?" Aunt Sarah asked.

"I don't want to fall in love with Lord Hatherly," Alice admitted. "It's not part of my plan. My friends told me that he's a rake, and incapable of love, so I must maintain the upper hand. Is it possible to give one's body without surrendering one's heart?"

Aunt Sarah gave a rich, melodious laugh. "I'm living proof, my darling. I may be scandalous and shunned by polite society, but some of the world's most powerful men have knelt at my French-heeled slippers."

"And you never fell in love with any of your . . . protectors?"

"I fell in and out of love, I suppose, but I never lost a moment of sleep over it. I was always in complete control." Aunt Sarah winked. "It's been loads of fun being a Lady Rake."

A Lady Rake.

Alice liked the sound of it. "But I'm not as sophisticated as you are."

"That's what the corset is for, darling. And you're my niece, are you not? I rather think you and I have more in common than you imagine."

"Do you really think I can manage it?"

"Of course you can." Aunt Sarah chucked Alice under the chin, her rings cold against Alice's skin. "Now then, what do you say?" She gestured toward the corset.

The shopgirl returned, looking expectant.

Alice exhaled sharply. "Wrap it up, please."

"That's my niece," Aunt Sarah said approvingly. "We'll make a seductress of you yet. First the corset . . . and then the soup."

Now she'd lost Alice. "The . . . *soup*?"

"You must keep him guessing. Always maintain control. Stay one step ahead," explained Aunt Sarah as the shopgirl wrapped up their purchases. "Think, darling. You're clearly an intelligent lady. How does he gain control over you?"

"He kisses me and my knees go weak."

"Precisely. And how do you regain control?"

"Um . . . find a way to make his knees turn weak?"

"That's right. Knock him off balance. And I've always found a hearty chicken soup does the trick. Men don't even know they crave it—warm, fragrant, simple, comforting—but a few spoonfuls and *voilá*! They fall at your feet. Think of this as a game of cards. Hatherly won the first hand by staying out all night. You will win the second hand with my two-part strategy. I promise."

Alice was still attempting to wrap her mind around the soup strategy. Why was she supposed to cook for him? But Aunt Sarah was undoubtedly an expert.

"I'll give it a try," Alice said. "Though I prefer not to cook with animal flesh."

"It's only poultry. Pluck that chicken, Alice. Bring him to his knees. He'll be your devoted love servant within days."

Alice frowned. "I don't want him to fall in *love* with me."

"Oh, of course not, darling," Aunt Sarah reassured her. "Of course not. We wouldn't want that. My strategy will merely assist you with maintaining control of the situation."

Alice studied her aunt's face for a moment.

Aunt Sarah spread her bejeweled hands. "Trust me, darling. I've never known it to fail."

The waiting footman gathered their parcels and they began the journey home.

"Now then, I'll return you straight to Lord Hatherly so your mother won't have anything to say about my methods." She winked. "It will be our little secret."

"I wish I'd defied my father and mother and come to visit you before now, Aunt Sarah," said Alice.

"Aren't I fun, dear?" Aunt Sarah said with a naughty smile. "You're a grand lady now. You may do as you please. Why should you listen to your pompous old father anymore? I never listened to my brother a day in my life. Why don't you come and see me again soon? I expect a full report."

Alice smiled. "I'd like that."

Before Aunt Sarah's carriage left Alice outside of Sunderland House, she stuck her head out the window. "Oh, and one more thing, darling. You must compliment his tool. Whether it's long or short, squat or thin as a taper, a man believes his prick to be womankind's greatest gift, and you must never disillusion him of his fragile convictions . . ."

Her instructions faded away as the carriage wheels jolted into motion, leaving Alice blushing on the front steps. Gracious. What had she agreed to?

Instead of running away, she'd purchased *armor.* But even though her mother and Aunt Sarah had the wrong idea about Hatherly's absence last evening, Alice could use their methods to maintain dominion over her heart and continue with her love lessons as planned.

Mr. March eyed her parcels with displeasure when he finally appeared to assist her. "Moving in to stay, are we? We'll see about that."

"Where's Kali?" she asked, ignoring his surly greeting.

"With Gertrude. I told her she should pester someone her own size, but she does love terrorizing that old lion."

Alice grinned. Despite his perpetually dismal humor, she rather thought March had a soft spot for Kali.

"Put those parcels in my room, March, and then meet me in the kitchens."

"The kitchens?" March gaped at her.

"That's right. And bring Bill with you. And wash your hands first, if you please."

It was time to prepare phase two of Aunt Sarah's plan.

Nick rarely slept alone, so where were the warm, womanly curves nestled by his side?

He lifted the velvet counterpane.

No upside-down-heart-shaped bum, either. No half ellipse of a waist.

Everything came flooding back.

He was sleeping alone right now because he'd made his wife angry.

Badly done, that. Why hadn't he simply told her the truth earlier?

They must share Sunderland for the next weeks, and he'd been hoping she'd share his bed as well.

Nick rubbed sleep from his eyes.

Felt like there was moss growing in his brain and cotton wool in his mouth. What time was it anyway? He thudded out of bed and pushed aside a curtain, wincing in the sudden slash of sunshine.

Already afternoon. He'd slumbered the whole day away.

He splashed cold water on his face and dressed hastily.

Alice's cat pranced into the room and rubbed against his boot, shamelessly angling for a scratching.

Nick knelt down. "Hello there, what's your name again? Kali? You like me, even if your mother thinks I'm a stubborn, heartless fool." He had to go and find Alice and apologize.

The noise of clattering crockery sounded from the direction of the kitchens and Nick noticed there was a tempting odor curling in the air.

More clanging from below stairs and the sound of muffled curses and feminine laughter. What was happening down there? Was Alice in the kitchens?

The sound of her laughter rippled cool and clear like lake water touched by a stone.

His stomach growled. It did smell good, whatever was happening in the kitchens.

The cat quirked her small, pointy chin, listening to the racket, and decided to investigate, bolting away as swiftly as she'd come.

His boots started carrying him out the door before his mind realized he was moving.

A bright flash of color in the corner of his eyes made him pause outside the kitchens.

Flowers.

Yellow daisies in vases on the tables.

A window open somewhere, carrying the scent of garden loam inside the walls.

It was jarring, the daisies and the fresh air. Out of place in his dark, decadent world.

When he reached the kitchens, the scene unfolding before his eyes was nothing Nick would have ever expected to find at Sunderland.

Alice had enlisted his men to her devious purposes. Bill peeled potatoes while Pigeon stoked the hearth fire.

And March, even March, was chopping carrots. Sullenly chopping . . . but still.

Consorting with his wife. The destroyer of his equilibrium.

Turncoats.

The cat watched everything with great interest from a position near the warm hearth.

Alice had her sleeves rolled up and was stirring the bubbling contents of a large black pot.

Nick hovered in the doorway, not wanting to disturb the scene, feeling that he would be out of place in the cozy room.

She smiled as she stirred, humming a happy song.

"'Ere's your carrots," March said, shoving a handful at Alice.

"Why thank you, Mr. March." She beamed at the footman. "Throw them in the pot, if you please."

March let the carrots slide from his hands into the soup.

Had he washed his hands? His wrists were suspiciously white and freshly scrubbed-looking.

"You know, Mr. March," Alice said. "Bill tells me you like marmalade, and I will receive a jar this month from my friend Thea who is traveling this summer to her estate in Ireland. The most marvelous orange marmalade in the world. I'm willing to part with a jar . . . for the price of a smile."

"Humph." March scowled.

Good luck with that, Alice, Nick thought. *You'll never force a smile out of Harold March. I've been trying for years.*

"Don't you like marmalade?" she asked.

"He does," said Bill. "It's his favorite. He ate three whole jars last month alone. I calculate he's eaten ten jars already this year."

"Then give us a smile," Alice wheedled.

"Might crack his face. He never smiles. He's smiled a total of . . . never," Bill finished with a surprised look. "He's never smiled."

Alice laughed. "Then he shall have no marmalade."

March stalked away, pausing when he noticed Nick watching from beyond the door.

At Nick's gesture he walked over.

"What's happening here, Mr. March?" Nick asked sternly.

"A bunch of utter nonsense. She"—he jerked his thumb at Alice's back as she bent over the pot—"is making the duke some chicken soup." "Were you chopping vegetables, March?"

March hung his shaggy head. "May 'ave been."

Alice turned around at the sound of their voices, and Nick's heart stopped beating.

The steam had curled her hair in tendrils around her face and painted her cheeks with roses.

Too beautiful.

Too wholesome.

Not mine.

His lovers would never soil their hands with soup ladles. They'd be too afraid of the scent clinging to their clothing. They were far too fine for peeling garlic.

They'd rather die than make their own soup.

He scowled at the cat, who smirked back. She'd

led him here knowingly, to this den of temptation and turncoat-ery.

When Nick entered the kitchen, his men took one look at his face and found hasty excuses to leave.

Alice stirred the pot, avoiding his eyes.

With every pass of the ladle through the rich, golden broth, the heavenly fragrance teased his nostrils and made his stomach clench with hunger.

"Now don't go thinking I'm cooking this for you, my lord," Alice said in a saucy tone of voice.

She scattered a handful of chopped fresh herbs into the soup and the aroma rose, fresh and clean.

"It's for the duke, and for Jane," she said. "She's doing much better today but she could use a restorative meal, and your cook only seems to know how to make unhealthful meals smothered in cream sauce and butter."

"Where *is* my cook?"

"I gave him the day off."

Nick blinked. The lady was taking charge of the household, it seemed. "I won't have you superimposing order here. I like the chaos."

"A few rules make life less uncertain. I don't usually cook with animal flesh," Alice continued. "But chicken bones, boiled for hours to release their marrow, will feed the soul as well as the body. Jane needs nourishment in order to regain her strength."

"Alice, about this morning. I know I should have told you the truth earlier."

"Stir this, will you?" She handed him the ladle she was using to stir the soup. His stomach clenched. He was ravenous.

Taking the ladle from her hand and setting it down, Nick caught her wrist. "Alice," he said softly. "You know you can't change me, right? Not with daisies. Or rules. I'm long gone. What's left of me is what you see." He held both her hands in his and brought them to his chest. "Not worth saving."

"I'm not trying to change you or save you, Nick. I'm only making soup."

She retrieved the ladle and dipped it into the broth. "What do you think, more salt?"

It smelled so good. His lips opened of their own accord, slurping the broth greedily.

At his entertainments he served expensive imported foods. Port wine from Portugal. Platters of cured beef and heavy cheeses from France. This was only a hearty chicken stock. The same soup served in every countryside tavern across England.

Rich with fat and flavored with a basic mixture of onions, carrots, and celery.

Only a simple chicken soup.

Only some woman, some warm, fragrant woman with hair curling around her face and clear, turquoise eyes.

"Do you want to know the secret ingredient?" Alice asked.

He squeezed his eyes shut. "No."

"I haven't added it yet."

He opened one eye.

"The secret is . . ." Alice reached into her apron pocket and brought out half of a lemon. "Lemons. From your father's lemon tree, the one in his conservatory. But you can't add it during cooking, or it may turn bitter. You have to add it right at the end, right before you're ready to eat. It's like a little squeeze of sunshine to brighten up the soup."

Alice squeezed the lemon over the soup.

Nick knew what the secret ingredient to brightening life was, and it wasn't lemon.

It was Alice.

His mouth watered for more soup and his hands itched to hold her, touch her, savor her warmth. He stopped fighting and wrapped his arms around her, nuzzling her neck. "You smell good."

"I smell like onions."

He captured her finger and licked it. "And lemons. And sunshine."

He had to taste her. Now. This moment.

Three things happened then: He crushed her into his arms and kissed her, which caused the soup ladle to crash to the floor, which startled the cat, who ran away and then returned immediately to lap up the spilled broth.

But Nick didn't notice anything but the warm, feminine curves in his arms and the sweet, soft lips beneath his mouth.

He lifted her into his arms, never breaking the kiss, and carried her to a kitchen counter, where he swept away a pile of onion peels and herbs and made sure there were no knives before setting her down.

He wrapped her long limbs around his hips, needing her to be closer, and she wound her arms around his neck.

She tasted far better than the soup. Sweet, wholesome woman, heated with steam and flavored with the tang of the basil she'd been crushing.

Moaning his desire, he deepened the kiss, using his tongue in the same rhythm his cock found against the layers of fabric between them.

She drove him completely wild with need.

He couldn't be in the same room with her without wanting to kiss her. Claim her.

Kissing his way from her lips down her neck, he pushed her bodice down greedily and tasted her nipples again, flicking them with his tongue until they were firm.

Alice wrapped her limbs more tightly around him, pressing her heels into his buttocks to draw him nearer.

A few buttons to unfasten and he could be inside her heat.

"Alice," he groaned against the smooth flesh of her soft breasts.

"I gather you . . . like my . . . soup," she gasped, as he sucked her nipples.

He wanted to tease her breasts while he slid inside her, slow and gentle at first, and then hard and fast.

Teach her that first lesson in love.

Make her come for him. Come around him. Her flesh clenching his . . .

Her cat stared with wide, alert yellow eyes.

Kitchen . . . counter.

Afternoon sunlight.

What's wrong with you? Can't you find a bed to seduce your new wife upon? And what happened to the roses and champagne?

He never lost control like this.

He broke the embrace and smoothed her skirts

down. He lifted her off the counter, avoiding her eyes.

This was completely uncharacteristic, and he had to regain at least a modicum of control.

"We'll continue this tonight. In my bed. We're going to make history, Dimples," he growled.

She smiled, pleasure still hazing her eyes like a cloudy summer sky. "I'll hold you to that, my lord."

He helped her assemble a tray of soup, bread, and tea for Jane. She stuck some yellow daisies into a vase and placed it beside the bowl of soup.

The simple, fresh-cut flowers glowed vibrant and bold.

Just like Alice.

Nick left her in the kitchens and sent March to help her carry the tray.

He needed to go out. He'd find Lear and they'd do manly things.

Drink in a pub.

Hunt down Stubbs.

Lear and he had made some progress, and Nick was increasingly left with the idea that the person who'd hired Stubbs to impoverish him was someone skilled at hiding his trail.

Probably someone he knew and interacted with.

He couldn't let Alice's intoxicating kisses and tempting soup distract him into losing his edge.

Chapter 16

◎◎◎

She should be born of a highly respectable
family, possessed of wealth, well connected,
and with many relations and friends. She
should also be beautiful, of a good disposi-
tion, with lucky marks on her body.

The Kama Sutra of Vātsyāyana

Aunt Sarah had been right. The soup had been
highly effective.

Nick had lost control, gathering her into his
strong arms and lifting her to the counter. He'd
been overcome with carnal longings and they'd
nearly . . . well, all of her questions had nearly been
answered in the *kitchens.*

It had made her feel powerful, confident, and
capable of regaining the upper hand.

Chalk up one round for the Lady Rake, she thought
with satisfaction as she entered Jane's chambers.
She'd taken the tray from March, so as not to startle
Jane with a male presence.

The effects of the laudanum were wearing
off. Jane's unusual light purple eyes were much

clearer and she didn't have such a bewildered, frightened air.

Jane made a motion as if she were going to tuck a lock of hair behind her ear, and then looked surprised when there was no hair to tuck.

It broke Alice's heart.

"How are you feeling?" Alice asked, setting down the tray on the bedside table.

"Much improved, thank you." Jane smiled shyly. "Your name is Alice?"

"You remembered. I wasn't certain how much you would recall of last night. You were very disoriented."

"My keeper drugged me. To keep me quiet." Her eyes hardened. "They tried to keep me quiet and docile. But I fought them."

"My husband told me where you came from. The Yellow House is a . . . lunatic asylum."

Tears welled in Jane's eyes. "I'm not mad."

"Of course not," Alice said briskly. "I brought you some soup." She indicated the tray. "Shall I help you?"

"I can manage." Jane lifted the tray into her lap, her hands wobbling only slightly. "I'm grateful for your attentions, Alice. Am I to assume this is your home?"

"You are in the Duke of Barrington's house."

Jane paused with her soup spoon raised. "The Mad Duke's house?"

Alice nodded. "The very one."

"Then who were the gentlemen who escorted me to safety last night?"

"One of them was a Captain Lear, whom I know nothing about. And the gentleman you met upon arrival was my husband, the Marquess of Hatherly, the Duke's son."

"I'm afraid I was rather rude."

"You were frightened and unwell."

Jane lowered her spoon. "They saved my life, Alice. I had been in that forsaken place one month. I thought I would die there, shackled to a bedpost, a hideous thing with tufted hair and bruised wrists."

Alice winced. "One month. You poor thing. Please, don't dwell on it right now. Eat some more soup. You need to bolster your strength."

Jane stared out the window, her eyes gone flat and cold. "My keeper hated me because I was highborn. She forced me to eat in a most cruel manner, shoving a metal feeding tube down my throat. Many choked to death under the care of a keeper. I was nearly one of them."

"Shh . . ." Alice said soothingly. She took a seat close to the bed. "Don't think of it. You're safe now. You'll never go back there."

Jane grabbed Alice's hand suddenly, spilling soup over the coverlet. "I'm not safe, Alice. And neither are you. I must leave here. My presence is a danger to you."

"Why? No one knows you are here."

"He will find me." Jane's shoulders quivered and the color drained from her cheeks. "He always finds me."

"Who?" Alice asked. "Who will find you?"

"My husband," Jane whispered.

A chill swept over Alice. The way she said those words was horrible to hear. "You fear him."

"He's the one who had me declared insane and committed to the asylum against my will. I was . . . inconvenient to him. Insubordinate, was his word for me, among other, less polite epithets."

"But, I don't understand. If you are highborn, was there no one to save you from such a fate?"

"I'm an orphan."

"Who is your husband?"

"I can't tell you."

"You must. Lord Hatherly will be able to help you if he knows the details. Tell me, Jane. Tell me your husband's name."

She shook her head. "I'm sorry. I can't risk it. I don't even want to say his name aloud."

"I understand."

Her violet eyes burned with hatred. "That shivering woman still chained to the bed in the Yellow House is married. Not me."

"You're not even alive," said Alice.

Jane frowned. "What do you mean?"

"Lord Hatherly told me that he and Captain Lear planted evidence of your drowning in the canal near the Yellow House, as if you had escaped and taken your own life out of desperation. I think they mean to help you begin a new life."

"If that is true, if they have given me this opportunity, I should leave immediately." Jane tried to push herself upright.

Alice placed a hand on her arm. "You're not

strong enough yet. You'll have to stay here until your strength returns."

"I don't want to be a burden."

"You're not." Alice settled Jane's pillows more firmly behind her back. "Now have some more soup, before it goes cold."

Jane relaxed against the cushions. "You're right. I'm too weak." She finished her soup with relish. "It's very good."

"Only a simple chicken soup."

"But it tastes like home. I grew up in the countryside. We weren't too elegant there."

"I grew up in the countryside, as well."

"Did you?"

"In Yorkshire."

Alice waited for Jane to reply and tell her where she'd been raised, but she remained silent. She truly was on edge.

"And how long have you been married?" Jane asked.

"Only a few days."

"No!" Jane wiped her mouth clean with a linen napkin. "Then this is supposed to be your honeymoon. And here I am, intruding upon it."

"Oh, it's not like that. It wasn't a love match."

"He's very handsome, Lord Hatherly. If my feverish rememberings can be trusted." Jane smiled. "Are you certain you don't want a romantic honeymoon with him?"

"Funny concept, honeymoon," Alice mused. "From the Old English 'hony moone' referencing the sweetness of honey and warning of the changes of the moon. The first month of marriage is rapturous . . . yet love inevitably wanes."

She and Nick only had one month. She knew the limits of their relationship.

"Alice?" Jane was looking at her with a worried expression.

Alice laughed softly. "There I go again, always delving into the origins of words when there's work to be done in the here and now. It's time you had a nice, hot bath."

Jane sighed. "That would be lovely." She touched one of the cheerful yellow daisies. "I used to hate this color. Now . . ." Her eyes filled with tears. "Thank you, Alice," she whispered. "I hope I have the chance to thank Lord Hatherly and Captain Lear as well."

"You will." Alice rose. "I'll go and see about that bath."

"𝓗e's in the carriage," Lear said tersely. "Tried to run so I tied him to the hand strap."

"Where'd you find him?" asked Nick. "I thought he'd be halfway to America by now." They'd been searching for a month and hadn't found a trace, but now Lear had Stubbs trapped inside a hired carriage.

He'd have his answers now, Nick thought grimly.

"He's been hiding in a hovel in Cheapside," Lear said. "Squandering the duke's winnings on gin. When his funds ran low, the landlady turned on him and contacted me. Heard I'd been looking for him."

Nick paused. "That doesn't sound like Stubbs. I

hired him from a respectable agency. I trusted him. He was a good caretaker and a gentle, sober man."

Lear snorted. "He's not sober now." He opened the carriage door. "Isn't that right, Mr. Stubbs? She sold you out the second you couldn't pay. No loyalty these days, I tell you. I've brought someone to see you."

Stubbs cowered into the corner when he saw Nick. "I didn't mean you to be gambled away, Your Lordship, I didn't know you'd have to marry the girl."

Nick climbed into the carriage.

"I'll stay outside," Lear said.

"Don't leave him in here with me alone," cried Stubbs. "Help! Murder!" he shouted out the window, though they were far from the crowds, in a quiet alleyway off Fetter Lane.

"There'll be no murder today." Nick balled his hands into fists. "Though you'd best start talking, or I may be tempted to use these on you."

Stubbs cringed. "I didn't harm the duke in any way. Just a bit of fun. He had a lark, the duke. Loved every second of it. Loved the gambling."

Nick paused. Could that be true? He'd always thought his father was happiest in the peace and quiet of Sunderland. The few times he'd taken him out, the duke had gone silent and wide-eyed with fear.

"Whether he enjoyed himself is neither here nor there." Nick grabbed Stubbs by the neck cloth and pulled him closer.

The man reeked like a distillery. It smelled like he'd bathed in gin.

Grimacing, Nick twisted his neck cloth tighter. "I trusted you, Stubbs. What made you do it? Did someone force you into it?"

"It was my idea," Stubbs said sullenly, his large, fair head lolling to the side.

He was definitely more than three sheets to the wind.

Nick threw him back against the seat cushion in disgust.

How could Nick have hired a secret drunkard to watch his father? Stubbs had never touched a drop of spirits before, not where Nick could see him, anyway. And he'd been so very mild mannered and trustworthy.

Nick could only surmise that Stubbs was lying, and someone had hired, or coerced, him to betray Nick's family.

"I don't think it was your idea," Nick said evenly. "Why don't you tell me who was behind this."

Stubbs's face crumpled and he began to blubber, fat tears streaking his face. "I can't tell you. If I do, he'll hurt her."

"Hurt whom?"

"I can't tell you. He's got her there and he'll hurt her. He made me do it to hurt you. He hates you."

"Who hates me? Stubbs," Nick shook him by the collar, rattling his blackened teeth. "*I'll* hurt you if you don't tell me."

"I can't, I can't," Stubbs wailed. "He'll kill her. He said he would."

So he'd been blackmailed. The man who'd forced him to it hated Nick and held some power over Stubbs.

"Captain Lear and I will dispense justice if you tell me who he is. You'll never have to worry about him again because he'll be behind bars."

"It's no good. You can beat me. You can even kill me. My life doesn't mean much anymore. I won't give him a reason to torture her more than he's already done."

Torture was a strong word. Maybe this person he was protecting was a prisoner and the man was her jailor. They could begin searching the prisons for a sister, a wife, a daughter, or a lover.

It was something anyway.

Nick could tell he wasn't going to get anything else out of Stubbs. Cheap gin had eaten him from the inside out. He was a rotting shell of a man now, with trembling hands and bloodshot eyes.

Nick untied Stubbs and swung the carriage door open. "Get out."

Stubbs scurried down, lurching out of the carriage.

Lear grabbed his collar. "If we need you again we'll find you." He shoved Stubbs away.

If he kept drinking like that, it would only be a matter of months for him.

Lear climbed in and pounded on the carriage ceiling with his ebony walking stick and they began to move.

Nick glanced at the sleek, expensive stick, the question flashing through his mind as to whether it concealed a sharp blade.

He wouldn't be surprised.

"Didn't know he was so far gone," Lear said. "The poor devil."

"You heard everything?"

"Unfortunately."

"Wasn't afraid of dying. They aren't, you know, once the gin takes hold."

"Where to now?" Lear asked.

"We start with the prisons."

Lear nodded. "I had the same thought."

Nick had been so sure that finding Stubbs would be the answer, but the man was too far gone. It hadn't felt right to beat him. He was harming himself enough.

"How is Jane getting on?" Lear asked.

"Alice said she's feeling better but needs to build her strength before she can leave."

"I swear she's a lady, Nick. She spoke like one. Hawkins didn't know much about her."

Hawkins was an underkeeper at The Yellow House, the private lunatic asylum they'd rescued Jane from.

"I'll speak with her tomorrow," Nick said. "Find out more about her circumstances. Then we can find a safe place for her to go. Although Patrick's gone to Brighton with his family, so he won't be able to help forge her papers."

"We'll think of something," Lear replied. "The main thing is to keep her hidden for now."

They rode in silence for a few moments.

"How's Sally, by the way?" Nick asked Lear.

"In my bed as we speak, waiting for me to come home." Lear smirked. "Has expensive tastes, your Venus. Had to buy her another bauble yesterday. But she's well worth the price. Won't cry when I leave though, Sally. Has a heart as hard as marble, she does. Probably already has her eye on the next prize."

That was the problem. Alice was too tender-hearted. Nick couldn't give her any reason to care for him.

The last thing he wanted to do was hurt her.

"Sally says you'll fall in love with your wife. She said she's seen it happen too many times to count."

"Never," scoffed Nick. "That's an impossibility."

"Why? You've married her, may as well settle down like your friends Osborne and Harland. Become a family man."

"Lear. We've known each other for at least seven years. Have I ever given you the impression of a man who might ever consider settling down?"

"Not until your wife tied you in knots," Lear said with an unrepentant grin. "I never saw you so eager to please anyone as the morning of your wedding."

"Because I needed to keep my house."

That's why he'd married her. Plain and simple.

"If that's what you need to believe, old boy."

Why did everyone keep saying those words to him? Was he deluding himself somehow?

"So," Lear gave him a sly look. "How's wedded life treating you thus far?"

The tart scent of lemons rose in his mind with a clarity that drove everything else away. Alice in the kitchens, steam flushing her cheeks pink, his kiss leaving her lips swollen and red-tinged.

"Never mind," Lear laughed. "Don't answer that question. Your foolish grin is the only answer I need."

Nick groaned. "This has to end, Lear. I'm losing my edge."

"What has to end?"

"This obsession I've developed for my wife. Ever since our engagement, I haven't even wanted to look at another woman. And I have these terrible, nearly uncontrollable urges to wear flannel waistcoats, smoke a pipe, and read sentimental novels."

Lear chuckled. "Not *novels*."

"Laugh all you want but this is serious. I've never been this strung up before. I feel as though . . ." he paused. "Did I just start to tell you about my feelings, for Christ's sake? Kill me now." He closed his eyes. "Just end it all now."

"Said you were in trouble, didn't I?" Lear chuckled. "I could see it the moment I met the lady. She's a magnificent creature, your new wife."

That was it.

She was so much more than he had bargained for.

Nick had sworn he'd seen Alice's slim figure disappearing down the street ahead of them as he and Lear had crossed King Street earlier.

He'd had to fight the urge to chase after the lady, who couldn't possibly have been Alice because she'd been holding the hand of a small child in a straw hat with ribbons streaming down her back.

For some reason, the sight of a trim-figured woman with light brown hair holding her little girl's hand as they crossed the street had set his heart humming with some strange new tune.

A wordless longing for something.

For Alice.

For her body and nothing more, he told himself.

"She's making changes, Lear. There are flowers blooming on every table. She wants us to eat vegetables. Even cooked the duke a chicken soup."

Lear chuckled. "The nerve of that woman. Invite me for supper and I'll eat your vegetables if you don't want them. Haven't had a good home-cooked meal in years."

"I don't think that's a good idea. She's very curious. She'd ask you twenty questions about who you are and how you know me and what we do together all day."

Nick didn't want Alice knowing anything about his more dangerous pursuits. And Lear was thoroughly implicated in those.

"I understand," Lear said. "You're keeping too many secrets."

"Exactly." Nick stared out the carriage window at the buildings full of ordinary people living quiet, ordinary lives. "I'm keeping too many secrets."

She had somehow wrested control away from him. Infected his mind with this need for closeness, intimate conversation, *feelings.*

And he couldn't do a damn thing about it because he was going to go mad and hurt her and then she would leave him, as his mother had left his father, and . . . oh hell. How had it come to this?

He couldn't stop thinking about her.

What happened to wed her, bed her, be rid of her?

Surely, after they made love this growing obsession would evaporate, like spilled whiskey.

She could share his bed, slake her curiosity on his body, but that's where it ended.

This obsession ended tonight.

Chapter 17

❦ ❦

> In the pleasure-room, decorated with flowers, and fragrant with perfumes, attended by friends and servants, the citizen should receive the woman.
>
> *The Kama Sutra of Vātsyāyana*

Nick had never made love to a wife before.

At least not his own.

He rubbed his chin. He should probably shave. He already had several days' growth of whiskers and they would scratch her soft skin.

Berthold was with the duke tonight. Nick had asked him to be his father's new caretaker, until he could find another one he trusted. Between the two of them, they would keep the duke safe from harm.

With no valet, Nick had to make do, untying his own cravat and tugging off his boots.

While he shaved by candlelight, always a tricky proposition, he thought about the night ahead.

He wiped his razor clean, splashed water on his jaw from the washbasin, and toweled himself dry.

If she was hungry, he had enough to satisfy her. He had oysters on ice and a bottle of champagne.

Strawberries and whipped cream. Rose petals.

He knew how to seduce a timid lady.

He grabbed a red rose from the vase on the mantelpiece and, with one firm twist, separated the head from the stem and scattered the petals across the silk counterpane, flinging a few on the pillows.

The door to Alice's adjoining suite was open. He heard the sound of a pen scratching across parchment from her study.

Such a studious scholar, so absorbed by her work she didn't even notice when Nick entered the room.

She wore the same modest gray gown with its lamentably high neckline.

No matter. He'd soon peel it off.

Tendrils of fine brown hair had escaped her chignon and she puffed them away with her breath from time to time.

She'd lit several candles, and the glow caught the gold strands in her hair and danced shadows over her face.

There was a pride in being her first lover, Nick reflected, as well as a responsibility.

No more shocking her with coarse language. She was putting on a brave act to hide her timidity. He would be gentle with her. Gentle and patient.

She would enjoy this as much as he would.

He cleared his throat but she took no notice.

He leaned over her shoulder, reading the words on the sheet.

He peered closer. Surely that didn't say . . .

"*Mouth congress?*" he asked incredulously. Had he read that correctly?

Alice startled, and her pen slipped. A blob of ink puddled on the parchment. "Now see what you've done!"

She blotted the ink and lifted the sheet, fanning it with her hand.

He reached for the sheet but she snatched it away. "This is a lady's private writing, I'll thank you not to pry."

She hastily gathered the pages into a pile.

"Is it writing or translation?" he asked, his curiosity aroused.

He must have read the words wrong. Must have been *months' progress* . . . or some such.

"A bit of both," she said vaguely, as she reordered the desk, everything in its place, pens here, inkpots there. "Third-century odes to the moon. That sort of thing."

He dropped the subject, as there were other aroused parts of him to satisfy tonight. "You've been working late."

"Is it late?" She glanced at the window. "I didn't even notice the moon rise." She stacked her pages with precision, lining up the edges. "Sometimes I lose all sense of time when I'm working. I was accustomed to studying through the night while my mother slept."

When the desk was spotless and her papers tucked away in a drawer, she wandered to the window, hugging her arms around her chest. "*You are pale, friend moon,*" she spoke, gazing out the window at the swollen yellow moon. ". . . *and do not sleep at night . . . and day by day you waste away. Can it be that you also think only of her, as I do?"*

He approached her and ran his hands down her shoulders. "I've been thinking of you all day, Alice. Have you been thinking of me?"

"Yes, my lord," she whispered. "I've been thinking of you."

"Then come, Alice." He held out his hand. "Come to bed."

Come to bed.

Three wicked little words.

But they were married before God, her parents, and half of London high society.

This was a *marital* bed. She wasn't breaking any rules. Still, her heart thumped almost painfully in her chest.

The idea of having an experienced rake answer all her many questions had seemed quite sensible as a solution for helping her translate the true meaning of the *Kama Sutra* fragment.

Oh yes, it was all quite sensible and logical until it became *real*.

Real marquess—really *large* marquess—smiling at her like Kali smiled at a field mouse before she pounced.

Smiling as if she were a bowl of cream and he'd relish licking her up.

Would there be any Alice left?

What if this experience changed her irrevocably?

Stop right there, Alice.

You're a Lady Rake. And you wed this large marquess for a reason.

You've a fine, sensible head upon your shoulders.

You're not about to lose it because a handsome marquess takes you to bed.

In his bed, all her questions would be answered. Well, perhaps not *all* of them in one evening. They did have several weeks of nights ahead of them.

She touched his hand, and his warm fingers closed over hers possessively.

The same crackling sensation kindled along her skin, like she were made of straw and he'd touched her with a burning torch.

As she followed him into the bedchamber, the unfamiliar sensation of the elongated silk-covered gussets shaping her midriff made her heart race even faster.

He had secrets to teach her but Alice had a secret, too.

A wanton, silken secret rustling beneath her serviceable cotton gown. *Oh, Aunt Sarah,* she thought. *You definitely knew what you were doing.*

She wasn't accustomed to wearing anything tighter than loosely tied cotton stays. The corset thrust up her breasts and squeezed her midriff smaller.

The knowledge that she was wearing a silk corset from Paris and fine Swiss lace-trimmed garters under her plain cotton gown made her feel more in control, more seductive and alluring.

This was a garment designed with only one aim: to inflame a man's lust.

Building fences required heavy hammers.

Writing needed a sharpened quill.

This corset was the tool Alice required to speak Nick's language.

She could satisfy her curiosity, and improve her translation, without losing her head . . . or her heart.

Nick led her to an excessively large bed framed by beeswax candles burning in tall candelabras. Were those rose petals strewn across the pale green silk counterpane?

He'd prepared.

"So this is the notorious bedchamber of the infamous Lord Hatherly," she said.

"This is where the magic happens, Dimples."

"That is, without a doubt, the most enormous bed I have ever seen. It's more of a small island than a bed. You could fit *ten* brides upon it."

"That's a few too many, even for me," he quipped, walking to a nearby table.

"You mean you've had more than one woman here at the same time?" She glanced at the bed with renewed interest, nervously twirling an escaped lock of hair around her forefinger.

"Occasionally." He caught her eye and winked. "One will do tonight."

"The first time I met you, you had a woman on each arm."

"Ah yes, the Satine twins."

"They were twins?"

"Not really, they liked to call themselves twins. They came from an opera house in Paris. I bought them passage to London for one of my entertainments."

"Perhaps you do have more in common with Eastern culture than I supposed."

"I never kept a harem. But I don't want to talk about my past."

"How many women have you had here over the years?"

"Let's not quantify such things."

"Ten?" Silence. "Twenty?"

"What's in a number?"

More than twenty? Good gracious. Alice felt light-headed.

Courtesans. Bored wives. Worldly, seductive ladies with sophisticated tastes. What was she doing here? All of a sudden it seemed almost ludicrous.

She was no practiced seductress. No French opera singer.

"What happens the next day?" she asked.

"In the morning they leave. Glowing and satisfied. I'm usually a stepping-stone for them. Sharing my bed is a badge of honor, of sorts."

"And then you forget about them."

"The women I choose never want or expect more than a night, or at most a few weeks of diversion. They know I don't keep mistresses for very long."

"A revolving door of pleasure. What if they don't want to leave?"

"I never allow a woman, or her possessions, to linger. No hairbrushes or perfume bottles. This room is strictly masculine. Look around you."

It was a very male sort of room. One large bed, really.

"My entire household is composed of males only, if you haven't noticed," he continued. "We're a sorry lot of bachelors and misfits, but we have our system. The chaos works for us. Alice," he said softly, "look at me."

She lifted her head and then wished she hadn't. His eyes were so intensely silver.

"I never made any pretense of being anything other than a rake and a bachelor. Confirmed in my hedonistic, reckless ways."

"Oh, of course," she said lightly. "Of course I knew your reputation. That's why I married you. You promised me one month of tutelage and then a lifetime of neglect."

She'd only been slightly fuzzy on the details. She hadn't thought it all the way through.

He grinned and lifted a curvaceous green bottle, unpeeled a wax seal, and wrestled with a cork for a moment.

There was a loud popping sound. Bubbles fizzed over the rim of the bottle. He poured the sparkling liquid into two tall, thin glasses.

"Champagne?" He held out a glass.

Alice had never tasted champagne before, but she was wearing a French corset and she was alone in a bedchamber with a notorious rake, so she might as well throw caution to the wind.

He clinked his glass against her glass, holding her gaze as she took a small, exploratory sip. The bubbly stuff tickled down her throat, making her sneeze.

He lifted the lid of a serving dish and uncovered a mound of glistening red strawberries. He dipped one of them into a bowl of whipped cream. "Strawberry?"

The tartness of the strawberry bursting in her mouth and the sugared cream mingled perfectly with the champagne.

She closed her eyes as he prepared another strawberry, placing it against her lips until she opened for him. He fed her another. And another.

She could become accustomed to this manner of dining.

"Now, how does this gown unfasten?" he asked, reaching for her.

She ducked away. She wasn't ready yet for the bedding portion of the evening.

"So, this is what you do then." She attempted a tone of careless sophistication. She ran a finger lightly over the silk counterpane. "This is your profession."

"My profession. My raison d'être. If it's lessons in love you want, I'm the man you require."

Pleasure wasn't his only reason for living. He did care for his father's happiness and well-being. And he'd rescued Jane from a horrible fate.

He probably told himself that everything he said was true, but Alice could sense deeper waters, something he strove to hide.

"Life's only an amusement, Alice." He drained his glass and poured another. "We'll drink it to the dregs, you and I. We'll suck the marrow out of our brief amour."

"I'm not sure I approve of sucking the marrow out of anything," Alice said primly.

He snorted. "I could make a comment about that, but I won't."

To calm her swiftly beating heart, she walked

away from him, exploring the rest of the large chamber.

"Feathers?" She brushed her fingers over the black ostrich feathers in the vase on his mantel. "Are you starting a millinery shop, my lord?"

He gave her an amused smile. "They sometimes serve a purpose during bed sport."

"Really?" She touched the waving fronds. They were soft, and made her palm feel ticklish. She flushed, imagining what Nick might do with feathers.

He approached and ran his hands lightly down her arms. "Why don't you have another glass of champagne?"

Once again, Alice slipped from his grasp.

Not yet, the nervous little voice in her mind urged. *Not just yet. You need time to compose yourself.*

"What are these?" she asked with puzzlement, indicating the two iron rings mounted on the wall.

"Tour's over, Dimples," he growled.

"Why is this wall padded?" She pushed her palm against the cushioned wall behind the rings, which looked like the padding on a divan. "What do you do here *specifically*?"

He stalked across the room and backed her against the wall.

He pushed her hands over her head and captured both her wrists in one hand.

"*Specifically* . . . I bind women with silken wrist restraints which are then threaded through these rings embedded in my wall. Then I pleasure them. It's not my specialty, but I cater to most desires."

Padded walls. Alice eyed the section of wall that

looked like it should be the seat of a sofa. *Whoever heard of such a thing?* There was nothing about padded walls or wrist restraints in the *Kama Sutra.*

Although there were some rather perplexing descriptions of the marks lovers should make upon each other's bodies with nails and teeth.

Alice wondered if that was something Nick liked his courtesans to do.

She regarded her nails. They were short because she kept them clipped with scissors so they didn't catch on the parchment or impede the progress of her quill.

"Why would anyone want you to bind their wrists?" Alice asked, shocked by the idea.

He pushed her wrists higher, pinning her back against the padding with the length of his body.

"Some ladies beg for it." His breath was hot on her neck, and his eyes, when he lifted them, shimmered with streaks of silver. "And I always give ladies what they want."

Alice had momentarily forgotten that she was a Lady Rake, and not at all easily shocked.

"I'm sure you do," she purred. "Maybe I'll ask you to bind me later."

Abruptly, he dropped her wrists and stepped away. "You don't need any of this." He waved toward the rings and the padding. "Simple is sometimes better. These pleasures are for people whose tastes have grown jaded. Not for you, Alice."

"Why not?"

"Because you're a sweet little innocent and you're making me feel like the big bad wolf."

"Sweet little innocent?" Alice huffed. "Don't patronize me."

"You're not sweet?"

"I'm not that innocent."

The silver of his eyes intensified. "Are you telling me you've had a man?"

"What? No!"

She'd been referring to the knowledge she'd gleaned from translating the *Kama Sutra*. And from her married best friends and her scandalous Aunt Sarah.

"Well then, there's a first time for everything, Dimples." He held out his hand. "And that time is now."

Chapter 18

⟨❀❀⟩

When a girl, setting aside her bashfulness a little, wishes to touch the lip that is pressed into her mouth, and moves her lower lip, but not the upper one, it is called the "throbbing kiss."

The Kama Sutra of Vātsyāyana

Alice allowed Nick to circle her waist with his hands and gently lift her onto the edge of the high bed. She perched there, her stomach tying into knots.

He wiped a spot of cream from her lips with his thumb, and the touch set her trembling.

He stood in front of her in his shirtsleeves with no cravat, while she perched on the edge of the bed, her legs dangling off the side. She was at a decided disadvantage.

He obviously preferred to control his liaisons completely.

She peered over the edge of the bed. No boots, either. He was barefoot, in breeches and a white linen shirt undone at the throat, giving her a nice view of his smooth chest.

He'd so clearly planned the view on purpose, to tantalize her.

And it was very effective. The triangle of chest made her want to see more. See everything she'd seen yesterday, when she'd watched him working in the gardens.

Ridged, sinuous lines of muscle rippling down his abdomen.

"Would you like some oysters?" he asked.

"No, thank you." *I'll try a marquess, instead.* Alice giggled softly because the thought was so very unlike her.

It must be the champagne. It had traveled straight to her head, and her belly, amplifying the fizzing sensation and making her feel reckless.

"What's so humorous, Dimples?" he asked in a low voice, sipping his champagne and regarding her with half-lidded moonlit eyes.

"You planned all of this, didn't you?" She swept her eyes over the rose petals, the champagne, the undone buttons. "You may as well scrawl some ink across your chest that says: 'Eat me.'"

He choked slightly on his champagne. *"Eat me?"*

"That's right. You're a large, satisfying platter of gentleman, enticingly displayed so that young ladies will want to have a taste."

He chuckled. "I had the same thought about you, Dimples, when I saw you that first day in your father's study. I thought the dress you were wearing was like a strawberry tart your parents were hoping I'd want to devour."

"My mother would be so pleased to hear it."

"Well?" he asked, his voice roughening. He

struck a wide-legged stance and squared his shoulders. "Is it working? Am I making you hungry?"

Oh, it was working.

She was probably staring at him right now in the same way he'd stared at her that day in her father's study.

Alice drained the rest of her champagne. When had he refilled her glass?

She handed him the empty glass. "I don't think I should imbibe any more champagne," she announced. "I'm not accustomed to spirits, and I haven't eaten much today." Her head felt light and airy, like it might fly off her shoulders.

He took the glass and set it down. "Very well." He finished his champagne and discarded his glass as well.

He kissed her then, positioning himself, still standing, between her thighs.

The effervescent, tart taste of the drink lingered on his tongue as he stroked inside her mouth. He dragged her bum to the edge of the bed and held her firmly against his hardness.

It must have been the champagne that made her part her limbs with barely any prompting. She'd forgotten that she wasn't wearing any drawers.

Spreading her legs brought her in direct contact with that part of him which pressed against her naked, intimate flesh through his breeches.

In a rush of near panic, Alice's stomach flip-flopped and she ended the kiss, pushing against his chest to stop him.

She pressed her knees closed.

She wasn't ready yet. Not yet. Maybe never.

Maybe this was all a dreadful mistake.

She wasn't a seductive, worldly Lady Rake. What had she been thinking?

It was all well and good to wear French lingerie and no drawers, but she was beginning to realize that a few chapters of an ancient erotic text and some bawdy anecdotes from one's friends did not a sophisticate make.

"Did you know, my lord," she said in a rush, "that champagne began as a still wine of a rosy hue? The cold winters halted fermentation entirely until the warming of spring produced bubbles, much to the monks' consternation. Why, even into the seventeenth century, winemakers endeavored to exorcise that characteristic effervescence! It wasn't until—"

"Alice," he broke in.

"Yes?"

"Is anything the matter? You seem distracted."

"If you must know, I'm rather flustered by you and by the thought of what is to take place upon this bed."

"Of course you are, Dimples. That's only natural. But you needn't be frightened. I'll do nothing against your will . . . and everything to please you."

He teased her lower lip between his teeth gently, kissing the corners of her mouth before moving to her neck.

She tilted her head back to give him access, but her mind wouldn't stop churning. "While I have conducted a thorough inventory of my person, from pate to toes and everything in between, I'm not at all sure that I understand how my person is supposed to accommodate your person and whether it won't at first be very painful and whether I might not like it as much—"

"Alice." He placed his hands on her cheeks, framing her face. "While I enjoy hearing your every thought, and your every thought is a unique revelation that no other lady could possibly express, there is a point at which language becomes superfluous."

Language was never superfluous. "You can't mean we are to be completely silent while we . . . that is . . . during the act of congress."

"Not completely silent. Short exclamations of the imperative variety and breathy moans are encouraged. The words *Yes, Nick, right there* and *Oh God, yes, don't stop* are allowed."

"Oh." Alice blinked rapidly, absorbing this new information.

Not supposed to talk?

Then what was she supposed to do? "But language, my lord, is how I make sense of the world. But if you request me to refrain from speech, I shall. If it's the sensible thing to do in these . . . situations."

His smile widened. "Do you ever do anything for a reason other than 'It's the sensible thing to do'?"

She thought about that for a moment. "No."

"You never let emotion carry you away."

"Never."

"This is going to be quite a challenge. But I've always loved a good challenge."

He ran a hand down the center of her gown.

"I've never seen wrappings like this on a gown," he said, sliding a finger beneath one of the crossed layers. "Are there buttons somewhere?"

"Hidden hooks."

"Mmm . . . another challenge."

He had her bodice undone in seconds flat, and a large hand burrowed beneath the fabric, sliding across the edge of the corset. He opened her bodice and inhaled sharply, his gaze traveling over her mounded bosom and the scarlet silk corset.

"What's this, Dimples?" The expression on his face was almost one of pain.

She'd made yet another error. "You don't like it?" she asked, biting her lip.

Chapter 19

❖◈❖

Some women enjoy themselves with closed
eyes in silence, others make a great noise over
it, and some almost faint away. The great art
is to ascertain what gives them the greatest
pleasure, and what specialties they like best.

The Kama Sutra of Vātsyāyana

"Ungh," said Nick.

He couldn't seem to form a coherent sentence.
The sight of her full breasts shaped into a mounded
offering, spilling over scarlet silk, had stolen all
words away.

Holy hell. He needed a moment to steady his
breathing.

He hadn't been expecting her to be dressed like a
high-priced courtesan under that schoolgirl gown.

The lady was full of surprises. Always toppling
him off balance, wrenching him away from control.

"I knew this was a bad idea." Alice attempted
to draw her bodice back over the corset. She lowered her large, aquamarine eyes, and dark lashes
fanned across her cheeks.

"No," Nick said, holding her arms at her side. "It was a very, very good idea. I was only caught off guard for a moment. I thought your undergarments would be as sensible as you are."

"You don't know everything about me, my lord."

"Apparently not." And he liked every new curve she threw his way.

Every luscious, rounded, tempting curve.

"Let's see the rest of it." He peeled her dress down her slim hips, lifting her off the bed to remove it fully. He pitched the gray cotton into a corner. She wouldn't be needing sensible gowns any more.

He might keep her in this corset for the next month.

Holy Mother of God. It just got more mouthwatering.

The boned corset ended at her natural waist, and a short, sheer shift barely hid anything below. He could even make out the patch of dark, curling hair over her sex. Below, her limbs were encased in rosy pink stockings held up by scarlet garters trimmed with fine lace.

Nick appreciated a woman in sensual lingerie.

Hell, she was the most gorgeous thing he'd ever seen.

Prosaic, pragmatic Alice from Pudsey.

Somehow she'd transformed herself, and it wasn't because of the silk and lace, although that was a nice addition; it was the tempting look in her sparkling turquoise eyes as she watched him soak in the sight of her in the scandalous garment.

"I'm glad you like it," she breathed, her lips curling into another coquettish smile.

He needed to regain the upper hand here.

Couldn't have her thinking he was a lusting beast whom she could bend to her will with a few scraps of silk and some lacy garters.

He stepped back a pace. "Undo your hair," he commanded.

Her eyes widened, but she obeyed, reaching around and deftly removing her hairpins, shaking her long, wavy brown hair over her shoulders.

Catching a handful, he brought her lips closer and drank his fill of her strawberry-and-champagne lips.

Damn, he was hard as the champagne bottle and he felt nearly as thick.

Slowly, so as not to startle her, he inched her knees apart with his legs until he was standing right where he wanted to be, in between her long, shapely limbs. Dipping his head, he captured one of her nipples between his lips and lapped greedily.

She laid a tentative, questing hand on his head, showing him that she approved.

He'd known she would be a quick study. Known without a shadow of a doubt that she'd be responsive and passionate, once her sensuality was awakened.

Although he could have licked and sucked her breasts all evening, there were other erogenous areas that required his attention.

He lifted his head, and she made a soft, moaning noise of disappointment that nearly demolished his control.

He dropped to his knees in front of her. She immediately snapped her knees closed.

Sable lashes shaded her cheeks. He couldn't read the emotion in her eyes, but he imagined it was half trepidation and half curiosity.

He reminded himself that she was innocent, despite her bold garments.

He placed his hands on her silk-covered knees. "Do you have dimples in other places, I wonder?" he teased. "Perhaps here?" He stroked the backs of her knees, and she squirmed.

"Ticklish?"

"Stop." She laughed. "I'm terribly ticklish, my lord. Fred used to torture me so when we were children."

"Nick," he growled, losing another inch of control. "From now on, you call me Nick."

He needed to taste her now, and his lips were on the perfect level.

He flipped the hem of her shift over her hips and she gasped, squirming in his hands.

He held her firmly above him; he wasn't letting her escape. He blew on the silky, soft curls between her thighs, and her breath caught on a surprised squeak.

"Wh-what are you doing, my lord—I mean, Nick?"

"Spread your legs," he ordered. "I never eat sweets, but tonight you're my dessert."

"I—I . . ." she stuttered. "I don't know if I can. It's awfully embarrassing. I surmise that you are about to . . . attempt a form of congress, with your mouth, but I must say that when I imagined our coupling, I hardly guessed this—"

"Do not surmise, guess, extrapolate or translate," he said sternly. "Don't even think. Just obey. Spread your legs, Dimples. Now."

She parted her thighs one inch. Then two. He slipped in the middle, finding his treat, holding her by the bum as he delved into her salty-sweetness with his tongue and one of his fingers.

Control yourself. Nice and slow.

Nice and easy.

Prolong the pleasure.

"Don't be ashamed," he whispered, against her thigh. "Your body is beautiful. You are exquisite."

She was still tense, still not allowing herself to enjoy his caress.

Her stomach muscles clenched. "I feel so exposed."

"You are exposed." He parted the lips of her sex, reveling in the curves and spirals of her. "I can see you, the heart of you, and goddamn, Dimples, you're so fucking beautiful."

"Nick! You can't say that to a lady."

He didn't apologize. There was something about the contrast between her innocence and her questing mind that shattered his control.

He followed words with his lips and tongue, worshipping her, working her. Bringing her closer. Her knees trembled on either side of his head. She was straining toward climax but holding back.

"This is made for pleasure." He touched her sex with his tongue. "Your whole body is made for pleasure. Let yourself go. Don't fight it, breathe deeply and jump. Like it's a river, a rushing, swollen river after a rain, and you'll be swept away."

God, he loved women. Their softness and their sighs.

The delicate flavor of them on his tongue.

This could take an hour. Sometimes it did.

He could do this all night. He loved tasting Alice, and listening to her breathing hitch and stutter.

She'd gone quiet for once . . . maybe for the first time in her life.

He focused on listening to her body; when she trembled, he followed the small movements, and when she tensed, he stopped until she quieted and he placed his fingers on her belly and reminded her to breathe.

He hadn't thought the idea of being her very first lover would be so exciting, but it was.

She trusted him enough to give him this gift.

He would make this so good for her.

He flicked his tongue lightly over her, only the softest touch.

"Yes, Nick." Her fingers tangled in his hair and she pressed his mouth between her thighs. "Right there."

He smiled against her intimate flesh. She'd followed his instructions about the words she was allowed to use.

Which deserved a reward.

He gave her exactly what she requested.

Hard and fast and steady.

Until her fingers clenched in his hair and she climaxed in a tremor and a quake of clasping thighs and soft belly and gasping moans.

Nick moved onto the bed with her, gazing down

with a rush of masculine pride at his flushed and dimpled wife.

"Oh, my." She grinned widely. "That was *highly* educational."

She's happy and satiated. I made her happy, his heart chirped like a damned songbird.

Nick decided he had a new goal in life.

Making Alice come, so he could see that approving smile and those delighted dimples.

You're hired, Alice thought, and nearly burst into laughter.

She flopped back on the bed, unheeding of the fact that he was still between her limbs and she was still exposed and naked.

The flood of pleasure had left her boneless. Senseless.

She had definitely chosen the right gentleman for the task. At least ten of her questions had been answered.

She'd touched herself before, and he'd touched her in the gallery, but she'd never felt such nearly violent, utterly overwhelming sensations.

She was still floating in the voluptuousness of it, carried downstream in a sun-warmed river, kicking lazily with her feet when the current faltered.

Nick rose and lifted her into the center of the bed, settling next to her. He shrugged out of his shirt. She placed a palm over his heart, as she had earlier, but this time he was naked under her fingers. Naked and warm and hers for the exploring.

The simple pleasure of touch.

The voluptuousness of skin on skin.

She'd been translating a passage from the *Kama Sutra* about how women experience pleasure in different ways than men.

She wanted to know how Nick experienced pleasure.

She could feel his stiff length jutting against her thigh.

She rolled to her side, facing him, and slid her hand to his breeches flap.

He froze.

She took a deep breath. "Let me see your cock."

"Alice," he moaned against her neck.

"Or am I not allowed to say things like that?"

"You are most definitely encouraged to say things like that."

He tugged his breeches and smalls over his hips, and his tool sprang free, looking very pleased to make her acquaintance.

A thick, long affair with a purplish cap, smooth and silky to the touch. Tentatively, she drew her finger along the length.

His breathing quickened.

"Did you know that there have been whole cultures formed around the worship of the phallus?" she asked. "Travelers to the jungles of Angkor have met hermits who describe whole riverbeds carved into hundreds of lingams as a tribute to the Hindu gods Shiva and Vishnu."

"I did not know that, Dimples," he said in a strained voice. "Are you making an anthropological study? Or do you mean to give this phallus his proper devotion?"

She curled her fingers around the base, watch-

ing for signs that he approved. She remembered
Aunt Sarah's last piece of advice. "It's so large."

"Are you . . . awed?" he gasped.

"Very."

He closed his eyes and thrust into her hand,
which she took as a positive sign. "How does
one . . . er . . . What does one do with it?"

He wrapped her fingers around him, showing
her how to stroke.

Up and down. Around the head, and back down.
He was hot and stiff beneath her fingers.

"You can finish me like this, if you want," he
said, with his eyes closed and his stomach muscles
straining. "We have weeks. This is enough of a
lesson for one night."

"But we are newlyweds and must consummate
the marriage. Though I've no idea how such a thing
will be accomplished given your girth and my lack
thereof."

He rolled on top of her, pinning her to the bed
with his body.

She felt him nudging there, between her legs,
hard and insistent.

She tensed her muscles, waiting for the pain to
arrive.

He smoothed his large palm over her belly and
dipped lower, his finger connecting with her still
swollen flesh.

"Oh." She jumped under his hand.

He stroked her and it began to feel nice again.

"That's the way of it. Breathe and relax." The
blunt, hard tip of him pressed deeper, and she
couldn't help contracting her muscles.

He was so large and she was so small.

But she could feel and see, when she lifted her head and glanced between them, that he was gently and slowly burying more of himself inside her.

He was raised on one elbow above her, his hand stroking her, his thumb making small half moons over her sensitive flesh while he sank deeper into her with each breath she drew.

"It's never perfect the first time between new lovers," he said. "There's a certain amount of exploration involved. But we'll learn the way of it. We'll find our rhythm."

He stretched her further, and groaned, deep and low in his throat.

She fell back against the pillows, her lips brushing one of the velvety rose petals he'd strewn across his bed for her.

She breathed deeper, consciously relaxing around him.

She bit into the pillow, stifling a cry.

He stopped moving. "Is it too much? I'll stop, Alice, if you want me to."

Smoothing her hands down his sweat-slick back, she shook her head. "Keep going."

He thrust deeper, filling her to bursting. "You're so beautiful, Alice. I want to stay inside you forever."

Forever was a long time.

They didn't have forever.

He moved more swiftly, strong thrusts that pushed her higher on the bed, and stretched her wider.

He dipped his head and closed his lips over her nipple.

His hand slipped out from between their bodies and he sank against her, suckling her breast while he pumped faster.

"Ah . . . Alice. So. Good."

She was beginning to agree. Not entirely. But there was the noise of that rushing river, off in the distance, a trickle, a tributary, but somewhere it rushed, strong and loud, beckoning her to follow.

"You're so quiet, Dimples. Now's the time to talk. Tell me what you want. Does this feel good?" He moved inside her, angling upward, and touched a place that did feel rather promising.

"Yes."

He smiled and kissed her cheek, moving inside her faster, angling up more, and her cheeks heated and her body felt flushed, like she had a fever.

It was so very raw and elemental. No wonder people wrote whole treatises on the subject; no wonder they wrapped it in poetry.

"That's nice, right there," she said shyly as the rushing noise in her ears grew louder.

"Alice. I need you to come now. I'm not going to last long."

"I . . . don't think I can. I mean . . . there are signs. But you'd best find your pleasure. I'm not sure how much more of this I can stand."

It was good but it hurt. And she needed breathing space.

The slide of him inside her grew deeper and more unguarded, and she wrapped her arms around him because even though there was discomfort, there was also an intense closeness.

With a gasp, he withdrew from her completely, holding himself by the base. He lifted her shift out of the way and spilled his seed over her belly.

He collapsed upon her breast, breathing heavily, pressing her into the mattress.

A sudden welling of emotion startled her. Was she . . . going to cry?

It was the same thought she'd had during their wedding ceremony. The feeling that maybe their union, this pledge with their words, and now their bodies, was supposed to have some deeper meaning, some transformative significance.

Nick didn't seem troubled by any such thoughts.

With practiced efficiency, he used his discarded shirt to wipe both of them clean, and then he drew her into his arms and placed her head against his chest.

"Did that answer some of your questions?" he asked drowsily, stroking her head. "You'll be quite sore tomorrow."

"Does that make you proud?"

"It might." He tilted her chin toward him. "Lovemaking gets better every time." He bent down and kissed her lips. "I didn't spring a fully formed rakehell from my cradle, instantly knowing everything there is to know about the ways of a man with a maid."

Alice hadn't considered that.

"For men there's uncertainty as well," he continued. "Some initial fumbling. I had to learn the right way to pleasure a woman. And that means time and practice. Lots and lots of practice. We should practice every night."

She smiled against his chest. "I think we should . . . for educational purposes only, of course."

"Of course," he murmured.

She felt his body go slack beneath her and she snuggled closer to his warmth.

She wasn't quite sure who'd won that round, or whether there even needed to be a winner.

Maybe this was enough, this intimate, wordless moment.

She rested her head on his chest, listening to his heartbeat.

"Nick?"

"Mm-hm?"

"Tell me about the Yellow House." She wanted to know more about why he'd rescued Jane.

"Thomas Coleman's private madhouse in Bethnal Green." His voice was soft and low but carried a hard edge. "Death house would be a more appropriate name. If my father were a pauper he could be there right now. Rotting."

"But Jane's not a pauper."

"Some are paupers sent to the madhouse by their parishes who pay nine shillings per week for housing. Coleman profits from their keep. Others are conveniently declared insane and committed against their will by unscrupulous relations."

"Yes, that's what happened to Jane. She said her husband committed her because she was insubordinate."

He lifted his head. "Did she tell you her full name or the name of her husband?"

"She refused. She thinks it would put us in danger."

His head dropped back. "I'll talk to her tomorrow."

"She told me that you saved her from near certain death. Her keeper hated her."

"I've never been inside the asylum. They chain the patients like animals. Keep them barely alive."

His body tensed and his voice rasped with emotion. "Alive enough to collect their rent from the parish. I don't understand how the good church-going folk rest easy in their beds when they've relegated their fellow humans to such a hell on earth."

"I had no idea this was happening."

"Most people don't. It's all hidden away so that society doesn't have to think about it. Some of the inmates truly are insane but the chief affliction of many of the inmates is poverty. I can only offer refuge to a select few."

"Mr. March." Now Alice began to understand. "Was he in the Yellow House?"

"Yes, and Bill as well. They have their oddities, that's certain, but they should never have been committed. I have a man, Mr. Hawkins, a paid informant who is an underkeeper in the asylum. He alerts me to cases such as theirs."

"I take it that you wouldn't normally accept a case such as Jane's."

"I've never accepted a female before. I only did so because you were here to make her feel more comfortable."

"Poor Jane. I can't believe she's been declared insane. What will she do? Where will she go?"

"Patrick Fellowes will be able to help when he returns from his vacation in Brighton. Jane will need a new name. Letters of reference. An entirely new identity. We'll find her a place somewhere far from London."

"I think it's wonderful what you're doing for Jane. What you've done for others."

"I can't save everyone," he murmured, stroking the back of her neck.

"Dr. Forster told me that he thinks your method of caring for the duke is highly effective for treating milder cases of lunacy and perhaps even for effecting a cure. He said he asked you to write about your method, for the benefit of others."

"I won't be publishing any study about my father, Alice. It would expose me too much. I wouldn't be able to continue helping other inmates."

She hadn't thought of that. "Yes, but you could at least record your observations of your father's behavior. Whether tending his orchids makes him less agitated, for example. Perhaps only for the eyes of physicians such as Dr. Forster."

"Perhaps . . ." His voice drifted off and his chest rose and fell beneath her cheek.

So Nick and his friends saved people from madhouses.

That didn't mean Alice had to fall in love with him. It only meant he was a better man than she had judged him to be.

And she had to make him see how much potential he had to do even more good.

Now she had two tasks during the remainder of her time here.

Finish the translation, which should flow better now that certain things were more clear, and convince Nick that he was so much more than he pretended to be. That if he'd only stop living in darkness, wallowing in the fear of going mad, he might have a bright, passionate, caring future.

No doubt he'd think her meddlesome, and he might refuse to begin keeping a journal on the subject of his father's illness, but Alice felt it her duty to try.

Of course, she had more than two tasks remaining.

She had sixty-four, to be precise. She snuggled closer to Nick, inhaling his spiced, masculine scent.

She could indulge in fleshly pleasures, while remaining in complete control of her emotions.

Because she was a Lady Rake.

Chapter 20

⊠⊠

Love which is felt for things to which we are
not habituated . . . is called love resulting
from imagination, as for instance, that love
which some men and women feel for the Au-
parishtaka, or mouth congress.

The Kama Sutra of Vātsyāyana

Alice woke with a start. Disoriented for a moment,
she lay still, rubbing her eyes.

Large body curled around her, holding her close.
Numb arm because his heavy form had her pinned.
A soreness between her legs, a throbbing ache.

Nick's breathing, deep and rhythmic, rumbling
close to her ear.

It was still early morning.

Kali hopped onto the bed and nuzzled her wet,
cold nose against Alice's cheek.

"Where have you been, Miss Kali?" Alice whispered. Kali looked smug. There was a feather sticking to one of her whiskers.

"Ah-ha," Alice said. "Terrorizing birds." She
should tie a bell on her cat.

Kali licked her lips and then licked her paw, climbing over Alice to investigate the sleeping marquess.

He certainly slept soundly.

Probably never left his bed before noon. Alice's favorite time of the day was morning. Even on the evenings she stayed up late working, she still rose early to snatch a few more minutes of calm and peace.

She had much to mull over.

She lifted Nick's arm and slipped out of bed. He muttered something and rolled over, crushing a pillow in his arms and curling up around it.

Kali decided he made a nice bed, and draped herself across his ankles.

Alice smiled. Kali wasn't scared of Nick, which was unusual. She normally didn't like large men. She'd loathed Fred, hissing whenever he came into a room, but she seemed to approve of Nick.

In the washroom, Alice soothed her soreness with soap and water.

The secret things they'd done during the night, aided by champagne and French corsets, were perhaps meant to stay in the darkness.

But the acts described in the *Kama Sutra* were equally voluptuous. So why didn't she balk at reading them? It was the remove between reading and doing.

Palm leaves and palms holding her breasts.

It made her pause. She'd been thinking of the text as a historical artifact, and a window into the minds and practices of an ancient civilization.

But they had been people just like her and Nick.

And today, because of sexual congress, she had a new awareness of her body . . . and the meaning of the *Kama Sutra*.

She stretched before the glass, looking at her body. She'd never truly studied her form before. Nick thought she was beautiful, or at least he'd said so last night.

She cupped her breasts, turning before the glass.

There was a power in knowing the intimate workings of one's body, Alice reflected. She felt sensual in a way she never had before.

She could weave that sensuality into her translation. This was still a scholarly pursuit of knowledge.

Nick was still the best man for the job.

And she was still very much in control.

Nick had slept late, as he always did, but Alice was already hard at work in her study.

There was a striking contrast, he thought, as he watched her pen dance across the parchment.

The scarlet corset-wearing wanton by night, and the prim, cotton-garbed scholar by day.

He liked her contrasts . . . and her moans of pleasure.

Last night had been extraordinary. And Nick wanted more.

He drew closer and leaned over her shoulder, intending to kiss her cheek until a word on the page caught his eye.

Surely that didn't say . . .

He stared at the page, reading and rereading.

After the fifth pass, it still said what he'd thought it had said: *When she raises her thighs and keeps them wide apart and engages in congress it is called the "yawning position."*

Good God. Was his prim, scholarly wife writing an erotic novel? Perhaps she wasn't quite as innocent and chaste as he'd assumed.

"Ahem." He cleared his throat, and she jumped.

"What are you working on, Dimples?" He tapped his bare foot on the rug.

Her eyelashes flapped rapidly. He knew by now what that meant. She was trying to think of one of her evasion tactics.

He grabbed the top sheet of parchment from the stack.

"Give that back," she cried, reaching for the paper.

He caught her wrist in his hand and leaned away, reading aloud, *"When a man wishes to enlarge his organ, he should rub it with the bristles of certain insects that live in trees, and then, after rubbing it for ten nights with oils, he should again rub it with the bristles . . ."*

He gaped at her. Her cheeks were rapidly turning bright pink.

"What in the name of all that is unholy is *this*?" he asked.

"A recipe," she replied defensively. "A lady's private recipe. Not for your eyes."

"Bristles?" he sputtered. "I have no need for bristles."

"Not everything is about *you*," she huffed.

"Then whom is it about?"

She let out an exasperated puff of breath. "This is the translation I'm working on. Now give it back." She reached for the sheet again but he held it out of reach.

"This is the translation? Of an ancient Hindu manuscript? But . . . I thought you said it was stodgy and staid."

Reverently, Alice touched the thin, elongated dried palm leaf pages which were bound together with a cord that looped through holes drilled in their centers.

"I never said anything of the kind. You made an assumption. It's a treatise on pleasure in all its many variations."

"Those bristles don't sound pleasurable to me."

"The recipes are quite antiquated, though there are some that hold interest for a modern reader."

Nick shuddered. "Not this reader."

"You happened to have read one of the more painful-sounding recipes."

"I'll say."

"There are some quite lovely and fragrant-sounding ones."

"Uh-huh." Nick wasn't convinced. He was still attempting to scrub his mind free from the mental image of rubbing his cock with insect bristles. Whatever that meant.

Although the oil part hadn't sounded that bad. He'd been known to rub himself with oil from time to time.

Alice stacked her pages with precision. "This is

only a fragment of a much larger work entitled the *Kama Sutra. Kama* means desire and *sutra*, taken literally, is sort of a thread that holds things together."

"So you've been translating a dirty book. I must say I'm shocked, Dimples."

"And awed?" she joked.

"Well, I did rather assume that it was my kiss that had kindled your latent libidinousness. Now I find that it was this dirty book all along. Rather pricks a gentleman's pride."

"It's not dirty; it's an important and illuminating glimpse into the minds of an ancient culture."

"More like a glimpse into the bedrooms. I mean . . . the *yawning* position?"

"The prurient sections will ensure the work finds a wide audience. But the *Kama Sutra* is also a philosophical meditation on spiritual and physical fulfillment, as well as a guide to virtuous and gracious living."

"Is this why you asked me for instruction in the art of sexual congress? Are you . . . are you *using* me? Am I merely the most convenient cock to practice with and nothing more?"

She stroked his arm. "You're the best, Nick. That's why I chose you, remember?"

He didn't know why any of this should bother him. After all, wasn't this what he was to every woman who passed through his bedchamber? A pleasure ride and nothing more?

But this was *Alice.*

Not just any woman.

He'd been so proud and smug, believing that his masterful powers of seduction had awakened her sensuality, when her curiosity had been sparked by a book.

Why did he feel so disappointed? And why was this moment complicated in a way that his relationships were never complicated? Because they were *married*?

She'd be gone in a month's time, for Christ's sake.

"I wonder if you've thought that contributing to the translation of such a scandalous work of literature could have consequences for your family's reputation, even if it's published under Fred's name and not yours?" he asked.

"Oh, I'm sure if he requested anonymity they'd grant him that. This is the missing portion of a much longer work. The Sanskrit professors I've been corresponding with think that with my chapters, they'll be able to compile a complete manuscript."

"So you're doing all of this not for glory but merely for the love of literature?"

"I suppose so. Someday I believe the *Kama Sutra* will be widely read. I think it could be very educational for naïve young ladies who are kept in ignorance of the workings of their bodies and the particulars of sexual congress."

"I've been forced to revise my opinions and preconceived ideas about young ladies several times since I met you, Alice."

"Is that a compliment?"

He smiled and touched her cheek. "It is. Of course, the fact remains that you're using me for scandalous scholarly research purposes. And I'm not sure how I feel about that."

"Oh please. Isn't the pursuit of pleasure your reason for living?"

"Well, yes."

"You're certainly not the first gentleman to make a lifelong study of sensual fulfillment. And we British didn't invent sexual congress, you know," she said with a purse of her full lips that for some reason drove him nearly mad with lust and made him forget all about his disappointment.

"No. But we're about to perfect it," he growled, hauling her from her chair, lifting her into his arms, and stalking toward his bedchamber.

He laid her across his bed and teased the edge of her bodice down enough for him to locate one pink nipple. He closed his lips around it, licking hungrily until she squirmed beneath him.

"Nick, I was working."

"Mmm," he answered, his mouth full. "So am I."

He noticed she didn't protest too much, so he shifted to the other taut peak. Soon she was sighing beneath his lips.

He raised his head. "We haven't made love in the afternoon yet."

She looked pretty in early afternoon light. Glowing and warm, her hair threaded with gold and her lively, intelligent eyes shifting with darker shadows and brilliant green like leaves dappled by sunlight.

"Lie back and raise your arms above your head," she said.

"What was that?" he murmured, back at his task of worshipping her glorious breasts.

"I said lie back and raise your arms over your head," she said in an amusing approximation of a growl.

Interesting, the lady wanted to play. "Whatever you want, Dimples."

He stretched lazily. He'd left the bed in only his smalls, so she had plenty to see.

He loved the way her eyes grew hazy as she watched him stretch his length across the bed.

He lifted his arms over his head and flexed his muscles. "Like this?"

"Wrists crossed," she ordered.

Even more interesting.

Nick complied, liking this new, forceful side of his wife.

She was full of surprises.

She reached up and . . . surprised him even more.

"Are you tying my wrists?"

"It appears so," she said, bending to her task, biting her full lower lip as she concentrated on wrapping silk cords around his wrists. Where did the cords come from? Had she been carrying them around, thinking about doing this all morning?

"You know I'll be able to break free easily, right?" he asked. "And then I'll have my way with you."

She smirked. "I've been practicing my sailor's knots, in the event the merchant ship to India is overrun by pirates, all the crew is killed, and I have to escape in a rowboat."

Nick burst into laughter. "And have you been practicing rowing then, too?"

She tugged on the knot around his wrist and calmly proceeded to secure it to one of the carved bedposts. "Oh yes. And I've also been practicing . . . riding," she said in a seductive tone, glancing down his body. "In the event I must make my escape by horse once I reach shore."

"Riding," said Nick, his voice sounding strained.

He twisted his wrists to test her knot. The lady could tie.

She gave him a satisfied smile. "You won't break free easily."

No, he wouldn't. And why was that so arousing? He'd never wanted to be tied before. He'd always been the one in control. He'd always been the *tie-er*.

Something about Alice's smile disarmed him so completely. He didn't mind being in her power. In fact, he could probably learn to like it. Especially when she looked at him like that.

"Why are you smiling at me so wolfishly, Lady Hatherly?"

"Because I just remembered something I read about in my manuscript," she replied, flinging her long, silky hair out of the way and down her back. She licked her lips, her gaze sliding lower, over his abdomen and down further.

Mouth congress. Nick remembered the words he'd read before and rejected as too preposterous. Now they made a lot more sense.

He immediately went as thick and stiff as he'd ever been. Stiffer. He was going to burst right through his smalls.

The lady had shed her inhibitions under his tutelage, he thought proudly.

And the result was thoroughly wicked.

"Now then. Do you know why I've tied you?" she asked.

Mouth congress, Nick thought hopefully. "Ah . . ." His breath rasped harsh and fast. "I don't know. You'll have to tell me, Dimples. Or you could . . . show me," he suggested.

Show me, show me, his mind screamed.

"I tied you up," the little vixen said, licking her lips again, "so that we could have a nice, long . . . *talk.*"

Nick's shoulders tensed and his arms strained against his bindings. "The nice, long object I was hoping you wanted *rhymed* with talk," he ground out.

"I'm sure it did," she purred. "And I'll pay attention to you soon enough, I promise," she said, in the direction of his tented smalls.

Nick always did love a woman who spoke directly to his cock.

"But right now," she continued, her gaze traveling back to his face, "I'd like to hear you tell me a few things."

Nick sighed. She really would be the death of him. "You know you don't have to bind me to have a conversation, right?"

"I know, but it's so much fun to bind you." She drew her hands down his biceps. "And then frighten you with the threat of conversation."

Nick narrowed his eyes. Was she . . . teasing him?

She was, the temptress.

"Alice, untie me right now." He wanted to flip her on her back, thrust her arms over her head, and have her twenty different ways.

She bent down to kiss him, her lips soft yet demanding, moving over him hungrily.

Her hair fell in a curtain around them, blocking out the world with the faint, evocative scent of lavender and lemon leaves.

He kissed her hard and strong, pouring all his longing into it, telling her that he needed her.

He wanted so badly to clasp her, to thread his hands in her hair and deepen the kiss, but the silken cord held tight around his wrists, keeping him immobile.

"Alice," he moaned. "Untie me, sweetheart, I have to touch you."

"Not yet. Not until I do some exploring."

She brushed her fingers down the trail of dark hair that led into his smalls. He instantly hardened again.

She tugged his smalls over his hips, and his cock sprang free, upright and eager for action.

"I think I'll serve you as you served me," she said breathily.

Nick held his breath, praying that what she'd said meant what he thought it meant . . .

She kissed her way down his chest, over his stomach, and still she kissed, lower, over the curly hair at the root of his cock.

She stopped.

He strained against the ropes. "Untie me, you vixen."

"I don't think so." She gave him a truly wicked wink, and her pink tongue darted out and licked the side of his cock. Then she took a swift breath, opened her mouth, and lowered her lips over the entire head.

He groaned, lifting his hips. He couldn't have controlled his response if he'd wanted to. It was the most erotic sight he'd ever beheld.

His ravishing, intelligent, until-recently-innocent wife with her lush, full lips closed around his hard cock. He moved inside her mouth slowly, carefully, and she held her ground, her warm, wet mouth surrounding him.

"Yes," he groaned. "Take a little more, if you can, only if it feels good." *Take it all,* he wanted to moan, but didn't. And holding himself back made it even better.

Her mouth slid a little bit farther and her tongue flicked out, tracing the rim of his cock. Her palms were braced on the bed to either side of him, and she had the most endearing little wrinkle of concentration between her arched eyebrows.

He pushed in an inch deeper. Her eyes widened slightly but she didn't balk. Instead, she relaxed her throat and made an effort to swallow more of him.

"You have to untie me now, Alice," he groaned. "Or I'm going to come in that luscious mouth of yours."

She made a garbled sort of response, her mouth full of cock, and he jerked beneath her, needing to slide, desperate and helpless with his wrists tied and his wife teasing him to the brink of ecstasy.

He'd never felt this mindless with desire before. He was so close to losing control. He couldn't spill down her throat. She was sensible Alice.

Prim Alice. Pragmatic lover of languages.

And skillful seductress.

She was learning this language very quickly, indeed. Her lips stroked him up and down, following the gentle thrusting of his hips, while her tongue kept swirling.

"Wrap your hand," he managed to say, "around the base."

"Like this?"

Soft fingers around the base of his cock.

"Grip it. Harder."

She did, and pleasure shot fast-growing tendrils from the root of his prick to the head. He wasn't going to last long.

"Alice, I don't want to spend in your mouth . . . if you keep doing that, if you . . . Alice, *lift your head*."

She didn't lift her head. Only kept working him with her fist and her mouth and he lost all control, climaxing with a loud, guttural growl, his vision spotting around the edges while he spilled into her mouth.

She swallowed some of his seed, her eyes gone wide with surprise.

She raised her head, her throat working. "Well," she said primly, wiping her mouth with her skirts. "I had no idea there would be so very much of it. I didn't see exactly what happened last night . . . down there."

His head fell back on the pillow as his orgasm subsided and the last bursts faded from his mind. "If you had unbound me when I begged you to, I would have bodily lifted your luscious lips away. Most women aren't keen to swallow."

"I've already told you, Nick, I'm not *most women*.

You have no idea what I'm going to do next . . . and that drives you wild, doesn't it?"

She could say that again.

And she could do what she'd done again. He'd never, ever grow tired of her plump, soft lips clinging to him as she took him deep in her throat.

And, just like that, he was instantly hard as oak.

She was having trouble untying the knot she'd made. He couldn't tear his eyes away from the sight of her round breasts bouncing over his face as she struggled with the knot.

"You pulled on it too much. It won't come loose," she said.

Well, this could be embarrassing. Wouldn't March grumble if he got an eyeful of *this*. He already thought Alice meant to exert her evil, female control over the entire household.

Nick grinned. "You shouldn't bind a gentleman if you don't have the strength to untie him afterward."

Her lips pursed as she tugged and worked on the silken cords.

She let out a frustrated sigh. "I'll have to cut you free."

"There's a knife in my boot," Nick said.

She paused. "Why is there a knife in your boot?"

"Never you mind. Just fetch it and release me. My wrists are going numb, Alice."

She found the small knife secreted in the hidden holster in the top of one of his Hessians and climbed back into bed.

When the knots finally came free, he did what he'd been longing to do the entire time. He hugged her close to his chest, wrapping his arms around her, holding her so close he could feel her heart beating against him.

God, it felt good to hold her.

Before he'd married her, he'd thought that she was his very favorite kind of trouble.

He'd been wrong.

She wasn't just his favorite kind of trouble.

She was the best trouble he'd ever had.

Chapter 21

❧

Pleasures, being as necessary for the existence and well-being of the body as food, are consequently equally required.

The Kama Sutra of Vātsyāyana

Alice pressed closer against Nick's chest.

What she'd done had been so very depraved, but for some reason she didn't feel ashamed.

It must be the tender light in Nick's eyes. The way he smiled as he smoothed his hand over her hair.

The *Kama Sutra* said that pleasure was as necessary to the body as food. Now she knew what the old sage had meant.

Being held by Nick . . . holding him back . . . fed something in her. Some desire for closeness that she hadn't even known existed.

Her belly tingled with warmth and with the awareness of him. His nakedness. She was still fully clothed and he was quite thrillingly not clothed.

She traced the whorls of hair in the center of

his chest. His body was so hard and angular, the complete opposite of hers.

His abdomen was ridged with muscle, unlike her soft, concave belly. She touched him there, and his belly rippled beneath her fingers and his . . . good Lord. Was his tool stiff again?

She glanced up swiftly.

"That's right, Dimples," he growled. "I'm aroused again. And do you know something else?" He riffled her hair and kissed her cheek. "You'll like it even more today. You may even like it quite a lot."

A quick, breathless wave of longing flooded through Alice at his words. She wanted him inside her again. She was as ready as he was. She could feel wetness between her thighs and ripples of the same pleasure she'd felt yesterday.

He rose above her. "This time I want you naked as well." He undid her gown and made swift work of her stays, petticoats, shift, and stockings until she was as naked as he was.

In full, glowing daylight.

With nothing to cover her but her hair and her hands.

She shifted her hair over her breasts. He caught her hand. "Oh no. After what you just did to me, I have a right to look my fill."

She closed her eyes as he made a lazy perusal of her body.

"Gods, you're beautiful, Alice."

She peeked out from half-closed lids. He was staring at her with awe and admiration writ across his face.

"Such high, firm breasts." He covered her breasts

with his palms, bouncing them lightly, starting a luscious, aching throb between her thighs. He pinched her nipples lightly, rolling them between his fingers.

"Slim waist," he said reverently, sliding his hands down her body and encircling her waist with his large hands, "and flaring hips, exactly how I like them. Were you made just for me, Dimples?"

He dipped his head and kissed the depression in the center of her belly, and then he worked his way lower. His toyed with the curls covering her sex, and then, when she was ready to beg him for it, one finger slipped inside her.

"You're so wet," he said on an exhale.

He pushed in farther and she gasped. It hurt a little, but it was also indescribably good. His thumb found the sensitive button of flesh at her core and rubbed over her, making her tremble and moan.

Without warning, he grasped her hips and reversed their positions, pulling her atop him with her knees spread to either side of his hips.

His hardness sprang up, between her legs, slapping against her belly.

"When Lear interrupted us in the gallery, you were on top of me, and I wanted so badly for you to do . . . *this*." He held her hips, positioning her core against his cock. "Lower yourself onto me."

Could she do that? Did she dare?

"That's right," he urged. "Guide him where you want him."

Alice curled her fingers around him and guided him into her body. She wanted him there. Right there.

His fingers tightened around her hips and he eased upward, entering her slowly.

She bit her cheek. It stung. But he'd told her it would feel better and better, and she trusted him completely.

With one, smooth, swift movement, she pushed down over him, burying him inside her.

"Alice," he cried. Hearing him say her name made her feel proud and powerful.

She felt him, solid and hot, filling her, stretching her.

She closed her eyes, braced her palms on his chest, and started to move.

Slowly at first, finding what felt the best, and then faster. Harder.

He moaned dirty, wicked things as she rode him. "Pump your arse," he commanded, and she did, losing all restraint and throwing her modesty away.

Her breasts bounced and she didn't care. Her bum slapped against his thighs and she didn't feel embarrassed.

His fingers dug into the flesh of her hips. "Hold a moment. We have all day. Let's make this pleasure last."

Rearing from the bed, he flipped her over and pinned her wrists above her head, still moving inside, slow and sure, and she loved it . . . she loved every second of it.

She loved him.

The thought stopped her cold and she tensed beneath him.

"Is something wrong, Alice?" he asked, halting his movements as well.

She couldn't love him.

That was against the rules of their contract. She couldn't love him because she had to leave him. And because he could never love one woman alone and she could never share him with anyone else.

She was confusing lust with love. Thinking that because he said her name in the heat of passion that he must be having these same feelings.

"Alice," he murmured, stroking her cheek, his eyes glinting silver in the sunlight. "Talk to me. Sweetheart. Tell me what's wrong."

Get a hold of yourself, Alice. You're a Lady Rake. You're far too sophisticated to fall in love.

Reaching for his neck, she pulled him down. "Nothing's wrong, Nick. I . . . it's all so new. But it feels amazing." And it did. And when he began to move again inside her, slow and sure, pleasure built in her mind and in her belly, sharpening to a pinprick of light like the North Star in a night sky.

He reached between their bodies, and his rough finger found that sensitive place, and then light burst in her mind and sensation rocked through her body.

He lifted her off him and clasped her so tightly she couldn't breathe, his smooth length sliding against her belly in swift, hard jerks as he found his pleasure.

As her pulse slowed and the glow faded, Alice rested in his arms, her moment of emotional weakness gone.

That had been much, *much* better, she thought, still floating on a frothing wake of pleasure.

He touched her lips with his thumb, and her body's reaction was immediate, and overwhelming.

She wanted him. Again.

Would she ever stop wanting him? The thought frightened her.

"You said you've revised your opinion on young ladies," she said lightly. "But I haven't revised my opinions on rakes. Arrogant, domineering, and quite convinced you are the world's best lover."

"You don't have anyone to compare me with, Dimples. So I'm definitely the best lover you've had."

"You do seem rather . . . expert."

"I'm going to keep you in this bed until *you're* the expert."

"I'm not sure I want to stay in your bed."

"You're the one who asked for lessons."

"Yes, but they don't have to happen all at once." She needed time to steel herself against these forbidden feelings.

"You mean I can't just keep you in my bed for the next month, wearing that scarlet corset?" he asked, with a wicked grin.

"I happen to believe that if one gorges oneself immoderately on pleasures of the flesh, one never truly tastes anything. It's only a gulping, a satisfying of an immediate need."

"Is that what you believe, sensible Alice?" He touched her cheek lightly. "That your needs and desires should be denied?"

She didn't know what she believed when he gazed at her with such hooded, sensual eyes.

"No . . ." How could she convince someone like him, whose immediate needs took precedence over all else? "Think of it this way. If you stopped eating desserts for one week, the next time you tasted a cherry tart, the flavors would burst in your mouth. You would savor the flaky, buttery crust and become aware of each grain of sugar in a new way."

"We can proceed as slowly as you want, Alice. But I never eat sweets. And you're all the sugar I need." His kissed the top of her head, squeezed her shoulders, and fell back against the pillows.

She was the one developing the sweet tooth.

Kali hopped up on the bed, and Alice gathered her into the crook of her arm. "How's my baby?" she crooned. "Been out stalking lionesses?"

Kali immediately began purring loudly and snuggled deeper into Alice's arms.

Nick scratched Kali's chin, and their hands rested together atop her cat's gray-and-brown stripes.

For some reason, the sight of their hands overlapping atop Kali made Alice's heart begin to ache again.

Chapter 22

◎ ◎

A man who is versed in these arts, who is lo-
quacious and acquainted with the arts of gal-
lantry, gains very soon the hearts of women,
even though he is only acquainted with them
for a short time.

The Kama Sutra of Vātsyāyana

The following weeks passed far too quickly. Alice's days were filled with her translation work and
with caring for Jane, who was nearly recovered.
Though Alice still hadn't been successful in coax-
ing her into divulging her true identity.

Alice and Nick read aloud to the duke while he
tended his orchids. He loved accounts of sea voyages the best of all, and pestered her with questions about every detail of her upcoming journey
to India.

She explained to the duke that the ship on which
she would sail was a respectable merchant vessel
from her father's fleet. She'd known the shipmaster
since her childhood, and while he had thought it
rather odd that she wished to voyage to India in

her brother's stead, and even more strange that Alice begged him not to tell Sir Alfred of her plans, the magic of being Lady Hatherly, and Duchess of Barrington someday, had convinced him to agree to giving her safe passage.

She'd considered hiring a respectable companion, or a lady's maid, to accompany her, but had decided against it. She'd been living for weeks with no maid and found she rather liked the freedom it afforded from prying eyes and gossiping tongues.

Alice encountered plenty of those when she accompanied Mama on her social calls. All the ladies of the *ton* plied her with questions about Nick, probably desperate to know when he would be back in the market for a mistress again.

Which was a subject Alice had no interest in either thinking, or talking, about.

Alice had sent Charlene and Thea on their way to their summer homes, with assurances that all was well and going according to Alice's plan.

And she enjoyed long, laughter-filled visits with Aunt Sarah, who no longer seemed quite so scandalous, now that Alice understood precisely what happened behind bedchamber doors.

By day she was a dutiful daughter, a devoted daughter-in-law, and a loyal friend.

By night, she cast all propriety aside and lived for pleasure.

Nick's bedchamber was a dream world that had nothing to do with the daylight.

They were swiftly moving through the sixty-four varieties of pleasure.

She'd married him for the freedom to achieve

her dreams and she'd also married him for this: unbridled sensual enjoyment.

She'd dreamt of this, alone in her room at night, before she met Nick, as she translated the *Kama Sutra*.

She hadn't dreamt of a mannerly professorial type.

She'd conjured a strong, confident lover who knew exactly how to stoke her fire until passion burned hot and uncontrollable.

While her body learned his heated language, she attempted to keep her heart cold.

Attempted . . . and failed.

She'd lost all control of the game.

Didn't know who was winning or losing.

All she knew was that she loved his arms around her, loved how tender he was with his father, and with her, and her heart had cracked wide open.

*N*ick thought, idly, that he should probably be spending less time with his brilliant, beautiful wife, and more time easing back into his former life of wild and wicked pursuits.

He should be drinking at his club with the usual crowd. Planning his next hedonistic entertainment.

Stalking the evil man behind Stubbs's betrayal.

He should be doing any number of depraved, unwholesome things.

But instead here he was, in the library with his wife, his head in her lap while she read a novel.

He told himself the reason was that she was leaving soon and he had to soak as much Alice in as possible.

That's what he told himself.

The truth was that the lust for revenge had died.

And the club was full of flatterers and fools, posturing and making pointless wagers about trivial matters.

And the truth was that the only entertainment he needed was right here.

He had a beautiful view of luxurious curves and sweet dimples as Alice smiled over a passage in her novel.

His body felt mellow and peaceful. He was warm and cozy and domesticated. He could allow himself to drift in this feeling because they were still following the plan.

She was leaving.

Nick had the rest of his godforsaken life to return to empty pleasures. Right now, he was going to fill his well so full of Alice that it would brim with the memory of her bright smile until the darkness swallowed him and the madness took hold.

Raising his head, he kissed the soft skin above her bodice and slipped beneath the fabric, searching for her nipples, the two reasons he had a tongue.

What else was it good for? Not talking. Not convincing her to stay.

His tongue was good at making Alice pause while she was reading.

He licked her nipple with long, lavish strokes.

He continued exploring and she continued reading, but her chest rose and fell rapidly and the blush he loved, the soft tinge of pink like the flush one found sometimes along the petals of cream-colored orchids, spread over her chest.

The book fell to the floor with a thud.

"Nick," she sighed, leaning against the cushions, arching her back and thrusting her nipple into his mouth.

He could do this for the rest of his life. Pleasure his wife. Make her sigh with contentment.

The noises intruded on his brain slowly. *No*, his mind said, *ignore them. Keep licking.*

"Nick, stop," Alice said. "There's someone coming."

A loud knock on the door.

Damn it. Nick rearranged his trousers and helped Alice restore her bodice to order.

They'd been doing a lot of those last-second adjustments lately because he couldn't keep his hands off her.

"Enter," Nick growled with a very bad grace because there were other types of entering he wished he could be doing at the moment.

It was Patrick.

"Hello there," he said cheerfully, bowing to Alice. His gaze darted between them, taking in Alice's pink cheeks and mussed hair and Nick's grimace. "I hope I'm not interrupting anything."

"Patrick," Alice said, walking toward him and holding out her arms. "You're not interrupting anything. Please, do come in."

Not interrupting anything? Nick begged to differ.

Patrick's green eyes danced with laughter as he

noticed Nick's sour expression. He bowed over the hand Alice proffered. "Lady Hatherly."

"Oh." She squeezed his hand. "You must call me Alice, as before."

"Apologies for my lateness," Patrick said. "The Dowager suddenly decided she wanted to go to Brighton to bathe in the sea water, and my son Van plagued me so that I gave in and we journeyed as a group."

"How was Brighton?" Nick asked.

"Van loved the seashore, and wanted to run free, but the Dowager watched him like a hawk every second of the day. She loves him so very fiercely."

"He's such a bright lad," Alice said.

"And mischievous. Always getting into some trouble, my Van," said Patrick proudly.

Alice smiled. "You must mean you are late in congratulating us on our marriage?"

Patrick lifted a sheaf of papers from the satchel he carried. "I'm late in delivering the contract you requested."

Nick's heart fell. He'd forgotten all about the bloody marital contract.

Chapter 23

A wager may be laid as to which will get hold of the lips of the other first. If the woman loses, she should pretend to cry . . . and dispute with him saying, "Let another wager be laid."

The Kama Sutra of Vātsyāyana

"The contract?" Alice echoed, her mind drawing a blank.

With a sickening lurch deep in her belly, she remembered the marital terms she'd asked Nick to have prepared. Patrick must have drawn them up for him.

She'd completely forgotten the existence of the contract.

How had she forgotten something so important? Had she changed so much in the span of a few weeks?

"The terms you asked for," Patrick replied. He turned to Nick. "You told me she stipulated very specific terms."

"Oh, she did," he drawled. "Very clear terms."

Alice avoided Nick's eyes. "Of course I did. I'm sorry, I was only confused for a moment. I didn't know that Nick had asked you to be his man of business in this matter."

"Oh, Thea sent you this." Patrick drew a jar from his satchel. "Some of her aunt's famous marmalade."

He handed Alice the jar and she held it to the window, watching sunlight tease the amber and orange into a rich glow. "March will be delighted," she said dully.

Patrick gave her a perplexed look.

"Mr. March. Our footman."

"I see," said Patrick.

"Care for a drink?" Nick asked Patrick.

"Don't mind if I have a small one," Patrick replied.

While Nick was at the sideboard pouring something golden into a glass, Patrick moved closer to Alice.

"Are you sure this is the right thing for you, Alice?" he asked in a low voice. "You don't have to sign the document, you know. Even if you asked for it. You've a right to change your mind."

Had she changed her mind?

Everything was still the same, wasn't it? She was still planning to leave. Her trunks were already packed. The ship sailed in six days.

"Nothing has changed," Alice said.

"This contract details a business arrangement, but the scene when I arrived didn't look like business to me."

"The contract is still required."

Intellectually, Alice knew that Nick could never be true to one woman, even if she wished the complete opposite were true.

Signing this agreement was the prudent, sensible course.

And Alice had been prudent and sensible her entire life.

Patrick's eyes searched her face. "You're signing away your right to bear him children. I thought that part was rather strange, and not something to be decided lightly."

She didn't have a chance to reply because Nick approached, handing the glass to Patrick.

"While you were away we had another delivery," Nick said to Patrick. "One that will require a new name."

He must be speaking of Jane, Alice thought.

Patrick nodded. "You can give me the details later. In the meantime, I will witness the signing of the contract. Unless . . . perhaps you don't wish to sign it anymore?"

Nick stared at her expectantly, waiting for her to say something. He lifted his hand, dropped it back to his side. "Alice?" he said softly.

Both men were waiting for her to speak, and Alice was never at a loss for words, so she squared her shoulders, found the fortitude to curve her lips into a smile, and grabbed the roll of parchment from Patrick's hand.

"Of course we want to sign the contract." She laughed carelessly. "Right, my lord husband? Nothing has changed. How could it in the space of only a few weeks?"

She untied the ribbon and spread the pages out over the desk.

> *I, Lord Hatherly, do solemnly pledge to allow my wife, Lady Hatherly, to travel. I will never seek to keep her in England for any reason, and I do hereby swear never to make demands upon her except that she be circumspect in her manner of living and she never seek to bear an heir by . . .*

The words on the page swam in front of Alice's eyes, marching in a line of stark, black letters spelling out precisely what she'd requested.

Shouldn't her heart be lifting? Here it was, her writ of freedom and her license to leave.

"Everything appears to be in order. Lord Hatherly?"

Somehow she couldn't call him Nick right now. Maybe never again. She had to stop allowing him beneath her skin and into her heart.

She must follow the plan, because it was the only part of her life that made sense right now.

Emotion swirled in the depths of his silvery eyes when he finally met her gaze. Regret. Remorse. Could there be . . . yearning?

Let's tear this up, she thought with a strong surge of emotion. *We don't need this. Let's start fresh. Forge a new contract. One where we promise to love one another until death do us part . . . and we truly mean the words.*

Her mind was playing tricks on her, and her heart as well.

Telling her she cared for Nick.

Confusing physical intimacy for love.

Lovemaking wasn't a language to learn. She couldn't master it with hard work and memorization. Her heart had been too unpredictable.

There were no rules to follow in this game.

And she'd already lost.

Nick watched Alice sign her flourishing signature to the contract, and his heart didn't do any of the things he'd expected it to when she'd demanded the document that day at Dalton's house.

Shouldn't he be gleefully contemplating a return to his bachelor freedoms?

No one waiting to question him if he came home late.

No one who cared.

Perfumed courtesans with no expectations. Empty pleasures that never satiated him in any lasting way.

Not like sweet, satisfying Alice with her naughty questions and bawdy sense of humor.

Caring, intuitive Alice.

Visiting the duke in his orchid conservatory.

Gifting her body to Nick with such abandon it left him breathless.

I don't want to sign the contract.

I don't want her to leave.

A selfish, dangerous thought to have.

You can't keep her here for your pleasure, when she has a wide world to explore.

For his pleasure . . . or for his heart?

She finished signing and glanced at him from under dark lashes, the brilliant turquoise of her eyes dulled to stone.

She signed the contract. Didn't even ask to speak to him in private first.

Just walked to the desk and dipped her pen in ink and signed the damned thing.

She still wanted her freedom and she must have her adventures. He wanted her to be happy. Her dreams could never be fulfilled in England.

He gripped the pen and forced his hand to make the necessary motions.

This was how it ended.

This was how it was always going to end.

His name there, next to hers. Their signatures would stay close when their bodies were oceans apart.

"Well, that's done, then." He couldn't muster his usual bravado.

Patrick gave him a pitying look, as if he knew exactly what conflicted thoughts were roiling through Nick's mind.

"You'll have to tell me more about your plans for India, Alice," Patrick said. "Van is enamored of all things adventurous. He'll want to know everything. Will you visit the Taj—?"

The door to the library suddenly burst open, crashing against the wall.

"Look who I found lurking outside! I knew there were lurkers about." March stalked into the room pushing a large man in front of him. "All my vigilance has been rewarded."

"Stubbs?" Nick exclaimed.

Stubbs stood, head bowed, shoulders hunched. "I'm ready to talk," he whispered.

Chapter 24

❦

The good perform those actions in which
there is no fear as to what is to result from
them in the next world, and in which there is
no danger to their welfare.

The Kama Sutra of Vātsyāyana

Nick knew immediately what Stubbs meant. He
was ready to divulge who had blackmailed him
into leading the duke to the gambling hells.

His former servant looked even worse than the
last time Nick had seen him in Lear's hired carriage.

Bulbous purple nose, red-veined cheeks, and
sad, bloodshot eyes.

"Come in, Mr. Stubbs," Nick said.

"You're just going to invite the sorry blighter in
like he came for a nice cup of tea? He betrayed us!"
March glared at Stubbs. "Why did you do it? Who
hired you?"

Stubbs hung his head. "I'm truly sorry for the
pain I caused."

"As you should be," Patrick said coldly. "I'm glad

to see you've decided to make amends. I have made a full accounting of every wager, every penny you forced the duke to lose. You left a messy trail to follow."

Stubbs hung his head even further. "I know. I wanted you to find it."

"So you thought you'd apologize and have your old job back, is that it?" March asked. "Tell him, Your Lordship, tell him he's going to prison for what he's done."

"Nick," Alice said.

He was glad to hear her call him by his name again. He inclined his head.

"Mr. Stubbs has something to tell you," she said. "Isn't that right, Mr. Stubbs?"

"Make 'im pay, make 'im pay," March shouted, hopping around, his fists in the air.

"We thank you for your vigilance, Mr. March," Alice said with a stern frown, "but you may return to your post now."

"Humph," grunted March, but he walked back to the entrance and stood to one side, as a footman should.

"We'll have a nice civilized conversation," said Alice. "Now sit down everyone. Please. You as well, Mr. Stubbs."

He sat gingerly on the edge of one of the velvet library chairs.

His neck cloth was gray and his cuffs frayed. His boots so scuffed and worn they were barely clinging to his feet.

"Why did you do it?" Alice asked in a gentle tone. "Weren't you happy here?"

"Very happy, milady. Some of the happiest days of my life."

"My husband trusted you. He thought you cared about your charge, and took your work seriously."

"I had to do it, see?" Stubbs twisted his hands into a knot. "He has her. Coleman has her, and he told me if I didn't follow his orders, she would meet with an accident. Accidents happen often at the Yellow House, they do."

He spoke in a rush, his face crumpled with anguish.

"The Yellow House?" Alice asked.

"It was Mr. Coleman who arranged for me to come here. I'm not proud of what I did but I had no choice." His gaze veered to Nick. "You always were too kindhearted, Your Lordship. I thought you'd be a nob living in opulence and caring for your servants less than you cared for a new pair of boots. I was wrong. You made it difficult for me."

"Why don't you begin from the beginning, Mr. Stubbs," Alice said. "I've always found that's a useful place to start. And then you'll have a nice hot cup of tea. You look as though you could use one."

At her kind tone, Stubbs's face crumpled, and Nick was afraid the man might begin blubbering, as he'd done in the carriage.

"Coleman has my Annie in that cursed place," said Stubbs. "Her uncle committed her to gain control of the property she was to inherit from her late father. My good, kind Annie who is no more mad than you, milady." He lowered his head to his fists. "Trapped in that pitiless place."

"So Mr. Coleman is the one who hired you?" asked Patrick.

"Didn't have to pay me," Stubbs said. "Just promised me he'd let Annie go free if I cooperated. He doesn't know everything about what you're doing, Your Lordship, but he has suspicions."

Nick's stomach lurched. Coleman knew? "So you were sent to spy on me."

"I was under instructions to interfere in any way possible. I was to steal, turn your other servants against you, force the duke to gamble away money, I was supposed to discredit you. I—I'm sorry."

He raised his head, and his brown eyes were so bleak and hopeless it made Nick angry enough to leap from his chair and ride straight to the Yellow House and send Coleman to hell.

Stubbs hung his head. "I didn't know the duke would gamble you away, honest I didn't."

"How could you have known?" Patrick said. "It sounds to me that you were only a pawn and cannot be held responsible for anything you did under coercion."

"You mean you won't have me arrested?" Stubbs asked.

"Of course not," Alice exclaimed. "You are quite safe here, Mr. Stubbs. And you are welcome to stay as long as you need." She took his huge fists in her small ones. "My husband and his friends will rescue your Annie. And you'll have your happy ending."

The belief in his ability to dispense happy endings stirred something in Nick's heart, but he didn't have time to examine his feelings. "We'll see what we can do."

"You have to hurry," Stubbs said. "That's why I'm here. Coleman promised he'd set her free, but he laughed in my face. Said I was a drunkard and I'd die before I had a chance to marry Annie. I've only been drinking because I was so hopeless. And Annie will be feeling the same. You must hurry. Please. If Coleman finds out I've spoken with you he'll harm Annie."

Alice put an arm around Stubbs's shoulder. "We'll save her." She turned to Nick, her eyes filled with such an unwavering belief that he drew himself up like a soldier before a commanding officer, attempting to appear worthy of the mettle that shone in her gaze.

"I'll send for Lear," he said.

"And Dr. Forster," Alice whispered. "I know Mr. Stubbs has been overindulging in spirits, but there's a deathly pallor to his skin that I don't like."

Nick nodded. "I'll send for the doctor as well."

Alice stood. "March, show Mr. Stubbs to a guest chamber."

"I will not!" said March indignantly.

"I'll sleep in the stables, milady," Stubbs said, rising and shuffling his feet awkwardly. "'Twill be a sight more comfortable than the places I've been resting my head."

"You'll have a chamber," Alice said, staring March down.

"Would you like to see the duke?" Alice asked

Stubbs. "He asks about you sometimes. He remembers you fondly."

Stubbs squashed his hat in his hands. "I couldn't speak with him, milady, not after what I did."

"Come," Alice said, holding out her hand. "I'll show you to his chambers. No protests now."

She placed a hand on his arm, and what choice did the man have? When Alice set her mind to something, there was nothing to do but follow.

When they were gone, Nick turned to Patrick. "It seems we may have another delivery soon."

Patrick nodded tersely. "There's no time to send word to Hawkins to help us free Annie. Stubbs thought she was in immediate danger."

"We must move swiftly."

Chapter 25

The following are the arts to be studied,
together with the *Kama Sutra*: solution of
riddles, enigmas, covert speeches, verbal puz-
zles, and enigmatical questions.

The Kama Sutra of Vātsyāyana

The war council had begun hours ago, and Alice
was heartily sick of listening to the four large, imposing men argue.

They sat in the library, drinking spirits and going
around and around and never deciding anything.
She was in a room with what surely must be four of
the most handsome men the Lord had created, and
they were all as stubborn and shortsighted as they
were pleasing to look upon.

Nick and Lear were advocating for the use of
force, Patrick and Dr. Forster erring on the side of
caution . . . and legality.

Alice was glad they were consulting Dr. Forster
as well. He'd pronounced Mr. Stubbs to be fine,
if malnourished, and prescribed some hot beef

tea. Alice hoped the doctor would be a voice of reason.

"We lure Coleman out and we torture him until he agrees to release Annie, submit to monthly inspections, and improve living conditions," Lear said, slamming a fist down on the table.

"That's what we do. No question." Nick's eyes were lethal and focused. The carefree rake was completely gone. "Wish Dalton were here. He's a good man to have on your side in a battle."

"We can't just beat him into submission," Patrick said.

"Why not?" Nick asked.

"Well, for one, it's not legal."

"Spoken like a lawyer," said Lear. When he shook his head, his long, dark hair fell around his collar.

"I have a patient inside the Yellow House," said Dr. Forster. "Physicians are allowed to enter if a patient requests a visit. Otherwise the patients there never receive any kind of medical attention. I can say I'm coming at his summons, and they'll have to let me in."

"Perfect," Nick said enthusiastically. "You and Patrick will rescue Annie and while you're inside, Lear and I will force Coleman outside and deal with him in our way."

"Nick," Alice scolded. "You can't solve all your problems physically."

Nick's gaze smoldered. "Oh, can't I?"

She knew how persuasive he was with his body.

"And then there's the matter of Jane," Alice continued, ignoring the momentary flicker of heat in her belly. "If Coleman finds out she's here, he may have already told her husband where to find her. She has to leave now."

"I hadn't thought of that," Patrick said. "I'd best gather her new identity swiftly."

"She leaves tomorrow morning," Lear agreed. "I'll see to it."

"But where will she go?" Alice asked, looking from one glowering face to the next.

They all started talking at once then, espousing their theories for where Jane should be sent.

It made Alice upset to see them deciding Jane's fate without once thinking to ask Jane what she wanted.

She left them arguing and slipped from the room.

She hadn't gone far down the hall when she ran into Jane. She was wearing one of Alice's cloaks and had a small valise in her hand.

"Where are you going?" Alice asked with consternation.

"I'm bringing too much danger to this house. I have to leave."

"Were you listening?"

Jane nodded. "I heard the shouting and knew it must have something to do with me. If Mr. Coleman suspects Lord Hatherly is involved in some way with my disappearance none of you are safe. I must leave immediately."

"But where will you go? What will you do?"

"I'll think of something."

"The men are attempting to come to a decision about your future right now. You must go in and tell them what *you* want."

Jane raised her head and her violet eyes shimmered with tears. "I'm too much of a problem. If they knew who my husband was . . . Alice, he's a ruthless, cruel man and not one to be trifled with. Even Lord Hatherly . . . even he might think twice."

"Please, Jane. You must go talk to them. If I've been any kind of friend to you, do this for me."

Jane held still for a moment and then she inclined her head. "I will listen to their proposals. But I leave tonight. Not tomorrow. Tonight."

Alice pushed the door open, and the two women walked into the center of the group of argumentative men.

They fell silent as Jane entered.

The hood of her cloak slipped back, exposing huge violet eyes and cropped black hair that had at least grown in enough to cover the bald patches.

"While you lot have been shouting and arguing, Jane decided to take matters into her own hands," Alice said. "I found her attempting to slip out the door. Now what do you have to say for yourselves?"

The four men all had the grace to look extremely sheepish. "We apologize, Miss Jane," Lear said. "Please don't leave. We want to help."

Jane stood in their midst and bravely lifted her chin. "I can't stay in London. If Coleman suspects your involvement, my presence puts you in grave danger. I have to leave."

Admiration shone in Patrick's eyes. "But without new papers you will be a fugitive."

"They think I'm drowned, do they not?" Jane asked.

Lear nodded. "Yes. But we don't know if they believe that for sure."

"What's clear is that my presence puts everyone in danger. I must leave tonight. So, gentlemen." She stared at each in turn. "Where should I go? I will consider your counsel carefully."

Alice was startled by her calm, commanding air. Where had this Jane been? The cowering girl who had arrived, so damaged and frightened, was gone and in her place stood a lady as composed and regal as a queen.

"I think you should go to the Duke and Duchess of Harland's cocoa manufactory in Surrey," Nick said. "They have a charitable concern that helps women in crisis."

Jane tilted her head. "I've heard of it."

Alice had a sudden idea. "Or maybe she could come with me to India! As my companion. We could hide her near the docks for the remaining days until the ship sets sail."

Jane turned to Lear. "Do you have a proposal?" Alice imagined that Jane's gaze softened slightly when she looked at Captain Lear.

"I think you should go to my friend the Duke of Bayne in Scotland. He's in need of a governess for his two young children. They're rather troublesome. It's a godforsaken bog of a place, but no one would think to look for you there."

"Will he want a governess with a shorn head?" Jane asked.

"Bayne won't care about any of that. He can't

pay governesses enough to make them stay at his moldy old estate. It's the perfect hiding place."

"How do you know this fellow?" Nick asked.

Lear shrugged. "Supply him with goods same as you."

"What's his story?" Nick asked.

"Scottish lord who unexpectedly inherited a dukedom and a tattered old castle."

"Duke of Bayne. Can't say I've heard of him."

"Wife died in childbirth. Has two children to raise and he refuses to move away from his god-forsaken, backwater village."

Alice caught Captain Lear's eye. "Will Jane be safe with him?"

"I'd trust him with my sister."

"Have you got a sister?" asked Nick with a startled expression.

"I've got five."

Alice smiled. Obviously Nick didn't know his friend as well as he thought he did.

"Does anyone else have an opinion about where I should go?" When no one else spoke, Jane stared into the fire for a moment.

When she turned back to face the group, Alice could see she'd made a decision by the fierce light in her eyes.

"While I know of the Duchess of Harland's charity work and admire her for it," Jane said, "if someone discovers that you harbored me, Lord Hatherly, they may think to find me there."

"That's out then," Nick said.

"And Alice," Jane continued, "while you've been kindness itself, and the idea of a long voyage to

India with you is delightful, I don't want to wait even one more day. I need to leave London tonight. Which leaves the Duke of Bayne."

Lear nodded tersely. "You'll be in a private coach this evening, Miss Jane."

Alice caught Jane's hands in hers. "Are you sure? It may be lonely in a moldering old castle in Scotland."

"The wilds of Scotland and a surly duke and his ill-behaved children will suit me perfectly. I'm a ghost, am I not? I don't exist. I'm no one except the person I will become. That person wants to do some good, and if I may use my education to help the Duke's children, I will. And my husband won't think to search for me in Scotland."

"It's decided then. I shall miss you, Jane," Alice said.

"And I you," Jane replied. "There's another thing, gentlemen. I know the women's wing at the Yellow House intimately." She shuddered but forced herself to continue speaking. "I know where they are keeping Annie. I'll draw you a diagram so that you may remove her more swiftly. I only wish . . ." Her eyes brimmed with tears. "I only wish you could save them all."

Alice placed an arm around her shoulders and led her from the room. "Come, we'll make sure you have everything you need in that valise of yours. It's very small. I think you might require more clothing in your new post."

When Alice returned, the men were talking over the options for their mission tomorrow, and Nick and Lear still seemed to be advocating for the use of violence to persuade Coleman to reform his ways.

Alice walked into the middle of the circle, to the spot Jane had vacated, and held up her hand. "Gentlemen, I believe I have a plan."

They stopped talking and stared at her.

"Why am I not surprised?" Nick asked. "Let's hear it, Dimples."

Patrick smiled at his use of her pet name. "Dimples?"

Alice wasn't going to let anyone distract her. She'd had an idea while she helped Jane pack a trunk with sensible governess dresses, since they were much of a size.

Jane had said again how she wished the men could rescue all of the inmates suffering from abuse at the hands of Coleman and his sadistic keepers.

And the answer had struck Alice. It was so simple, really.

"Nick, your friend the Duke of Harland is a respected member of Parliament. He could request a select committee be convened to investigate the deplorable conditions in private madhouses, could he not?"

"I see," Nick said. "Very clever, my dear. We use the threat of such a report to bend Coleman to our will. Augment that threat with a few well-thrown jabs, am I right?" he asked Lear.

"Hear hear," said Lear, and the two reprobates clinked glasses. "I'm thinking smash his nose and break his kneecaps."

"Why make it only a threat?" Alice asked.

"Nick, don't you see? You should inspect the Yellow House and you *should* write a report for Parliament. Then Harland can present it as evidence when he convenes the select committee. It's a way to not only seek your revenge and rescue Annie, but help hundreds of other patients in similar asylums as well."

Patrick cocked his head. "Of course, Alice. Why didn't we think of it before?"

Dr. Forster nodded emphatically. "There's no incentive for Coleman to treat his patients well. He is paid by how many he keeps. A Parliamentary investigation would expose his cruelty and cause a public outcry. I will be happy to sign your report, Lord Hatherly."

Alice clapped her hands. "It's all settled then. Tomorrow, we all visit the Yellow House. The more witnesses, the better."

Nick shook his head. Why was he shaking his head? He had a stubborn look on his face as well.

"I won't visit the Yellow House. That's not my method."

"Maybe it won't be as satisfying as beating him until he begs for mercy," Alice said, "but it will have much larger and more lasting consequences. You will wield far more power working within the confines of the law."

"The man needs to be completely shut down," Dr. Forster agreed. "This evil can't be allowed to continue unpunished and unabated."

"I won't go inside the asylum," said Nick, his voice icy. "I can't. Don't ask me why. I just can't."

Why was he being so obstinate? If he visited the

asylum in Bethnal Green, and wrote the report, he could help far more people than he did now. He could save hundreds of women like Jane.

She had to make him see that this would be even more effective than helping people one by one, under cover of darkness.

Bring the larger problem into the light. Illuminate its ugliness for all the world to see and abhor.

"Gentlemen," Alice said. "Allow me to speak with my husband in private."

Chapter 26

❦

If she tries to prevent him doing this he should
say to her, "What harm is there in doing it?"
and should persuade her to let him do it.

The Kama Sutra of Vātsyāyana

"𝓘t's no use, Alice. You won't convince me." Nick
didn't want her to think him a coward, but visiting
the Yellow House was out of the question.

"I seem to recall saying those exact same words
to you. And here I am. Married to your obstinate
self."

They were in his bedchamber. Alice had held
out her hand and he'd followed.

They sat upon the bed but their bodies weren't
touching.

Nick heaved a sigh. "I won't do it, Alice."

The panic clawed at his chest. Darkness rolling
in at the edges of his eyes. "I won't enter that place.
I can't. Don't ask me why."

"Why?"

He should have learned these things by now:
Alice never followed instructions. And he would

never stop wanting to please her. But he couldn't. Not this time. "Let me do things my own way."

"With your fists?"

"If necessary. They've served me well in disputes before."

"Giving Coleman a thrashing won't convince him to change his ways. You need to utilize a more civilized method of persuasion."

"This is how men solve problems, Alice. And I plan to make sure that he knows if he doesn't improve conditions at the asylum there will be worse in store for him."

"But could you give my method a try first? If it doesn't work then you have my blessing to beat that horrible man until he's bloodied beyond recognition."

"So bloodthirsty, Dimples." Nick caught her hand and stroked his finger across her palm. "I'd like to give your method a try but it's not me. It's not the way I do things."

He wanted to tell her the truth: he was frightened that if he entered the private asylum, if the maw of madness swallowed him, he might never re-emerge.

The fear that ate his soul away.

The fear that made him live for pleasure, live each moment as if it were his last, as if he had no future.

But he couldn't admit any of that to her. She thought he was strong. He didn't want to disillusion her.

"Why won't you go?" she persisted.

"I don't play by society's rules. I thrive in darkness. I'm not the kind to blare my trumpet for bloated, corrupt politicians. They wouldn't listen to me, anyway. If you hadn't noticed, you married a notorious rogue."

"Oh, I noticed, Nick," Alice said, raking her gaze across his powerful frame. "But that's precisely why they'll listen to you. You come from a notorious line of madmen. But Dr. Forster believes your kind, permissive treatment of the duke could effect a cure for his lunacy. Your report can detail the contrast between your methods and the madhouse's corruption."

"My father's case is very mild."

"Yet you've been with him the whole time. You've borne witness to the ebbs and flows of his illness. You were on the ship with the duke when the mania claimed him."

"How do you know that?"

"Your father told me. You must have been young then. Weren't you in school?"

"I was at Cambridge with Dalton and Harland. I didn't know my father was going mad when he arrived in the dead of night and forced me to pack a bag. He would brook no protests. Didn't even have a chance to say good-bye to my friends."

One moment he'd been hard at work on his studies and the next day he was traveling across the ocean with his father on an insane hunt for a nonexistent orchid.

Wind on his face on the deck; salt spray in his eyes and salted cod for dinner.

Hold of a ship. Smell of candle wax and sweat. Father gripping his arm. Hadn't washed in days. Eyes blazing with the mania.

I'll never go mad, Nicolas. Because of this. Waving the dried stump of an orchid.

The sadness of the memory never waned. Evergreen and fresh each time.

Nick had been so helpless. He'd been unable to keep the madness at bay and had been forced to watch as day by day his brilliant father descended into the depths of his obsession.

There had been periods of relative calm since then, but his keen-eyed father had never returned.

In his place there was this affable, sometimes bumbling, courtly old man who believed orchids whispered secrets to him.

"Nick?" Alice asked softly.

He raised his eyes. The tenderness in her gaze nearly undid him.

"That must have been so difficult for you, to watch him go mad on board a ship."

"After that miserable voyage I swore I'd never set foot on a ship again." He shuddered. "That was the coldest, darkest, most miserable time of my life, and it's best forgotten."

She rested her head on his shoulder. "Nick, this mission tomorrow, it's a way for you to restore power over those painful memories. If you help improve conditions for lunatics, and you open an inquiry into better treatment methods and wider access to physicians, you're helping all the sons and daughters, mothers and fathers, who witness the torment of their loved ones and feel helpless."

She was right, of course.

He was tired of keeping the walls up between them. He might as well admit to himself that he wanted more than her body.

He wanted that tender light in her eyes. He wanted her to know that he was better than the wastrel she'd thought him.

She believed in him, and when he looked into her eyes, he began to believe in himself as well. He could do this. Visit the Yellow House. Face his demons. Send them yelping into the night. He could do this for her.

"I'll go," he said.

"You will?"

"I will. I'll help write the report. I'll try things your way."

She hugged him and the clean scent of lavender washed over his senses.

"You'll see, Nick, this is the right way. This is the only way to make a lasting change."

"It's not a good idea for many reasons, but I'll go. For you."

"It's not a good idea, it's a brilliant one."

"You're insufferably arrogant, you know that, Lady Hatherly?"

She caught his face in both her hands. "And you love it."

He did love her confidence.

She was this wholly strong and independent woman who stood in the center of a group of powerful men and informed them that *her* way was best.

He wanted to believe that he was strong enough

to face his fears. He wanted to make her proud of him.

She kissed him hungrily, drawing him into her arms. He bunched the fabric of her skirts in one hand, desire pounding through his skull. He unbuttoned his breeches.

When he buried himself inside her, swift and deep, she rose to meet him, wrapping her legs around his hips, urging him on with her hands grasping his buttocks.

He loved her.

His mind pushed the thought away. It was easy enough to think you loved a woman when you were buried deep inside her.

That's not it, and you know it.

Don't think that thought. Pin her wrists with your hands. Take control.

And ride to sweet oblivion.

He held back until she reached orgasm, her inner muscles gripping his cock.

Then he shouted her name as he found his own release, spilling into the covers instead of inside her, where he wanted to stay forever.

With Alice in his arms, he was fearless and invincible.

She'd asked him what he would do with his life if he knew he had ten years, or even twenty. He'd never considered that question because he'd been telling himself for so long that he'd go insane, so nothing mattered.

He was a man with no future.

If he had a future, if the madness spared him, what did he want from life?

Alice.

The answer was there, reverberating through his being.

He wanted Alice. Not just for physical gratification. Not just in his bed.

He wanted her light and her laughter all for himself.

She made him want to have a future.

Chapter 27

⟨◎⟩⟨◎⟩

A horse having once attained the fifth degree
of motion goes on with blind speed, regardless of pits, ditches, and posts in his way.

The Kama Sutra of Vātsyāyana

Nick's heart sped as he stared up at the ivy-
covered façade of the Yellow House. Dressed in so
much green, you couldn't tell the old girl was dripping with the pox and rotten as they came.

"How are you doing?" Alice whispered.

Nick nodded in a way he hoped was reassuring,
not trusting his voice.

The yard was large and well maintained. A
group of patients huddled against the wall with an
attendant watching over them.

They were all clothed but their faces were vacant
and slack-jawed.

It was indescribably sad, and Nick's chest con-
stricted.

Patrick and Dr. Forster had gone ahead to find
Annie and bring her to safety while Coleman was
occupied with Nick and Lear.

Nick strode through the door with Alice on one side and Lear on the other.

If her way didn't work, Nick and Lear would be ready to use their fists.

A keeper stared at them, but he had his hands full with an unruly patient.

There was a smell in the baseboards that no scrubbing would remove. The smell of desperation and fear and lives curtailed.

He'd expected there to be shouting, but the eerie silence was worse. Black lines danced at the edges of his vision, but Alice slipped her hand into his, and that gave him the courage to go deeper into the cursed building.

Coleman met them as they crossed from the hallway into one of the dining halls.

"You can't just come here as you please, Lord Hatherly," he said loudly. "You've no invitation and I've been given no advance notice of your visit."

"I have an invitation." Nick thrust a paper at Coleman, hoping he didn't examine it too closely. Patrick's forgery had been hastily done. "A writ to visit this institution on behalf of the Duke of Harland, who plans to present the report of my observations to Parliament at the next session."

"I've heard nothing of this."

"Why don't you want us to come in?" Alice asked in an imperious, duchesslike tone. "What are you hiding, sir?"

"Is this your wife, Lord Hatherly? You bring a lady into these walls? There are things here that are unsuitable for a lady's eyes. Nakedness. Depravity."

"She's not any lady. She's Alice," Nick said. Was that the right thing to say? He felt confused. His breathing labored. His thoughts muddled.

"And we're not just any visitors. We're the ones that will make your life a living hell if you refuse to let us enter," Lear said.

Coleman took one look at Lear, with his narrowed, dark eyes and clenched fists, and decided to comply.

"There's no problem here, gentlemen." Coleman held up his hands. "There's a visiting physician here right now, in fact. A Dr. Forster. I freely allow legitimate visitations. I have nothing to hide. Follow me, please."

The abrupt about-face didn't fool Nick. He knew the second their backs were turned, Coleman would send a message to his keepers to sweep the worst offenses under the rug before they arrived.

Alice threaded her arm through his elbow, and it wasn't so that he could support her.

She wanted to show him that he could count on her.

He wasn't sure it would be enough. His mind was muzzy with panic. He knew the hideous secrets these walls his from the world.

Ringing sensation in his ears.

Breath coming in puffs. Heart racing. Numbness in his fingers.

They followed Coleman into a large dining hall.

"Hello there." A plump, matronly woman with white hair that matched her starched white apron greeted them.

"This is my wife, Mrs. Coleman," Mr. Coleman said.

"More visitors, dear?" Mrs. Coleman asked. "Shall I fetch some tea?"

"We don't want any tea," Lear growled.

"I'm afraid many of the rooms are locked," Coleman said smoothly. "I need to go and fetch the keys for your tour."

Nick saw the deceit dripping from his smile, like blood welling from a fresh wound.

"Have some tea," Alice whispered to Nick. "It will do you good; you look very pale."

Mr. and Mrs. Coleman left and Nick, Alice, and Lear inspected the empty dining area. It seemed ordinary enough. Long wooden tables and benches. A sideboard with water pitchers and baskets of bread.

Nick didn't like the idea of drinking tea at the Yellow House as if they were on a social outing in a parlor in Mayfair, but he'd promised Alice to try things her way first, before he started flinging his fists around.

Nick hadn't come here to be led like a lamb through the carefully choreographed presentation that Coleman had no doubt assembled to fool visitors into thinking his operation was above-board.

The truth had already been told to Nick over and over by the inmates he spoke with after they made their escape. This was a house of death and suffering.

He sat on a bench beside Alice, trying to remain calm and not succeeding very well.

Mrs. Coleman returned with a tray of teacups and biscuits.

Nick finished his tea in one swallow and set the teacup down so hard the handle cracked.

Everyone stared at him.

"Now," he said through tightly clenched teeth, rising from the table. "We wait no longer. Fetch your husband," he said to Mrs. Coleman. "The tour begins now."

Something was very wrong.

Nick's mouth was strained around the edges, his shoulders hunched in on themselves like broken wings.

Even the way he walked was all wrong—no confident striding, no nonchalant, careless stroll.

His steps were tentative and faltered ever so slightly, probably unnoticeable to the rest of the company, but to Alice it was beyond troubling.

Coleman led them into a long, narrow room with rows of high-walled cribs, large enough to fit grown men. "This is one of the sleeping chambers," he said.

Chains fitted to the railings of the beds. A few inmates wearing the chains, trapped in their beds. The stench in here was worse. Alice put a sleeve over her nose.

Coleman didn't seem too interested in hiding anything from them. He didn't even comment on the loathsome stench or try to divert them away.

A sullen, greasy-haired attendant was scrubbing the wooden floor. A rust-red stain.

Alice laid a hand on Nick's arm. When he turned his head, his eyes were as vacant and cold as those of the man scrubbing the floor. Flat gray of cold metal frosted over so that all the shine was gone. Crystals of fear and hatred in his eyes.

She must take him away from here.

This was why he hadn't wanted to come. He was afraid.

More than afraid, terrified and faltering in the darkness of his mind.

"Nick," she whispered, tugging on his sleeve so they lagged behind the group, which was moving to the next room. "Nick, let's leave. Patrick can write the report. Come, you need fresh air."

Nick was shaking, staring about him in confusion. She held his hand so tightly she knew she would leave nail marks.

"You were right. This was a mistake. I can see now that it wasn't a stubborn whim—that you honestly can't do this. It's deeper than that."

"Too late," he said. "Too late, Alice. It's beginning. I can feel it."

"Nick?"

He staggered like a drunkard, lurching ahead, away from her and toward the group. She raced after him, but his legs were so long he quickly caught up with them.

Nick heard the shuffling of feet, he heard the thoughts of the asylum patients in the room, he heard their apathy and their outrage, dulled into resignation.

He heard everything with such sharp clarity.

Alice calling his name.

Coleman's swift intake of breath, like a man's dying gasp.

An elderly man with white hair that stuck straight up held out his hand.

"Barrington?" Nick asked.

The man spit in his face and Nick didn't even care.

"Stay back," one of the attendants said. "Old Mason is dangerous."

Another man, younger, chained to the wall in a loincloth and nothing more, scraggly hair and mottled skin, purple with bruises.

This is me, Nick thought. *This could be me.* He laughed then, a wild, desperate sound that spiraled to the rafters.

An answering clamor arose from the patients.

Laughter and shouting, a sound like the battle cry of an army.

A clanging of spoons on tin cups and the rattle of labored breathing.

Coleman with his arms crossed watching with ill-disguised glee.

Where was Lear? Where was Patrick?

Alice at his side.

Alice with the turquoise eyes and the tender smile.

She wanted something from him. "Nick, please, talk to me. What's happening?"

He averted his gaze. No tenderness for him. No hope.

"Maybe instead of writing reports, Lord Hatherly should be committed," Coleman said with a jeering smile.

Nick had thought the onset would be more gradual, as his father's was . . . losing memory here, feeding himself on delusions, imagining the voices getting louder.

Now there was only this roaring in his ears and the darkness closing around him.

He'd thought he would have years to crumble slowly, but this was no slow fade, this was a landslide and it swept everything away.

Madness dragging him down. Smothering him.

Clawing to the surface only to be dragged deeper and deeper.

Dr. Forster arriving.

Lear. Patrick. Shaking him by the shoulders. He thrust them off and threw himself at Coleman.

"You animal!" Nick slammed his fist into Coleman's nose, and his vision exploded to red.

"He's insane," Coleman screamed.

Not a fumbling, bumbling descent but a rushing, roaring one that consumed from the inside out and left nothing but a husk of a man, a man who used to be able to feel the blood pumping in him and then nothing, darkness, and he would have nothing, no one to care for him.

His heart galloping so fast he clutched at his chest, trying to slow it. He staggered and hit a wall. His head pounding, pounding, his mouth like cotton wool.

Alice so blurry now, he could see nothing but a faint streak of blue-green eyes.

Everyone disappearing, fading like light from the gathering dusk.

He had one final thought before true darkness descended:

He loved Alice.

And now he would never have the chance to tell her.

Chapter 28

❧❧

The following are the men who generally
obtain success with women: Men who are celebrated for being very strong (bull-men) . . .
enterprising and brave men.

The Kama Sutra of Vātsyāyana

Her fault.

Nick had experienced a delirium induced by his
fear and by the unwholesome atmosphere of the
madhouse, and his mind had broken.

Lear and Patrick had taken charge, half carrying
Nick to the carriage.

His huge frame was convulsing. Dr. Forster instructed Lear to pin him down. Alice sat across
from him and held his hand.

At Sunderland they rushed him to bed.

"Tie him to the bed," Dr. Forster instructed.
"Close all the curtains. Instruct the servants to be
absolutely silent."

Alice raced from the room and down the stairs,
bursting outside into incongruous sunlight. She

frantically searched through the kitchen garden for lavender to calm him.

"What's wrong?" Bill asked, following her down the garden path.

"Lord Hatherly is having an attack. We must all be very quiet. Please inform the other servants."

"What are you looking for?"

"Lavender."

"Here." He plucked some and handed it to her.

"Thank you, Bill."

She rushed back to the bedroom. Nick's convulsions were so strong they shook the bed. Dr. Forster had stripped him to the waist.

Alice crushed lavender between her nails and rubbed it on his temples. "Please," she whispered. "Please come back to me."

"He's convulsing!" Dr. Forster shouted. "Leather for his mouth."

Lear slit a chair cushion with a knife he produced from somewhere in his clothing, and tore a strip of leather free. He worked Nick's jaw open and stuffed the leather in his mouth to keep him from biting his tongue.

Nick mumbled something incoherent, thrashing against his restraints, straining, the muscles bulging in his arms, his veins popping blue against his tanned skin.

Alice held tight to Nick's head, trying to keep him still.

"Nick, shh." She smoothed lavender over his temples. "Listen to my voice, Nick. Follow my voice. I'm here with you."

The duke and Berthold came to the door. "What's happening?" the duke asked, his voice trembling. "Nicolas, my boy, what did they do to you? The orchids warned me something bad would happen. They said you would suffer for my sins."

Berthold placed an arm around his shoulders. "We can't do anything, Your Grace, best to wait in the other room."

Oh Nick, she thought. *I should have listened to you. You were trying to tell me. But you didn't want to admit to any weakness. You big, stubborn fool.*

"He told me he didn't want to go," Alice said. "It's all my fault. He knew this might happen. He knew he might go insane."

"He's not going insane," Dr. Forster snapped. "He's been poisoned."

Poisoned? Not insane. *Poisoned.*

Alice and Lear exchanged a glance. "The tea," she breathed.

Nick's cup, shattering when he set it down. A red handle; she saw it in her mind. Her handle had been . . . blue. Coleman must have poisoned Nick's teacup.

Alice recalled thinking it was odd that the tea had already been poured.

"Oh, thank God," said Alice.

Poison they could control, couldn't they?

"I wouldn't thank him yet," Dr. Forster said. "He's not out of danger. It was a very large dose. Belladonna, if I'm not mistaken; look at his pupils."

Alice raised one of his lids; his eyes were nearly black the pupils were so enlarged. No silver visible.

"A large enough dose to kill an ox, but he's strong and I think he'll survive. Everyone must be quiet. He needs absolute silence and darkness. And we've got to stabilize him. Hold him down, Patrick and Lear. Keep him covered. Lady Hatherly, you keep speaking to him in a soft voice, he seems to like that, his eyelids flicker when you speak."

Alice held his face in her hands, her tears falling on his cheeks as she bent over him.

"Nick, she whispered. "I love you. Nick, please come back."

She didn't even care that everyone in the room must have heard her say she loved him. She didn't care if he knew it.

If only he woke up, if only he wouldn't die, she would tell him again and again.

"Nick," a voice cried from far away.

Scent of lavender.

A soft voice.

Alice.

Was she down here with him? Had he dragged her into the abyss?

Arms holding him, encircling him. "Come back."

Tears wet on his face. Her tears. Her soft voice calling.

A stern voice now. "I've had about enough of this. Now follow my voice and come back to me."

A thread spooling before him.

Laughter. Dimples. A body. Not a body. Her body. Alice. She wasn't here with him; she was in the sunlight, trying to save him from the darkness.

You can't save me, Alice. He couldn't breathe. Fear clutching at his throat. Taking away his breath.

"I love you, Nick."

The words pierced through him.

She loved him and he would never emerge from this prison.

He'd gone mad. No other explanation for this darkness and these delusions. For the rest of his life, he'd always be searching for the lavender scent of her hair and the turquoise color of her eyes.

Not knowing why.

Just searching, as his father searched for orchids everywhere.

Finding orchids in the cotton stuffing of chairs.

Mistaking dandelions for rare blooms. Or even, once, a tuft of white hair the duke snatched from his hairbrush. Holding it up, so proud.

Lovely things, the coelogynes, he'd said, stroking the puff of hair.

Soft, yet hardy. I brought these back from eastern India. Tolerate drought and neglect, and flower faithfully—snow-white or emerald-green with black stripes. Scent like a freshly peeled orange.

Nick had dutifully sniffed, gulping back emotion. Wanting to cry.

Never allowing himself to cry.

That's how Nick would be with Alice. He'd see her everywhere. Hear her voice everywhere. He'd feel her soft hand on his cheek.

She kissed him. Holding him like a punishment for everything bad he'd ever done. It was a punishment because her love would torment him the most. Her love was his final error.

The darkness came again then, blotting her out, snuffing her voice to silence.

His bright, curious Alice. His greatest mistake.

Chapter 29

It is only, moreover, when she is certain that she is truly loved, and that her lover is indeed devoted to her, and will not change his mind, that she should then give herself up to him.

The Kama Sutra of Vātsyāyana

The next few days passed in a blur of carrying on with life, while her heart and mind lay sleeping in the bed with the still unconscious Nick.

Patrick came to report that he'd had Coleman arrested for attempted murder and he was being held in jail awaiting trial.

Lear assured her that Jane was halfway to Scotland now and safe from pursuit.

Alice sat with Nick every day, as she was sitting now, in a chair beside his bed, holding his hand, reading to him, crushing lavender and soothing it over his temples.

Kali liked to sleep curled up against Nick's side. She was here now, sniffing Nick's cheek inquisitively.

"He'll come back to us, Kali," Alice said. "He must."

Dr. Forster entered the bedchamber for his daily visit. Even though his medical specialty was lunacy, Alice wouldn't allow another physician to tend Nick. She trusted the doctor completely.

"How is he today?" Dr. Forster asked.

"The same."

"Please go out, Lady Hatherly. You'll make yourself sick and he needs you strong and healthy when he recovers."

"You think he will come out of this?"

"I have seen patients in a comatose state for months that suddenly recovered. Now go outside. The sun is shining. You'll do him no good if you are weak with an illness."

Reluctantly, Alice left the bedchamber.

She walked the path to the orchid conservatory.

She hadn't been out of doors in days. The sun felt like a kiss on her cheeks.

She found the duke in the conservatory with Berthold, tending his orchids.

"How is he?" Berthold whispered with worried eyes.

"The same. But the doctor said I needed to come outside and enjoy the air. So here I am."

"It will do you good, my dear," said the duke. "Remember the orchid you helped me water last week? See what you did? Isn't she lovely?"

Alice knelt on her knees to have a closer look.

The orchid's beauty almost hurt her.

The perfect swooping formation of the five overlapping petals, the cup in the center with its two symmetrical tendrils, the small bud inside bordered by very precise marking like the stripes on Kali's flanks.

The petals weren't uniformly purple, but crisscrossed with a spider's webbing of violet veins, like the veins visible beneath the skin of her wrist.

She loved those flowers with the fierce awe of possession.

She had helped create this beauty and now it was here, in this world, a burst of velvet purple and a secret spiraling darkness inside.

Several more small buds, as long as the distance from her nail to her knuckle, were close to opening. The power to form blossoms surged in the roots of the plant, replete with life and possibilities.

The duke handed her a watering can. "Why don't you water it, my dear? Remember, only a small amount of water. And don't leave even one drop on the petals or the leaves. They don't like that."

Alice tended the orchid, giving it a nice soaking drink and wiping the waxy green leaves dry with her skirts.

Some of the root tendrils curled straight up into the air instead of down.

Dr. Forster had been right. Being here with such beauty was good and right.

Nick was too strong to succumb to poison.

He would wake soon.

Alice leaned back on her heels.

Today was the day her ship sailed. And she wasn't on board.

How could she be, when Nick lay inside the house, unconscious and dreaming, growing paler every day?

Here in the humid air, with the trickling sound of water dripping from the plants and the scent of vanilla, she listened to the orchids whisper of new beginnings.

Of new adventures.

The duke lifted his head and stared straight at her. "Can you hear them, my dear?"

"Yes." Alice's eyes filled with tears that spilled over, streaking her cheeks. She was careful not to drop any tears on the orchid leaves.

"I can hear them," she whispered.

Chapter 30

───────── ❧❧ ─────────

When a lover coming home late at night kisses his beloved who is asleep on her bed in order to show her his desire, it is called a "kiss that awakens."

The Kama Sutra of Vātsyāyana

"Brandy," Nick croaked.

"Oh my God." Alice clutched his hand. "You're awake. Nick, you're awake! Send for Dr. Forster," she shouted at March.

March, who had been hovering by the bedside more often than not during Nick's illness, immediately bolted for the door.

Nick tried to sit up, but Alice laid a hand on his chest. "Don't try to move. Lie still."

"Alice?" His eyes drifted open. "Where am I?"

Dr. Forster had told her that it wasn't uncommon for the delirium induced by belladonna poisoning to be accompanied by a temporary state of amnesia. He'd said Nick probably wouldn't remember anything about what had happened.

"I'm so thirsty," Nick said. "I need brandy."

Alice laughed, so happy to hear his voice, even if it was a croaking shadow of its former bass rumbling. "I'll find some brandy but I'm going to weaken it with water."

"Water my excellent brandy?" he said. "That would be . . . a crime."

He was still weak; she could see by the way he struggled to breathe.

She handed him a glass. "Sip this slowly."

He obeyed her orders, taking small sips. He fell back against the pillow. "Good brandy."

"Lear brought you another case yesterday."

"Good man."

"Nick, you scared me so much." Alice squeezed his fingers. "Don't ever do that to me again."

"What did I do?"

"Do you remember going to the Yellow House?"

"No. I don't remember . . . anything. I remembered your name, though, didn't I? Alice, have I gone mad?"

She threaded her fingers into his fingers. "No, and you never will."

"You can't know that for certain."

"I don't have to know it. I feel it." She brought his hand to her heart. "*Here*."

"We went to the Yellow House?"

"We did. You were very anxious and I knew I never should have asked you to go. And then Coleman poisoned you with belladonna and you had a violent delirium with paroxysms. You lunged at Coleman and beat him."

"Excellent," Nick said with satisfaction. "At least I landed a punch."

"Coleman's being held on suspicion of intent to murder. So we won after all. And Mr. Stubbs has his Annie. Lear helped them book passage on a ship bound for America where they will start a new life."

"I remember one thing." Nick smiled. "The scent of lavender, seeping through the darkness. You sat with me, didn't you? All day and all night."

"I was so frightened. I didn't know your fear of going mad ran so deep. You should have told me. Why didn't you tell me?"

"I didn't want to appear weak."

"You're not weak, Nick, you're so strong. Any other man would have died with a dose of poison that lethal. Coleman was trying to discredit you, and perhaps if he'd administered a smaller dose, no one would have been the wiser. People would have thought you had a manic episode, triggered by visiting the asylum, but the dose he used was too strong. Enough to kill an ox, Dr. Forster said. And you survived."

She kissed his knuckles. "I knew you would wake up."

He wanted her to keep touching him.

Bringing their joined hands to his lips, he kissed the center of her palm, inhaling her clean, womanly scent.

Lavender. Lemon. A hint of salt spray.

A hint of adventure.

A disquieting thought gripped his throat. "Alice. How long have I been asleep?"

She smiled warily. "Five days."

"Five days . . . but that means your ship . . . has it already sailed? What are you doing here? You have to go to India."

"I wasn't going to leave you when you might die, Nick. How could I leave and spend six months on the ocean wondering if you were alive or dead?"

"But you won't be able to give the scholars your missing chapters of the *Kama Sutra*. They'll be waiting and no one will arrive. I never wanted to come between you and your dreams, Alice."

"I know that, Nick. You've encouraged my dreams at every turn. Outfitting my study. Finding me a tutor."

Nick shook his head. "You should have gone. You can't abandon your dreams for me."

"I should have listened to you. You had a very good reason not to go to the asylum. I blindly forged ahead without thinking that you might have a legitimate reason. I should never have forced you to go."

"You didn't force me to do anything. I made the choice. And you have to find another ship. Is there another in your father's fleet that will be leaving this month? You've worked so hard on this, Alice. I won't let you give everything up for my sake."

"You want me to leave?"

"Of course I do. You must follow your dreams to India."

Dr. Forster arrived. "Awake, are we?"

"And obstinate as ever," Alice said.

She dropped his hand and rose from the bed.

Nick heard the hurt in her voice and he didn't know how to make anything better.

She was fearless and unconventional and she wasn't his to keep.

She was something of the wind that blew through his life and lifted the dust from his heart. He could never be the one to destroy her dreams.

"Good to see you in the land of the living," Captain Lear said, shaking Nick's hand. "Scared us there for a moment, Hatherly."

"Lear, I upset Alice. She left in a huff."

"What did you do, you fool?"

"She missed her ship to India. And I told her she should find another one. That she should leave and she became agitated."

"Of course she did. The lady loves you. She said so while you were sleeping."

"I know, and that's terrible."

"Is it?"

"I've hurt a young, innocent lady, and my dark, scarred heart is bleeding. I have to find some way to make this better."

She'd said she was the one lady in the world who was immune to his charm and he'd believed her because he'd wanted to believe her, and because she had a convincing way of saying things, as though she were the authority on the topic.

He'd known she was inexperienced and easily hurt. He'd wanted to believe that she had shed her inhibitions so easily and entered freely and mindfully into a mutually pleasurable physical relationship with convenient time restraints.

What was it about her that made him want to be a better man?

He'd never had a twinge of conscience. Not once in all these years of debauchery. This was his destiny and he was merely fulfilling what was prescribed for him by his father and grandfather.

If this experience showed her nothing, hadn't it shown her that he was unstable?

"I need to ask you something," Nick said.

"You want me to take Lady Hatherly to India."

"How did you know?"

"She missed her ship. And I know how much it means to her to go. And I also know how much you love her."

"I don't—"

He was going to deny it. And then he shut his mouth.

"Uh-huh. That's what I thought," Lear said with a smug smile.

"How did you become so all-knowing?"

"Always wanted to see India. Long passage around the Cape of Good Hope, though. Five, six months. Of course, it will give you time for that honeymoon you never properly had."

"I'm not going. I can't leave the duke, you know that."

"Uh-huh," Lear said skeptically. "Well, if I'm outfitting one of my ships for India, I'd best be going to make the preparations."

"She'll bring her cat with her."

"That's fine. I need a new ship's cat. Mrs. Peebles perished, sadly, when she slept in the wrong barrel."

"Kali will be an excellent ship's cat; she loves to hunt mice and she's not afraid of anything. When can you be ready? I'll pay all costs, of course. She needs to be in Calcutta by December."

"Two days. Do you want to tell her, or should I?"

"I'll tell her," Nick said.

Lear nodded and left.

I'll tell her, Nick thought, *and I won't shout: Don't go to India.*

Even having that thought seemed sacrilegious. This was Alice's goal. All her hard work and scholarship would be for naught if she didn't follow her heart to India.

She would leave, and his life would descend back into chaos and emptiness.

She'd left a book behind on the chair by his bed. A memory penetrated the darkness of his mind. She'd read to him for hours, sitting by his bedside.

He touched the ridged spine of the book, thinking of Alice's supple spine, the feeling of her smooth skin beneath his hands.

Think this through, Nick.

What if he convinced her to stay? She would resent him, maybe not right away but eventually, for ruining her dream.

What if she went to India and he convinced her to come back to him? They would spend years apart. Her requirement was fidelity. He could be true to her, but what if she forgot about him? She'd probably find her affable professor in Calcutta. And then what would Nick be? Just the wild ride she left behind.

Good for sexual gratification but not exactly the makings of a safe, stable partner.

There was nothing stable about his life. He lived

on the edge of life, always testing its limits. Ride hard. Drink hard. Don't care too deeply about anything because it'll all go to hell sooner rather than later.

The duke will die.

Mother only wants her allowance.

No brother, sister, no bonds of flesh. Escape into pleasure because that's the best hiding place.

Alice's light and power should never be dimmed. She'd been held back by her mother trying to hedge her into a domestic, conventional role, but she'd found a way to escape.

She read poetry in Sanskrit. She took charge of difficult situations. She was kind to his father. She lightened Nick's heart.

When he'd agreed to their arrangement, he'd known that bedding her would be pleasurable. He hadn't known that it would change him.

She smiled, and he believed that life held some meaning and that he had a future.

You're getting older, Nick. Flannel waistcoats and quiet nights by a fireplace reading with his wife didn't sound so pathetic anymore. Maybe that's what he wanted.

Sometimes I fall in love six times before breakfast. I worship every woman I bed and I adore them until the moment they leave.

The words he'd so glibly spoken only two months ago. The problem was he'd tumbled into infatuation with Alice and he'd never climbed back out again.

He was still there, mired in this need for her, this wanting that never waned, never grew cold.

Kali hopped onto the bed, and Nick caught her in his arms and scratched between her ears.

At first the cat stiffened, not sure how she felt about his big presence next to her on the bed, but then, when he found the right spot with his nails, she sighed and stretched her little paw out to touch his arm.

"Kali," he said, feeling foolish for talking to a cat, but needing to tell someone. "I care for your mother. I don't want to, but I do. But I can't tell her because it would seem as though I were trying to make her stay here in England, when I want her to have her adventure."

Kali's tail thumped against the bed and her eyes closed.

Nick picked her up and cradled her in one palm while he scratched under her chin. What a sweet thing she was when she was in the right mood.

"We have to follow the plan, Kali," he whispered into her ear.

Kali raised her head and flattened her ears.

"We have to," Nick protested. "She'd think I was trying to keep her here for selfish reasons."

You are trying to keep her here for selfish reasons.

"You want me to tell her? Let her make her own decision?"

Kali purred approvingly.

Nick kissed the top of her head. "Thanks for the talk." He set her down, and she blinked sleepily and settled back into the covers.

Could there be anything more heart melting than a big, strong man holding a fluffy cat, scratching its chin, and whispering in its ear? Alice thought as she watched Nick and Kali.

People express love in different ways.

Some people don't say anything; they use actions to speak their heart.

Had Nick been trying to tell her he loved her when he did those nice things for her?

Now what was he doing? Crooning a nonsensical ditty about lion tamers and fearsome huntresses to Kali in an off-key voice.

Drat! Alice wished he wouldn't do things like that. It wrung her heart out like wet linen and hung it out to dry.

He glanced up and saw her watching. He sat up straighter, Kali still curled in his lap. "Alice, come here." He patted the bed next to him.

She sat in the chair instead. She didn't want him to touch her anymore. Every time he touched her would make it more painful when she left.

"I'll see if there are other ships going to Calcutta tomorrow, Nick."

"No need," he said. "Lear will take you."

"He will?"

"He's mounting an orchid-hunting expedition and a trip to India fits well with his plans. There's no way I'm allowing you to throw all your goals aside. You were always going to India. This was always ending with you boarding that ship."

Yes, that was the way it was supposed to end.

Sailing off for adventure.

But the taste for adventure had gone flat in her mouth.

"I forbid you to stay here, Alice. But perhaps

we'll see each other again in the future." He smiled. "Maybe we'll become the kind of lovers who meet for a week once a year. Or a month, maybe. I've heard of such arrangements. Husbands and wives who are the best of friends. I never thought it possible but we could . . . we could be friends."

He needed a friend. He didn't need another lover. Was that what he was trying to tell her?

"We follow the plan, Alice. We honor the contract. You go your way and I stay right here."

Traveling was her dream, not his. He had to stay here with the duke. And he'd said he would never set foot on a ship again. He didn't want to travel; he'd made that clear.

But it hurt so much.

"You want me to leave," she accused. "You can't stand the idea that you might begin to care for me and you want to push me away and make me leave so that all your fears can be realized. You want me to be like your mother. Just another wife who leaves after a madness scare."

"I do want you to leave. I want you to go to India and present your manuscript to the professors."

"It's only a pile of palm leaves with some scratches."

"Don't say that. You know that's not true. This means everything to you, and you can't suddenly not care about any of it. You're so passionate about your work, and that's something I love about you."

He loved how devoted she was to her work.

He didn't love her.

"It's time to stop hiding behind your gambits and ploys, Alice. Time to be yourself, and who cares if anyone doesn't approve? Break some rules, see where it leads you."

"Nick." It was on the tip of her tongue to tell him that she loved him, and what? Beg him to let her stay? That was ridiculous. She would never compromise herself or her ideals in such a way.

She would not swoon at his feet.

She never had and she wouldn't start now. She rose on unsteady limbs. She wouldn't cry.

Even though she knew this longing for Nick would never go away.

He was etched upon her heart, like stylus scratches on palm-leaf pages, and she'd never be rid of this wanting.

"Go forth, Dimples, go forth and conquer the world."

She managed a wan smile. "I will, Nick." She'd begun to dream a new future. A life with Nick. What a wonderful dream it had been. But it was over now.

Chapter 31

◎◎

> She should give him something capable of
> producing curiosity and love in his heart,
> such as an affectionate present, telling him
> that it was specifically designed for his use.
>
> *The Kama Sutra of Vātsyāyana*

Alice gathered her manuscripts and her clothing.

She marshaled her emotions and locked them deep inside her heart.

She would have long months at sea to examine this pain. To dissect it. And to speak its language.

The only item she left behind was a worn edition of her favorite novel.

She'd read it to Nick while he was unconscious. He had no memory of her reading to him.

As it turned out, he'd been right.

Her Darcy did not exist. And she'd been foolish to think she would find him someday.

What need had she for girlish dreams? She'd known who she was the day she'd arrived at Sunderland, but she'd changed many times since then.

From now on she'd be all business. She would

live for her scholarship, and she would become an esteemed linguist. Why shouldn't she? No one could dispute the fact that she spoke the languages she did.

She said good-bye to Nick without crying; how she managed that, she'd never know.

She said good-bye to the duke, and to Berthold, March, and Bill.

She made her farewells and she left.

Climbed into a carriage wearing a sensible traveling dress with Kali in her wicker basket.

The carriage met some sort of obstruction and couldn't seem to move around the blockage in the road. Alice sat, dully, watching the light fade.

She would be terribly late.

But Captain Lear would wait for her. He'd been charged by Nick with delivering her to India.

Follow the plan. Honor the contract.

And never look back.

*L*ike a damned coward, Nick watched Alice's carriage leave from his window.

Because if he'd gone down to see her off, he would have broken down and begged her to stay.

And that wouldn't be fair to her. She might think she loved him, but if she stayed here, eventually she would resent him for ruining her dreams and subsuming her goals.

She'd left nothing behind but a book. Fitting for such a studious lady.

He slipped the leather-bound novel into the inner pocket of his coat and headed for the duke's orchid conservatory.

March blocked his way as he attempted to leave the house.

"You're still 'ere?" he asked, his wrinkled face filled with confusion. "Thought you would have gone after her by now."

"I had to let her go," Nick said, trying to convince himself he'd done the right thing.

"Won't miss that furry rodent of hers," March said, sticking out his lower lip. "Not one bit."

Which was a very unconvincing lie.

Nick already missed her.

They would all miss her.

When he reached the front door, he saw Berthold walking down the pathway from the conservatory.

Bill came running downstairs behind Nick.

"Forgot I was supposed to give you this," he said, handing an envelope to Nick. "It's from the captain."

"Open it," March urged. "What does it say?"

Berthold joined them on the front steps, and the three men crowded around, closer and closer, waiting for him to open the letter.

Nick lifted the sheet into the sunlight.

Maybe Alice had been right. Maybe he needed spectacles.

Because he thought it said: *There's a special chamber for orchids on my new ship,* The Huntress. *And the duke's already in it. If you want him back you'll have to come and fetch him, you stubborn arse.*

"What the hell is that supposed to mean?" Nick asked after he read it out loud to the group. "The duke's in the conservatory, isn't he?"

Berthold gave him a guilty look.

"Isn't he?" Nick repeated.

Lear kidnapped the duke?

March grinned widely. "Bully for the captain!"

Nick couldn't believe it. "Are you smiling, March?"

"I might be," March replied sheepishly, the grin never leaving his face.

Then Bill's lips curved upward slightly.

Now Nick had seen everything.

Berthold joined in the group mania, chuckling loudly.

"You're all mad," Nick said.

"That's right," March said proudly. "And you're in love with that daft lady."

He *was* in love with her. And he'd let her go. *Why* had he let her go?

Would she have him? The one thing that he never could have planned for in this convenient arrangement was Alice.

No one could plan for Alice.

She was so completely and utterly her own person, you never knew what she would do or say. And if he laid his heart at her feet, she could tell him that she didn't want him with her on her voyage.

But he meant to convince her that he had his uses on long sea voyages.

"I have to pack," Nick said urgently.

Bill indicated a small trunk sitting on the steps. "Here you are, my lord. All packed and ready to go."

"I had one assignment, men," Nick boomed.

"Love and honor my wife. And I mucked everything up."

"That you did," Berthold said cheerfully. "That you did, my lord."

"Well, don't stand there gawking," Nick cried. "Saddle Anvil!"

"Already saddled," said March with another delighted grin.

They were all in on it, Nick realized.

Turncoats, he thought with affection.

You need someone to love. The duke's words leapt to mind. Had it only been two months ago? He'd been such a blind, stubborn fool. Why had he let her go alone? He needed Alice. If she'd have him, he'd spend the rest of his days making her smile. And blush.

Within minutes, he was swinging onto Anvil's back with his trunk strapped behind.

Anvil whinnied, ready to fly. "Trample anyone who stands in our way," Nick instructed. "We've a ship to catch."

Chapter 32

❧❧

... happiness is secured by the possession of excellent qualities in her husband, joined to a love of enjoyment.

The Kama Sutra of Vātsyāyana

𝒥t had taken hours to reach the docks because of the snarl of carts and carriages blocking the road.

The afternoon was misty and so were her eyes.

"There's no use crying like that!" said Alice to herself rather sharply. "I advise you to leave off this minute." She always gave herself good advice but rarely followed it.

Captain Lear joined her at the ship's railing. "Nice day for a voyage to India, isn't it?"

Alice nodded, unable to muster the excitement she should be feeling at the fulfillment of her long-held desire.

"Watching for someone?" Lear asked with a sly smile.

"Of course not."

She'd been watching for Nick. Hoping to see him galloping along the docks on his big, black stallion.

Coming to beg her not to leave. Telling her he loved her madly.

But there was no Nick, and no stallion.

He wasn't coming.

Of course he wasn't coming. This wasn't a romance. It was an adventure story. The intrepid heroine sets off for a lifetime of adventure on the high seas and in foreign climes.

Throwing everything away for some man, even if that man was Nick, wasn't an option.

"Come below when you're ready, Lady Hatherly," Captain Lear said as he left. "It's starting to rain. Yours is the first cabin to the left."

A drop slid off her bonnet brim and hit her cheek. Still no black stallion hurtling down the pier.

Sailors moving, shouting, huge ropes being untied, anchors lifted.

Alice dashed tears from her eyes.

It was ridiculous to stand here and wait for something that would never happen.

She lifted the lid of Kali's basket. "I was rather hoping he might come after us, Kali," she whispered.

Kali stared at her indignantly, more than ready to be released from her wicker prison.

Suddenly Alice glanced up, staring at the docks.

They were receding from view.

The ship had begun to move.

And her final hope died.

Her heart plummeting, Alice descended the ladder.

First cabin to the left. She opened the door and stopped abruptly, her heart pounding.

There was a man in her room.

Lounging in the very center of the bed.

Nick.

He was reading a book. Not just any book. He was reading the novel she'd left behind.

"What took you so long?" Nick grinned. "I've been waiting for ages. This is really quite a good book upon a second read. Though I don't much like that Caroline Bingley. Bit of a witch. And that arrogant Darcy. Who does he think he is?"

The sight of Nick lying in her bed had rendered her temporarily mute.

He was so beautiful.

And so unexpected.

Her heart expanded like the sails of the ship catching in the wind.

"Nick, what are you doing here?"

"I'm one step ahead of you, Alice. For the very first time. And probably the last."

"How did you arrive before me?"

"I rode Anvil. I told him I had to be early this time, instead of late."

"But . . ."

"Lear somehow created that obstruction in the road so that your carriage would be delayed. I've no idea how he does these things, but he does. Worked like magic. Are you going to stand there gaping?"

His eyes lost their teasing edge. "If you want me to leave I'd better go and tell Lear to turn this ship back, I believe we've already begun to move."

"But the duke . . ." Alice said. She seemed to only be able to manage sentence fragments. Very uncharacteristic of her.

"He's in the ship's orchid conservatory, happily making an inventory of his new blooms. I was the one who was afraid to leave London, not my father. I clung to the idea that he needed Sunderland when really it was me who was too afraid to leave."

"This ship has an orchid conservatory?"

"To store the orchids Lear will hunt for his wealthy investors."

"You don't like ships. You said you'd never set foot on one again."

"That was before."

"Before what?"

"Come here and I'll tell you, Dimples." He patted the bed beside him. "We'll talk this through in comfort."

Kali yowled in her basket, and Alice hastily set her down and opened the lid. Her cat hopped free of the basket in one leap and jumped onto the bed, flopping down beside Nick.

Nick propped himself up on one elbow to scratch behind Kali's ears.

He wasn't wearing a coat. Or a cravat.

"Do you have breeches on under those covers?" Alice asked suspiciously.

"Come and find out," Nick said, with a wicked grin.

Alice snorted. "What did I do to deserve this?"

"Married beneath you. Now come here, Dimples. I have an apology to make."

Nick's heart beat swiftly as he waited for Alice to say something . . . do something.

Why did she just stand there, watching him? Why wasn't she already in his arms?

Maybe he hadn't completely thought through the no-trousers thing. He wanted to go to her, take her in his arms, but he needed her to make this decision without any physical persuasion on his part.

Alice closed her eyes for a moment, and when she opened them again, they shimmered with tears. "Nick," she said, her voice faltering. "You can't uproot your whole life to follow me across the globe."

"What life? I was living for empty pleasures, stumbling moment to moment. Living in fear."

"But what of the report for Parliament?"

"Coleman's behind bars and the Yellow House is in his son's hands now. Patrick tells me the lad has a kind heart and has already made vast improvements."

"What of March and Bill and Berthold?"

"My ragged band of misfit servants will be fine without me."

Finally, she walked toward the bed, a little unsteady on her feet because of the motion of the ship.

When she was near enough he reached for her and tumbled her into the bed, sending an indignant Kali leaping away.

Smoothing her hair away from her face, he gazed tenderly at his beautiful wife. "I've made many mistakes in my life, Alice, but the biggest mistake I ever made was allowing you to leave without telling you I loved you and begging you to take me with you on your wonderful adventure."

"Nick." She closed her eyes. "You love me?"

"More than anything, Dimples."

He kissed her eyelids. Then he kissed her dimples, because she was smiling.

"I love how you plunge headlong into life with the belief that you can conquer anything. Speak any language. Translate any text. You've conquered me, Alice."

She opened her eyes and the clear, deep turquoise stopped his heart from beating.

"I can't tell you that you won't go insane, Nick," she whispered. "That you won't forget my name or forget me entirely. No one can assure you of that."

"I know. And I can accept that now, if you can."

She nodded. "Yes, Nick. I will always love you. No matter what happens."

"All I can do is be here with you right now, Alice. Right here. We can create memories so vivid that they weave themselves into the fabric of the universe. Into the light of the stars. The memory of this moment. You holding me. The memory of our kisses."

He kissed her then with all his heart and soul.

Because she wasn't just any fever dream of a woman.

She was Alice.

His wife. His lover.

His future.

Epilogue

※◎◎※

Six months later . . .
Calcutta, India

"**H**ere." Nick pointed to a spot on the map spread before him on the table in the study of the house they'd rented on Council Street in Calcutta. "We'll find the *Cymbidium aloifolium* blooming in the forests of the Himalayan foothills."

"*Aloifolium*. Does it resemble an aloe plant?" Alice asked.

"It has elongated leaves which resemble aloe," said Nick. "The Nepalese believe its roots cure paralysis and treat vertigo and insanity."

The duke glanced at his son, his gray eyes clear and focused. "I know this cymbidium, don't I?"

"We searched for it together once, you and I," Nick said gently.

Alice's heart brimmed with pride as she watched father and son pore over the map.

The months-long voyage had brought back painful memories for Nick, but he'd been writing in a diary, observing the duke and recording their conversations.

For his part, Barrington was growing sharper and less confused every day. Hunting orchids was his favorite thing in life and it gave him a focus and purpose.

"Will it be blooming in winter?" Captain Lear asked, scratching Kali's head. She was cradled in the crook of one of his arms with her head nestled against his chest and her hind legs spread in a thoroughly unladylike manner.

Nick nodded. "It's a hardy plant adapted to mountain conditions. It'll survive the voyage back to England."

Kali squirmed out of Lear's arms and jumped on the table to sniff the map. She'd proven a fearless companion on the voyage, and the sailors aboard *The Huntress* had adopted her as their ship's cat, even making her a miniature berth and a tiny sailor's cap to wear.

Captain Lear pushed back his long black hair, which he'd allowed to grow unchecked on the voyage. "My investors will care only for the beauty of the blooms, not its medicinal properties, I'm afraid."

Nick drew Alice to him and wrapped an arm about her waist. "Oh, she's a beauty, all right. Blooms in clusters on long, slender pendant stalks. Has small, perfect scarlet-and-cream petals with an hourglass mark in the center."

He gave Alice's waist a squeeze when he said the word *hourglass*. Why did everything he say have to sound so very suggestive?

Her heart skipped a beat recalling the wicked things she and Nick had done last night, and every sultry, languid night of the voyage. She was quite certain some of the things they'd done weren't even described in the *Kama Sutra*.

"It must be nearly time," she said to Nick.

They had an engagement today with the Sanskrit scholars from Fort William College. She was nervous about handing over her translation, even though she still intended to present it as Fred's work.

Outside, the air was warm and humid and filled with the fragrance of the coconuts, pineapples and oranges being hawked by street vendors.

They didn't need to take a carriage because Mr. Carey had suggested they meet at the nearby Government House, as the buildings housing the college were currently under renovation.

"How strange to think that it's December, and our friends in London are huddled in front of their fireplaces," Alice said.

"I never thought I'd leave England," Nick said. "But now that I have . . . I'm not sure I want to go back."

Alice smiled at him. "India is everything I dreamt it would be."

A surfeit of new sights, smells, and sounds; a feast for her senses. Around the docks, Alice had caught snatches of German, French, Spanish, and Portuguese, and what she guessed had been Arabic and Chinese.

She'd dreamt of traveling for so long, picturing all the languages she would hear, and the new sights she would see.

But she'd never imagined the tall, handsome man walking next to her, carrying her valise filled with the ancient manuscripts she would donate to the college.

A companion on her journey. Someone to share the wonder of each new discovery.

Government House was an imposing, white colonnaded structure, built by Lord Wellesley in 1803 at great expense. The entrance on the north side had a handsome stone portico and Ionic white columns.

"Are you ready for this, my love?" Nick asked as they mounted the steps.

"I'm ready." Ever since she'd saved her grandfather's collection of manuscripts from the fire, she'd been ready for this moment. She knew returning them to India was the right thing to do.

Mr. Carey and Mr. Vidyasagar met them in an inner room paved in dark gray marble with cut-glass chandeliers suspended from a blue and gold painted ceiling.

"Lord Hatherly," Mr. Carey said, bowing slightly, his spectacles sliding forward on his long nose. "I met your father many years ago."

"Then you'll have to call upon us and say hello again."

"He's here?" exclaimed Mr. Carey. "But I thought . . ." He squinted at Nick. "I thought he was . . ."

"Mad?"

"That is to say—"

"He is mad," Nick said calmly. "Mad as a March

hare. But that doesn't mean he should be locked away."

"Oh." Mr. Carey cleared his throat. "Quite right, Lord Hatherly. I would enjoy speaking with him again."

"You have brought your grandfather's manuscripts, Lady Hatherly?" asked Mr. Vidyasagar, his brown eyes gleaming with scholarly fervor.

"I have. I'm only sorry my brother Fred couldn't be here to present them himself."

"I should like to meet him someday," said Mr. Vidyasagar. "The translation he sent us was an extraordinarily erudite example of scholarship for one with so little experience in the Sanskrit language."

Alice and Nick exchanged smiles. They'd sent the translation ahead by post. Alice was thrilled to hear the learned scholars approved.

Mr. Vidyasagar never took his eyes off the valise. "May I?"

Alice nodded and Mr. Vidyasagar immediately opened the latch on the valise. With great reverence and care, he lifted the silk-wrapped palm leaf manuscript and laid it on the dark wood of the table.

"Can it be, Mr. Carey?" Mr. Vidyasagar addressed his colleague. "Can it truly be the long lost chapters from the *Kama Sutra*?

He and Mr. Carey bent close to the manuscript, examining the script etched into the palm leaves.

"Remarkable!" exclaimed Mr. Vidyasagar.

"Extraordinary," sighed Mr. Carey.

"Then you think it's authentic?" Alice asked eagerly.

"I will need to perform some testing," said Mr. Vidyasagar, "but my initial examination leads me to believe it is the original text."

"I concur," said Mr. Carey, trailing a long, slender finger along the text. "I don't suppose your brother told you anything of the subject matter of the work. And I'm certain he never allowed you to read his translation, Lady Hatherly."

Ha! Alice longed to reveal the truth, but she knew that that was not the prudent course of action. "Fred's in Paris right now and sent me as his emissary, as I had always wanted to visit India. He told me nothing."

"Quite right. Quite right. But you, Lord Hatherly?"

"Oh, I've read it. And I approve, gentlemen. I approve."

Mr. Carey peered at Nick over his spectacles. He didn't appear to have a playful or salacious bone in his thin, creaky body. Alice rather suspected the man had parchment for skin and ink running through his veins.

"Fred never allowed Lady Hatherly to read his translation, gentlemen," Nick continued, "because he didn't write it."

Alice stared at Nick. What was he doing?

"And what do you mean by that, Lord Hatherly? Are you saying that Mr. Fred Tombs did not author the translation we received?"

"That's exactly what I'm saying."

"Nick, please," Alice whispered urgently. "What are you doing?"

Nick was going off script.

Way off.

"How remarkable," exclaimed Mr. Vidyasagar. "Then who translated it?"

"A Hatherly," Nick said with a smug smile.

Alice kicked his shin under the table.

"Are you saying that *you* translated it, Lord Hatherly?" Mr. Carey asked.

Nick completely ignored her frantic signals. "The erudite example of scholarship you praised earlier was produced by none other than my wife."

Mr. Vidyasagar's jaw dropped, and Alice half-started out of her chair. "Nick—no!"

This was *not* what they'd agreed upon.

"Alice," he whispered, "I'll be damned if Fred, or I, take the credit for all of your hard work."

Mr. Carey stared over his spectacles. "Do you mean to tell me, Lord Hatherly, that *Lady* Hatherly translated this manuscript?"

"That's precisely what I'm telling you." Nick leaned back in his seat.

He obviously thought he was doing something noble but now her scholarship would be buried, passed over . . . her translation would never see the light of day.

"Nick," she said sternly, "may I have a word?"

He blithely ignored her. "Old Fred and I, we don't have a way with words. But Lady Hatherly here? Words are her bread and butter and foreign languages are her cup of tea."

"You're having us on," scoffed Mr. Carey.

Alice's shoulders stiffened, her ire centering on

a new target. "You don't think me capable of such a thing?"

Nick grinned. "That's right, you show them, darling."

The cat was out of the bag, so to speak. She may as well admit to it now.

"Frankly, no," replied Mr. Carey.

Mr. Vidyasagar looked more circumspect. "Perhaps you helped your brother with the translation, Lady Hatherly? As his amanuensis?"

Alice narrowed her eyes. They didn't think she could read the text?

She'd show them.

She spread out one of the long, thin palm leaves. Drawing her finger across the etched black text, she began to read and she didn't stop until both of the scholars were gaping at her with shocked expressions.

Mr. Vidyasagar raised his thick, dark eyebrows. "Well, this does change things."

"My turn," Nick said gleefully.

Alice gave him a withering glance, but he spread out a new page. He made a show of peering closely, and hemming and hawing.

"Ah, yes," he said in a scholarly tone. "Scratch, scratch, squiggle. Flourish, little snake, big snake, big squiggle—"

"Nick!" Alice suppressed a smile.

"Well it's all snakes and squiggles to me."

Mr. Carey stared down his long nose disapprovingly. "Why do I feel as though you two planned this little episode?"

"I wasn't planning to seek any credit," said Alice.

"The prurient content of the manuscript would bring scandal to my family if my connection were discovered."

"We will only publish for a select group of the Friends of India," Mr. Vidyasagar said. "Your work could remain anonymous."

"Of course, we had no idea a female completed the translation. We'll have to re-examine it," said Mr. Carey, wiping his spectacles with a square of cloth and looking very uncomfortable about this turn of events.

"Why should you re-examine it?" Nick asked.

"Er, well . . . it throws a new light on everything," Mr. Carey said. "The *Kama Sutra* was written by a man on the subject of desire. I hardly think an elegant lady would possess the vocabulary, much less the . . . *inclination* for describing some of the more . . . *enthusiastic* portions of the text."

Drat! "May I remind you, gentlemen," Alice said, "that you have already pronounced my translation to be erudite. You can hardly consider it worthless now."

"You know, gentlemen," Nick said. "My wife will be the Duchess of Barrington one day."

As if they hadn't considered that fact, the two professors drew themselves up in their chairs.

"And from what I hear, your college could use a new roof," Nick continued. "Must be very damp here during the monsoon season."

"Indeed," said Mr. Vidyasagar.

"Let's leave it at that, shall we?" said Nick.

A look passed between the three men, leaving Alice bemused.

The matter had just been decided, in the wordless way that gentlemen decided things. Her translation would be accepted. Her heart lifted.

"It was a pleasure and an honor to meet you, Lady Hatherly," said Mr. Carey. "We are so very pleased to accept your gift of your grandfather's manuscripts."

"They belong in your library, for others to study," she said. "They belong in India."

Mr. Vidyasagar nodded emphatically. "And we will be pleased to take your translation into consideration when we begin the process of seeking to publish portions of the *Kama Sutra* for a small, select audience."

"Thank you."

"Shall we be going, my love?" Nick said.

Alice rather thought they should. The two scholars still appeared shocked and dazed by the news that a woman had written about such *enthusiastic* subjects.

As they left, Nick reached behind her and squeezed her bum.

"Nick! We're in a public building. There are learned professors about."

"I forgot." He leaned down. "I'm so completely and utterly in love with you, Dimples, that sometimes I forget I can't make love to you whenever and wherever I please, and spectators be damned."

They emerged from the cool, stone building into the humid heat. "I think we've shocked everyone enough for one day," Alice said.

Nick threaded his fingers through hers as they walked along the banks of the River Hooghly.

"Why did you do it, Nick? It wasn't what we agreed upon."

"Because someone needs to know that the most brilliant linguist in the world decided to marry the likes of me."

Later, lying in bed, with Nick's arms twined around her, Alice dissolved into giggles.

"What are you laughing about, Dimples?"

"I was remembering the look on Mr. Carey's face when I began reading from the *Kama Sutra*."

"You were magnificent."

She kissed his cheek. "So were you."

"Does that mean I'm forgiven?"

"I didn't say that."

His mouth claimed hers with an urgency that took her breath away.

"How about now, Dimples?" he asked, several minutes later.

"Not yet."

Several hours later they lay exhausted, slick with sweat and breathing heavily, limbs tangled together in the center of the bed.

"Now?" Nick asked.

"I'm not sure . . ."

Nick groaned. "You're insatiable, Dimples."

Alice's heart sang with happiness as she drifted to sleep in Nick's arms.

They were in love.

They had a whole wide world to explore. And Alice was ready for their next grand adventure.

And don't miss the first sparkling romance
in Lenora Bell's Disgraceful Dukes series,

HOW THE DUKE WAS WON

*The pleasure of your company is requested at
Warbury Park. Four lovely ladies will arrive . . .
but only one can become a duchess.*

James, the scandalously uncivilized Duke
of Harland, requires a bride with a spotless
reputation for a strictly business arrangement.
Lust is prohibited and love is out of the question.

Four ladies. Three days.
What could go wrong?

She is not like the others . . .

Charlene Beckett, the unacknowledged daughter
of an earl and a courtesan, has just been offered a
life-altering fortune to pose as her half sister Lady
Dorothea and win the duke's proposal. All she
must do is:

- Be the perfect English rose [Ha!]

- Breathe, smile, and curtsy in impossibly
  tight gowns [blast Lady Dorothea's
  sylphlike figure]

- Charm and seduce a wild duke [without appearing to try]

- Keep said duke far, far from her heart [no matter how tempting]

When secrets are revealed and passion overwhelms, James must decide if the last lady he should want is really everything he needs. And Charlene must decide if the promise of a new life is worth risking everything . . . including her heart.

Do you love historical fiction?

Want the chance to hear news about your favourite authors (and the chance to win free books)?

Mary Balogh
Charlotte Betts
Jessica Blair
Frances Brody
Gaelen Foley
Elizabeth Hoyt
Eloisa James
Lisa Kleypas
Stephanie Laurens
Claire Lorrimer
Sarah MacLean
Amanda Quick
Julia Quinn

Then visit the Piatkus website and blog
www.piatkus.co.uk | www.piatkusbooks.net

And follow us on Facebook and Twitter
www.facebook.com/piatkusfiction | www.twitter.com/piatkusbooks

piatkus